QUICKSAND (#3)

"Charming characters, a hint of romantic conflict, and just the right amount of danger will garner more fans for this cozy series."

– *Publishers Weekly*

"*Quicksand* has all the ingredients I love—intrigue, witty banter, and a twisty mystery that hopscotches across France!"

– Sara Rosett,
Author of the Ellie Avery Mystery Series

"With a world-class puzzle to solve and riveting plot twists to unravel, *Quicksand* had me on the edge of my seat for the entire book...Don't miss one of the best new mystery series around!"

– Kate Carlisle,
New York Times Bestselling Author of the Bibliophile Mysteries

"A joy-filled ride of suspenseful action, elaborate scams, and witty dialogue. The villains are as wily as the heroes, and every twist is intelligent and unexpected, ensuring that this is a novel that will delight lovers of history, romance, and elaborate capers."

– *Kings River Life Magazine*

PIRATE VISHNU (#2)

"Forget about Indiana Jones. Jaya Jones is swinging into action, using both her mind and wits to solve a mystery...Readers will be ensnared by this entertaining tale."

– *RT Book Reviews* (four stars)

"Pandian's second entry sets a playful tone yet provides enough twists to keep mystery buffs engaged, too. The author streamlines an intricate plot....[and] brings a dynamic freshness to her cozy."

– *Library Journal*

"A delicious tall tale about a treasure map, magicians, musicians, mysterious ancestors, and a few bad men."

— Mystery Scene Magazine

"Move over Vicky Bliss and Joan Wilder, historian Jaya Jones is here to stay! Mysterious maps, legendary pirates, and hidden treasure—Jaya's latest quest is a whirlwind of adventure."

— Chantelle Aimée Osman,
The Sirens of Suspense

"*Pirate Vishnu* is fast-paced and fascinating as Jaya's investigation leads her this time to India and back to her own family's secrets."

—Susan C. Shea,
Author of the Dani O'Rourke mysteries

ARTIFACT (#1)

"Pandian's new series may well captivate a generation of readers, combining the suspenseful, mysterious and romantic. Four stars."

— RT Book Reviews

"If Indiana Jones had a sister, it would definitely be historian Jaya Jones."

— Suspense Magazine

"Witty, clever, and twisty... Do you like Agatha Christie? Elizabeth Peters? Then you're going to love Gigi Pandian."

— Aaron Elkins,
Edgar Award-Winning Author of the Gideon Oliver Mysteries

"Fans of Elizabeth Peters will adore following along with Jaya Jones and a cast of quirky characters as they pursue a fabled treasure."

—Juliet Blackwell,
New York Times Bestselling Author of the Art Lover's Mysteries
(written as Hailey Lind)

Quicksand

The Jaya Jones Treasure Hunt Mystery Series
by Gigi Pandian

Novels

ARTIFACT (#1)
PIRATE VISHNU (#2)
QUICKSAND (#3)

Novellas

FOOL'S GOLD (prequel to ARTIFACT)
(in OTHER PEOPLE'S BAGGAGE)

QUICKSAND

A JAYA JONES TREASURE HUNT MYSTERY

GIGI PANDIAN

HENERY PRESS

QUICKSAND
A Jaya Jones Treasure Hunt Mystery
Part of the Henery Press Mystery Collection

First Edition
Trade paperback edition | March 2015

Henery Press
www.henerypress.com

ISBN-13: 978-1-941962-27-5

Printed in the United States of America

For my mother

ACKNOWLEDGMENTS

What would I do without my incredible publishing team? Huge thanks to my editor Kendel Lynn for giving me one of the greatest insights into this book, back when it was a messy rough draft. Thanks to Stephanie Chontos for the gorgeous cover art, and the whole team at Henery Press for the creative ideas and enthusiasm. And as always, thanks to my agent Jill Marsal for always supporting me and my crazy ideas.

I also don't know what I'd do without my insightful early readers, who helped turn a cool idea into a fully realized story: Diane Vallere (art heists!), Emberly Nesbit (French!), Ramona DeFelice Long (a keen eye that saved the intro), Nancy Adams (overall awesomeness I can't imagine being without), and my mom (all things big and little).

Thanks to my writer pals who inspire me and keep me going. Local writers Em, Michelle, Mysti, Rachael, Julie, Sophie, Adrienne, Martha, Lisa, Lynn, Mariah, and the Sisters in Crime NorCal chapter; and all my remote writer pals, especially Brian, Nancy, and the Sisters in Crime Guppies. And my co-workers Catrina and Rebecca, who probably think I'm crazy but are amazingly supportive anyway.

Because I use real history as a backdrop for my books, discovering the true history of a place is essential. I'm indebted to Mont Saint-Michel tour guide Helene Cneude, who made French history come alive and continued to help with my follow-up questions from across the world.

And deepest gratitude to my parents, who are my biggest champions and the reason I believed I could be a writer in the first place. And James, who put up with the long hours I spent writing even before I dragged him along to France and other far-flung destinations for my research. I believe he's starting to have as much fun with these books as I am.

CHAPTER 1

"Is that the hilt of a sword sticking out of your purse?" Miles asked.

"No." I shifted the weight of the hefty tabla case in my hands to glance over my shoulder. I'd forgotten to take the dagger out of my bag when I swung by my attic apartment to pick up my drums. I was more distracted than I'd thought.

"But then—"

"It's not a sword. It's Tipu Sultan's jeweled dagger. And more importantly, this isn't a purse." My red messenger bag was the casual San Francisco equivalent of a briefcase.

"A dagger, Jaya?" This time it was my Russian landlady, Nadia, who spoke. She and my neighbor stood on the shady front porch of the Victorian house. "Is this what the city has come to? Young women resorting to carrying daggers for self-defense?"

"It's a plastic replica. The real one is in a museum in London. It was a nice prop for the Intro to World History lecture I gave today." I rested my tabla case on the steps and lifted the dagger from my bag. The jewel-encrusted hilt reminded me of the ruby artifact from the Mughal Empire that turned my life upside down the previous year.

"Oh." Nadia's lips puckered in disappointment. To a woman standing in front of her bright red front door in a black velvet evening gown, a prop to inspire students wasn't nearly as interesting as stories of maimed criminals.

"Cool," Miles said, taking the dagger in his ink-stained hands. He swooshed it through the air like a sword, a book of poetry falling from his jacket pocket in the process. "I came by to see how your first day of class went."

After knowing the twenty-something poet for over a year, I was convinced Miles selected leaky pens on purpose, thinking his temporarily tattooed hands made him look more artistic and earnest. His auburn beard fuzz also looked suspiciously uniform whenever I saw him.

"Class went so well that a lot of the students stayed to ask questions," I said, picking up the fallen poetry chapbook. "Now I'm late for the restaurant."

I should have been pleased my first lecture of the spring semester had gone so well. It was only my second year teaching at the university, and it already felt like home. My students were even more engaged than I'd hoped, and one struggling student I mentored the previous year did so well she decided to apply for history graduate programs.

But as the months of the fall semester had gone by, I'd become increasingly aware that something was missing in my life. I had my dream job as a tenure-track professor of history at a prominent San Francisco university, a cozy apartment in a great location, family not too far away, and a few good friends. After my uprooted childhood, it's what I'd always wanted. The response to my first lecture of the semester was gratifying, but it didn't make me as happy as it should have. What was the matter with me?

"Before you go," Nadia began, but instead of finishing her sentence she disappeared into the house. I was left to watch Miles pretend to be a master swordsman.

Nadia emerged a moment later with a stack of mail. My apartment didn't have a separate mailing address from the main house, because the dwelling wasn't strictly legal. My landlady had bypassed San Francisco bureaucracy when she turned her attic into the apartment where I lived.

I was in a hurry, so instead of dropping off my mail and the plastic dagger upstairs, I shoved both into my messenger bag, then slung my tabla case over my shoulder and headed to my car. I eased out of my parking spot between a pristine hybrid car with stickers from three universities on its back window, and a weathered sedan with its tailpipe dangling precariously close to the ground—the two sides of modern San Francisco.

I didn't give a second thought to that stack of mail as I drove across town to the Tandoori Palace, or as I played sets of tabla background music for diners at the upscale Indian restaurant with my best friend Sanjay accompanying me on the sitar. On a break, I had only a few minutes to eat a mouth-watering fish curry that the chef made extra spicy for me. The pile of mail didn't cross my mind until after we wrapped up our last set.

My phone buzzed faintly from deep within my bag. I found it buried underneath my pile of mail. It was a text message from my friend Tamarind, asking for an urgent favor. Tamarind wasn't one to ask for favors. This couldn't be good.

Instead of sticking around to chat with Sanjay and the restaurant staff as I usually did, I rushed to my car. But when I reached it, I found I was trapped. Double-parked inches away from my roadster was an empty car with its hazard lights blinking, blocking me in. I ran back to the restaurant and explained to Sanjay that I needed to stop by Tamarind's apartment to bring a box from her medicine cabinet to her "first day of the semester" party.

"Wait, why does Tamarind care that it's the first day of the semester?" Sanjay asked as we left the restaurant. "I thought she was a librarian, not a professor."

"That's the point." I climbed into the sleek black pickup truck. "Without this party, she doesn't get the same symbolic start to the semester as the rest of us."

Sanjay put the car in gear and we set out from the family-friendly Inner Sunset to the trendy Mission District.

"I haven't driven with you in a while," I commented after he let three perfectly good openings in traffic pass us by. "I'd forgotten you're a ninety-year-old man trapped in a thirty-year-old's body when you get behind the wheel of a car."

"Hey, I don't turn thirty until next year. And what have you got against ninety-year-olds? My friend Sébastien is ninety and he loves racing cars."

"Who's Sébastien?"

"A magician I know in France. Though I suppose he's not *technically* a magician. He's an engineer who helps magicians with their acts."

Sanjay was a successful stage magician who sold out seasons of shows in a Napa Valley theater each year. A Las Vegas venue approached him after he was named one of the up-and-coming magicians under thirty, but he loved his home in northern California. He'd been my best friend since the day I moved to San Francisco nearly two years before. Two nights a week, Sanjay and I played background music at the Indian restaurant. It was a relaxing hobby for both of us. I could play my tabla drums expertly even in my sleep, and Sanjay enjoyed playing the sitar—though he did it excruciatingly badly. Not that anyone could convince him of that fact. The Tandoori Palace's owner, Raj, had long ago given up gently suggesting he take additional lessons. Instead, Raj turned down the volume on the microphone in front of Sanjay's sitar, and left my mic on high to pick up my rhythmic drumming. That way, everyone had a good time.

"Anyway," Sanjay continued as he finally merged from the side street onto Lincoln, "it's called *responsible driving*. Something this city is sorely lacking."

"Well, at this rate at least I have time to look through my mail before we get there."

While Sanjay drove the speed limit along the south side of Golden Gate Park, I turned to the most interesting-looking envelope, one made of thick vellum paper with a postmark from France. It was the kind of expensive paper used for wedding invitations. None of my friends were getting married, as far as I knew, so I was curious. I slipped my car key under the envelope flap to open it.

My name jumped out at me. I did a double-take. This couldn't be what my first glance told me it was. The cab of the truck was dark. I had an overactive imagination. That was it.

"What is it?" Sanjay asked.

Even while paying attention to the road—too much attention, it could be argued—Sanjay knew me well enough to detect the slightest change in my emotional state.

"Nothing," I answered, scattering the contents of the envelope across my lap.

I wasn't imagining things.

It was a first class plane ticket from San Francisco to Paris, departing in three days. The name printed on the ticket: Jaya Anand Jones. The ticket was for me.

I'd been busy preparing for the start of the semester, so I'd ignored certain aspects of my life. Still, I knew I hadn't absentmindedly agreed to speak at any academic conferences in Paris. Or anywhere in Europe, for that matter.

I unfolded the other two sheets of paper. The first was a print-out of a hotel reservation for an upscale hotel in Paris. The second was a hand-written note.

My insides tensed as I began to read. As the streetlights cast multicolored streaks of light through the windshield like a slow-moving strobe light, I stared at the familiar handwriting, wondering if I could believe my eyes.

Five months of silence. *And now this.*

CHAPTER 2

Sanjay glanced sharply at me. "What's the matter?"

A combination of relief, curiosity, and anger swept over me. I was fairly confident that relief was the dominant emotion, but I couldn't be sure. The note meant so many things, I didn't know where to begin to answer Sanjay's question.

Jaya,

You know my reasons for needing to lay low and not communicate by email. I'm sorry that's the way it had to be. Now that I've taken care of some things, you could come to me.

I thought of you when research led me to the East India Company—and couldn't stop thinking about you. I know it's a lot to ask, but I hope we can pick up where we left off. Spend a few days with me in Paris?

L

I met Lane Peters the previous year while researching an Indian artifact. I'd fallen for him, even after learning about his past on the wrong side of the law. He understood me in ways nobody else ever had. The connection surprised both of us, and continued to confuse me. Without him in my life, I felt as if a chunk of me was missing. A piece of me I hadn't realized was missing until I'd met him.

My only clue to his whereabouts suggested he might have returned to India. Two weeks after I'd last seen him, a six-foot-high box arrived at my office, the customs slip informing me it had been sent from Kochi, India. Inside the sawdust packing materials that made such a mess I felt compelled to bring the janitorial staff donuts for a week, I found a granite statue of Ganesha—the remover of obstacles. In this carving, the elephant deity cradled a set of tabla drums in his arms. Though there was no accompanying message, the scratch across Ganesha's trunk told me it was the exact statue I'd fallen in love with when Lane and I visited a master craftsman's store in Kochi. I hadn't realized at the time that Lane noticed my reaction to the carving.

I believed Lane when he said that his past was in the past. Even though I hadn't heard from him in months, I still did. Unfortunately, other people didn't want Lane's past to stay buried. That's why I'd been so worried when I hadn't heard from him all this time.

And now this invitation.

"Jaya, what is it?" Sanjay repeated.

"It's a note from an old friend," I said, breathing a sigh of relief that Lane was safe, but simultaneously shaking with anger that he'd waited so long to get in touch.

I flipped back to the plane ticket. Even if I'd been inclined to drop everything for Lane, I couldn't possibly leave at the start of the semester.

As we came to a stop at a red light on Oak, Sanjay plucked the plane ticket from my hand. Using his skillful sleight of hand, the ticket was out of my hand before I realized what he was doing. I tried to grab it back, but my seatbelt prevented me from reaching it.

"Paris?" he said. "You're going to Paris?"

In the brighter light from the intersection, I saw something I hadn't taken note of earlier. It was normal for Sanjay to wear a tuxedo while practicing for his stage show, so it hadn't surprised me that he'd worn it at the restaurant. But under the glare of the streetlights, I noticed how wrinkled it was. His patent leather shoes were coated with gray powder, and a small clump of white paste stuck to his thick black hair.

"Were you attacked by a mob of your fans after our set?" I joked.

"What? You mean this mess?" He handed the ticket back to me, then ran a hand through his hair. He gave a start when the glop of paste transferred to his hand. He pulled a bright red handkerchief from an inner pocket to wipe it off. The red handkerchief disappeared from Sanjay's hand as quickly as it had appeared, and I had no idea where it went. He wasn't trying to impress me. Sleight-of-hand was second nature to him.

"I was practicing for a new act," he continued. "This new illusion is giving me grief, so we ran longer than I meant to. Why didn't you tell me you're going out of town? And who gets printed plane tickets mailed to them anymore?"

"I'm not going to Paris."

"Then why do you have—"

"The light's green."

"Oh." He gave me a quick scowl before tapping the accelerator so gently I nearly screamed.

"It's an invitation to do research on colonial history in Paris," I said, tucking the ticket, note, and hotel reservation back into the envelope. I wasn't exactly lying. Okay, maybe I was lying, but not by much. The letter *did* mention an East India Company. Since Lane was in France, I assumed he meant the French East India Company, one of the colonial trading powers from centuries ago. Though less successful than the English, the French once had colonial settlements in India and fleets of ships bringing home treasures not found in France. My historical expertise was colonialism in India, especially the British East India Company and the British Raj. I knew the histories of the companies as well as I knew which spots on my calfskin drums made which resonant sounds beneath my fingertips. But without further details from Lane, I assumed he wasn't after my research help. He was after me.

I didn't have the mental energy to go into Lane's note with Sanjay. He knew a little bit about my relationship with Lane, but I felt uncomfortable going into the details with him, even though we were so close. Or, more accurately, *especially* because we were so close. My best friend had always been like a little brother to me, until things got complicated the previous summer. Now there was no way I was going to share details about my love life with him. I was glad we were driving. Sanjay seemed content to pay attention to the road.

I, however, was far from at ease with my thoughts.

There was no question the letter was in Lane's handwriting, but there was something different about it that I couldn't place. Then again, giving up your life—not once, but twice—had to change a man. But underneath everything, we knew each other well. *That's* what was wrong with his letter. He knew I'd be worried about him, but he hadn't addressed my concerns in the note. Why did he think I would drop everything and meet him for a romantic tryst in Paris?

Oh. What single woman in her right mind would pass up a first class ticket to Paris to get back together with a guy she was incredibly attracted to, was desperately worried about, and had parted with on good, if enigmatic, terms?

Normally, I would be the woman to turn it down. But on that crazy first day of the semester, it was glaringly obvious that my seemingly perfect life wasn't all I thought it was.

Now that the initial shock was over, it occurred to me that Lane hadn't included a way to get in touch with him. Even if he thought his electronic communications were still being monitored, surely he could tell me to contact him at a new email address, using a new email address of my own. Why not? What was going on?

Sanjay double-parked while I ran up to Tamarind's apartment and used her spare key to retrieve a small wooden box from the bathroom medicine cabinet, then dropped me off outside the venue where Tamarind's party was taking place. He didn't come inside with me, claiming he was overdressed for it because of his tux. As soon as I got inside, I saw how wrong he was. The back room of the bar had been transformed into a 1980s prom, complete with streamers hanging from the ceiling and '80s music blaring from the speakers. I spotted Tamarind in a pink polka dot strapless dress with black lace fringe. I never knew what color her hair would be, but that night it was her natural jet black, with the exception of hot-pink bangs, matching her dress. I was relieved to see her laughing and raising a martini glass to her lips.

Before I stepped into the crowd, there was something I needed to do first. I raced to the sidewalk and dialed the number of the Paris hotel on the reservation. The sidewalk was crowded with people leaving upscale restaurants and inexpensive taquerias, spilling out of trendy pubs and dive bars, and walking home from the BART station to the apartment buildings that filled the neighborhood. I pressed my phone to my ear and ignored them.

I don't speak French, but as I expected, the man who answered the phone switched to perfect English.

"I'm sorry," he said in response to my question. "Mr. Peters isn't here yet. He's scheduled to arrive in three days time."

Damn. If I used the plane ticket, I'd be in the air when Lane arrived at the hotel. It wouldn't help to leave him a message. I had no way to get in touch with him. If I ever wanted to see him again, even for closure, all I could do was get on that flight.

CHAPTER 3

I thanked the hotel receptionist and headed back inside, my whole body sagging.

"Jaya!" Tamarind cried out. She zigzagged through the crowd of faculty and staff, holding her martini glass above her head as she made her way to me. I recognized a few faces from the history department and the library, but there must have been more than fifty people packed in. Not everyone was dressed up, so I wasn't out of place in my black slacks, sweater, and heels.

I handed the box to her as soon as she reached me.

"You are a *life* saver," Tamarind said, keeping her voice raised so I could hear her over the music. She opened the box and extracted a skull and crossbones necklace. "I can't believe I forgot this at home! It's perfect with this dress, don't you think?"

"You worried me over *a necklace*? And who keeps a necklace in her medicine cabinet? They're for medicine."

"Shut. Up. *I* had the unflappable Jaya Jones worried? Maybe that'll snap you out of the funk you've been in."

"What funk? I'm fine."

"Right. Whatever you say. Anyway, order the Librarian's Lexicon or the Dewey Daiquiri. Those are the drinks the bartender made up especially for my party tonight. I'm drinking the Lexicon. It's tequila, lemon, and some secret ingredients Hugh won't reveal. Good stuff, Jaya. Good stuff."

Tamarind Ortega was a librarian and one of my few good friends in San Francisco. She'd only received her MA in Library Science a couple of years before, but she'd secured her job at the university library through a combination of the two sides of her personality. First, she was brilliant. Whenever I hit a wall in my research, Tamarind could get me past it. Second, she knew how to deal with the vast array of people who came into the library. She was a punk who had a soft touch with the many homeless people who tried to come inside to sleep, but she wasn't afraid to use her size to intimidate people when her people skills didn't do the trick.

"I don't know what you said to those kids," she said, "but half a dozen of your students checked out history books this afternoon."

"That's great," I said, but my heart wasn't in it.

"Hey, what gives? Don't you like my dress?"

"It's lovely," I said, smiling. I meant it. The cut of the flamboyant dress flattered her sturdy figure. "I'm just distracted from my busy day. What's with the high school prom theme?"

She shrugged. "When I found this dress, the party pretty much planned itself."

I threw my arms around Tamarind. What can I say? It had been an emotional day, and I still had no idea what I wanted to do about Lane's invitation.

"You're worrying me, Jaya," she said, once I let go of her. "This isn't like you. Let's get you a drink."

At the bar, I ordered a Scotch whisky while Tamarind snagged bar stools from two women who were departing.

"A toast," I said, sitting down on the empty bar stool she was fiercely protecting for me, "to new beginnings." We clinked glasses and I scanned the room. Four thirty-something professors were dancing in one corner, but the rest of the crowd's attention was focused on drinks and conversation.

"Since your boyfriend has been MIA, I wasn't sure if you'd show up for the party."

I groaned.

"Something I said? I thought you'd be over that guy by now."

"It just got complicated." I took a large sip of my Scotch.

"Shut. Up. He's back?"

"Not exactly." I reached into my bag and handed her the fat envelope. "Talk me out of this."

"Shut. Up." She stared at the letter and tickets. "Why on earth would I talk you out of this?"

"Um, because you're a feminist punk?"

"I'm a post-feminist post-punk if you want to get technical about it, but that has nothing to do with free first class tickets to Paris. *Paris*, Jaya."

"Yeah, but you realize who this is from?"

"Your hottie boyfriend who you for some inexplicable reason wouldn't introduce me to before he left the Bay Area. I saw his picture, you know. I know what I'm missing out on."

"That's the problem," I said. "*Everyone* saw his picture. That's exactly why he had to leave."

"It's not like he's James Bond," Tamarind said. "Although I bet he could play him in a new Bond movie series. Especially since he needs a new career. Jaya, do you think he can act?"

"Tamarind?"

"Yes?"

"Focus, please. We're talking about this invitation to Paris."

"There's always more to see and do in Paris."

"I've never seen *anything* in Paris."

"Wait, you've never visited Paris?"

"Why would I have been to Paris? I did research in Britain and India during grad school, and backpacked through Asia one summer."

"And you're seriously entertaining the notion of turning down a free *first class ticket* to *Paris*?"

"I thought I had something real with Lane, but he hasn't contacted me in more than *five months*."

"For your own protection—"

"Are you listening to yourself?"

"Yeah, that sounded pretty weak, didn't it?"

"It certainly did."

"Well," Tamarind said, running her index finger around the rim of her glass. She appeared lost in thought for a moment, her eyes following the black nail polish on her finger tip, or perhaps the chunky silver ring in the shape of a book. "This is a real ticket, right?"

"So?"

"*So* forget him. He didn't ask if you wanted to go before buying this ticket. That means you've got a round-trip ticket, free and clear. Who says you have to meet him at the hotel? You've got a first class ticket to Paris to do anything you want."

"Tamarind."

"Yes, thinks-too-much-Jaya?"

"It's the beginning of the semester. I can't just fly to Europe and miss all of next week."

"Fine. Be practical." Tamarind pursed her lips and looked thoughtful for a moment. "I've got it! The letter."

"What about it?"

"It says he's onto something with the East India Company— you think he means the French Company?"

"Probably, but that's not exactly what it—"

"Close enough." She dismissed me with a wave of her hand as she polished off her drink and set it on the bar. "This is like totally related to your research. You're not blowing off classes. You're on a mission to discover the secrets of the French East India Company! A quest for higher knowledge! A—"

"I get it."

"Well, it's pretty damn perfect."

"Except for the part where there's no way I can skip classes right now."

"Uptight much?"

"You remember there's a thing called tenure that as a second-year assistant professor I'm not yet close to achieving?"

"You worry too much, Jaya. The dean loves you. The coolest librarian this side of the border loves you. Everyone except for Naveen Krishnan loves you. Oh. That last part is going to be a problem, isn't it?" She paused and whipped her head around. "He's here, somewhere, just so you know."

"It'll definitely be a problem."

"Fine," Tamarind said, stuffing the ticket back into the envelope. "Hey, can I borrow this?"

"What are you holding?"

"A little book of poetry you handed me along with the mysterious envelope. *The Thin Monster House.*"

"It's not mine. My neighbor Miles dropped it. I must have forgotten to give it back to him. I'm sure he wouldn't mind if you borrowed it."

"Sweet."

"The cost for borrowing it," I added, "is changing the subject away from Naveen."

"Speak of the devil..."

Dressed in a three-piece tweed suit, Naveen Krishnan walked stiffly in cap toe Oxfords that must have pinched his feet. He wasn't in formal attire for the party; that was how he always dressed. He was a linguistic prodigy who was overcompensating for being one of the youngest professors at the university.

"I'm glad to see you, Jaya," he said, pausing to acknowledge Tamarind with a slight nod. "I thought you'd want to hear that my symposium was such a success I've been asked to put on a similar one next year."

"Congratulations, Naveen." I smiled more broadly than I had all evening. I wasn't acting. Out of his line of sight, Tamarind stuck out her tongue and rolled her eyes at Naveen.

"It's a great accomplishment, I'm told," Naveen said. "Don't feel bad, though, Jaya. Not everyone can be such a success."

The strongest argument in favor of going to France might have been that I wouldn't have to see Naveen Krishnan for a week.

I caught a cab back to where my car was parked. The double-parked car blocking me in was gone. I got home quickly, but couldn't calm down enough to sleep well. There were too many unanswered questions. Why had Lane gotten in touch now? If it was safe to contact me, why not give me a way to get back in touch? What was he researching? And most importantly, could I trust my feelings? It was well after midnight by the time I got to sleep, and I tossed and turned all night.

In the morning, I went for a run to clear my head. It had the opposite effect. As I ran through the park to bhangra beats on my headphones, my subconscious insisted on pushing my thoughts back to the strange invitation, full of contradictions.

After my run and a quick shower, I picked up a large coffee and a breakfast burrito with added hot sauce and honey, then headed for campus. As I unlocked my office door, my six-foot Ganesha statue greeted me. Like all proper Ganeshas, he had a broken tusk, a reminder not only of the sacrifices we make in life, but also of all that can be overcome. That morning, he made me think of criss-crossing south India on a motorbike with Lane.

I had a little over an hour before my first class of the day. It was enough time that I couldn't resist opening my computer to do a little digging.

No, I could resist. I slammed my laptop shut.

Damn. I couldn't resist. I opened it back up.

The French East India Company formed in 1664 to compete with the British and Dutch trading companies. It was one of the least successful European companies that held trade and colonial interests across the world. It couldn't even hold onto the Indian city of Pondicherry, losing it time and time again to the British. After a series of scandals, it went bankrupt in the 1790s, a little over a hundred years after it was founded. The British East India Company and the British Raj lasted the longest of any colonial powers and exerted the most control over India, only ceding control when Indian Independence was achieved in 1947.

I stood up from my desk and grabbed a book on colonialism from my bookshelf. In spite of my better judgment, I was taking this idea seriously. I wanted to use the ticket to Paris. Now the challenge was figuring out how to pull it off.

A knock on my office door startled me. The dean was knocking on the door frame, a scowl on his face. He gave a disapproving click of his tongue. "Jaya, why didn't you tell me about this great opportunity?"

"Uh..."

"The invitation to consult on the French East India Company documents in Paris?"

"Oh, *that*," I said. *How had he heard?* "I didn't think it was worth mentioning, because it didn't seem practical. It's later this week, and I have classes—"

"Already taken care of," he said.

"It is?"

"Naveen Krishnan will be covering for you."

Oh, no. "Naveen can't—"

"His lectures won't be the same, of course, but he knows the subjects just as well."

Naveen would also do everything he could to turn my students against me. Naveen and I had rubbed each other the wrong way from the day we met, even before we realized we were both in untenured positions at a cash-strapped university. With similar expertise, it was likely only one of us would get tenure. Our rivalry grew stronger the previous year when I got the university's history department a lot of positive publicity because of the historical treasures I'd discovered.

"Isn't he busy planning a new symposium?" I asked.

The dean dismissed that notion with a wave of his hand. "He said he'd be more than happy to help out."

I bet. "How did you find out about my, um, consultant invitation?"

"A librarian you consulted came to me this morning."

"Tamarind?"

"She recognized what a great opportunity this was, and she was concerned you were too focused on your day-to-day responsibilities to see the big picture, and how this could be another fruitful experience."

"But—"

"Relax, Jaya. Pack your bags for Paris."

CHAPTER 4

Pampering me with everything from extra pillows to melt-in-your-mouth warm cookies and free-flowing champagne, the flight from San Francisco to the Charles De Gaulle airport in Paris should have been the most relaxing eleven hours I'd spent in months. But even first class wasn't enough to make me forget about the strange circumstances of my visit.

Part of my apprehension came from the fact that I hadn't made up my mind about what I was doing. I was going to see Lane with an open mind, but on my own terms. Since I didn't yet know if I'd stay in Paris longer than a day, or whether I'd be spending my days eating at romantic French restaurants, researching inside library stacks, or trekking through the wintery outdoors, I didn't know what to pack. Instead of packing everything, I packed very little. This was France, not rural Kashmir (which, for the record, you need to pack well for). I shoved a few items of clothing, a pair of running shoes, and toiletries into the well-loved brown leather backpack my father gave me years ago. I figured I could get whatever else I needed once I got there.

From the back of my closet I'd pulled out the long black coat I bought when I was living in London to complete my dissertation, and a small shoulder bag for items I didn't want to fall to the bottom of my father's old backpack, including my magnifying glass and music player. I didn't want to be helpless, so I'd downloaded an intensive French-language program to listen to on my headphones in the days leading up to the trip and on the flight.

In the airplane seat, I kicked off my three-inch-high black stilettos, noticing that my choice of shoes wasn't so out of place here in first class. In those shoes, I'm just shy of five foot three. Still shorter than almost everyone besides kids, but tall enough to maneuver in a world that's made for people much taller than me. The first class seat was especially spacious, but try as I might to pay attention to my French lessons, I couldn't stop myself from trying to puzzle out the meaning of this invitation.

Lane Peters was an art historian, so it made sense he could have been looking into one of the many artistic treasures plundered by colonial powers. Undersea divers periodically recovered treasures from sunken Company ships, but oceans were so vast that there was still a lot of history out there to be discovered. A few decades before, a sunken ship had been found off the coast of the Cape of Good Hope. The ship held "Lord Clive's Gold," the treasures of Robert Clive of the British East India Company. I couldn't remember anything recent, and a news search before I left San Francisco told me there hadn't been any new discoveries of note.

But why would Lane have been looking into something like that? He'd been forced to leave his graduate program, which had been his attempt to start a new life. If he'd started anew, he'd managed to keep his name off the Internet. There was no way to find out more before I saw him in person in a few hours. I willed myself to concentrate on my French. *Je m'apelle Jaya Jones...*

Lane hadn't said anything about meeting me at the airport, so I wasn't expecting him there. But in the area where we were herded like cattle as we exited Customs, a man in a suit held up a sign with the name "Jaya Jones" printed on it.

His cold brown eyes made me hesitate to approach him. This wasn't someone I wanted to share a car with. Was it a cultural difference, I wondered? No, that wasn't it...I instinctively looked straight ahead and kept walking, caught in the flow next to a large

Indian family whose patriarch had an especially ample belly that shielded me from view. I wasn't sure if the driver had been shown my picture, but I didn't want to find out.

I don't believe in signs, but I trust my intuition. I'm good at martial arts, especially jiu-jitsu, courtesy of my father who insisted on getting me lessons when I hadn't yet reached five feet in high school. One of the first things you learn is that it's best to never get yourself into a situation where you need to use your fighting skills.

I figured Lane must have been caught up in the research he mentioned in the letter and therefore sent a car service to pick me up. The driver was probably harmless, but it wouldn't hurt to play it safe. I took the Paris metro to the hotel.

A dozen illuminated globes hung from the high ceiling of the hotel lobby. Above them, the ceiling was lit with pin pricks of light in the shape of constellations. At the front desk, two hotel employees were speaking to each other in rapid French, but they broke off their conversation when they saw me approach. A clean-cut man with sandy hair greeted me with a wide smile.

"Bonjour," I said.

"Checking in?" he replied in English with a thick Australian accent. My accent clearly needed some work.

I gave my name and he handed me a key card. The room had already been paid for. I declined the offer of assistance to help with my small bag, and stepped into the mirror-lined elevator. I felt odd letting myself into the room where Lane was presumably staying. After locating the room, I took a deep breath—okay, five of them—then knocked on the door.

My knock was greeted with silence. I double-checked the number the Australian desk clerk had written down for me. This was the right room. A moment later, I heard footsteps followed by the sound of a lock unlatching. The door opened, and Lane Peters stood in front of me.

He looked nearly the same as when I'd seen him last—the tall, lanky figure, and the handsome, angular face he hid with glasses and floppy hair. Time stood still in that moment as relief flooded through me. The last few days hadn't been a dream. I stepped inside and closed the door behind me. It was a single room, but couches and a table formed a living room in front of the king size bed.

"Jones?" he whispered. His eyes lit up and his lips formed a priceless smile, but the reaction only lasted a couple of seconds, cut short by the sound of another voice.

"Oh good," the voice said. A man in a tailored suit stood by the window. His accent was neither French nor American, but upper-class British. "Dante called to say he didn't see you at the airport. I was worried."

"The driver?" I asked, seized by confusion.

"You sent *Dante* to get her?" Lane asked, then shook his head. "Of course you would."

"You're proving to be every bit as intelligent as I imagined you to be," the man said to me. "I anticipated nothing less."

"Lane, what's going on?" I asked.

"You shouldn't have involved her," Lane said to the Englishman. I had never before heard such raw anger in his voice. It scared me.

"*You* invited *me*." My voice shook with anger and confusion.

"What?" he croaked out. The word was barely above a whisper, and his eyes were earnest. He had always been skinny, but he'd lost weight. "I'm sorry, Jones."

"Fine," I said, swearing under my breath. I turned to go. I was ridiculously curious as to what on earth was going on, but my pride won out. I wasn't about to stay there and listen to Lane explain how he was so busy with whatever he was doing that he'd forgotten about me.

"Miss Jones," the British stranger said. "I don't think you'll wish to leave when you hear what we have to say."

"Let her go," Lane said. "I'll do it."

"What are you talking about?" I asked. "Why wouldn't I be free to go?"

"Nobody is holding anyone against their will," the British man said. "Why don't you two relax and have a drink while we talk? I don't think you'll be so eager to leave once you've heard what I have to say."

"Who *are* you?" I asked.

"Forgive me. My friends call me North. I hope you'll do the same. I'm an associate of Lane's. We go way back."

"You don't have to do this," Lane said to North. "I told you I'll do the job."

"I'd feel much more convinced in the strength of your word," North said, "if there was more at stake that you care about." His gaze shifted to me.

A wave of panic washed over me, starting in my gut and radiating to every inch of my body. I knew what those words meant. It was what Lane had been afraid of. When he turned his life around, he broke all ties with his old life—his life as an art thief.

But breaking ties with the past hadn't worked. Because of me, they'd found a way to get to him.

CHAPTER 5

"If you're talking about me," I said to North, "you've got the wrong girl. Lane doesn't care about me. I haven't heard from him in over five months."

"I know," North said. "That made it quite difficult to find his weak spot. I had to dig deeper into his activities than was convenient. He tried to deny it at first, but for someone who's such a good actor, he failed in this part. He couldn't cover up his feelings for you."

"Wait, Lane really wrote the letter about wanting to see me?"

Lane groaned. "That's why my shopping lists disappeared before I left Berkeley. I didn't think I'd thrown them away."

"It was much easier to obtain handwriting samples," North said, "in the days when people wrote letters and kept journals on paper. Luckily, Lane considers himself a cook, so he writes nicely detailed lists of ingredients along with recipes he's trying out."

"He's a forger," Lane said. "A forger and a con man." Behind his glasses, his eyes were full of so much sadness that it took some of the sting out of knowing I'd been tricked. "I'm so sorry, Jones. I had no idea he was bringing you here."

"That's what was wrong with the letter!" My shoulders slumped as I realized my mistake. "I *knew* there was something off about the letter, even though it matched your handwriting perfectly. I told myself I must not have known you as well as I thought I did, because the tone sounded off. But that wasn't it. It was what you called me in the letter. You call me Jaya in casual conversation, but when there's emotion involved—"

24

"Jones." Lane grabbed my hand. "I'm sorry to all of your names, Jaya Anand Jones." He pulled me closer, but stopped short of holding me close.

"I feel like a third wheel," North said. "Terribly embarrassing to have gotten in the middle of a lover's quarrel. I have one last thing to ask of Jaya, and then I'll let you two get caught up."

Lane gripped my hand tighter.

"No need to worry, Lane," North said. "I merely wish to have Jaya authenticate some old documents from India that have fallen into my hands."

"No need for euphemisms," Lane spat out.

"Quite. Now then, I'll leave you these documents I *acquired*." North paused and picked up a stack of worn pages in protective plastic sleeves. "I'll return in thirty minutes."

In spite of myself, the sight of the worn, faded papers sent a little thrill through me.

"Not a chance," Lane said.

"It's okay," I said. I wasn't planning on telling North whatever it was he wanted to know, but if he had historical documents, I wanted to see them.

"You can look at them," Lane said. "But not here. I know North. Whatever we say in this room, he'll hear it."

A flash of anger crossed North's face, but the emotion disappeared as quickly as it had appeared. He tossed back his head and laughed heartily. Deep laugh lines creased his forehead. This was a man used to enjoying himself. I wondered how long he'd been in this line of work. He had a full head of dark brown hair that was starting to grey around the temples. I placed him in his mid-forties, about ten years older than Lane. If he hadn't been manipulating me, I would probably have described him as quite handsome.

"You mean the room is *bugged*?" I asked.

"I knew I chose the right man for the job," North said, wiping a tear from his eye as he got control of his laughter.

I felt on the verge of hysterical laughter myself. Here I was in an opulent hotel in Paris where I'd been lured under false pretenses, having a civil conversation with an ex art thief and a forger, unsure of whether I was free to go, all while under surveillance. It was one of those situations where I really needed to laugh so I didn't cry.

"Of course the room is bugged," North said. "But I don't see any harm in letting you two catch up in private before we get to work. If you'll leave your cell phones with me, you can choose any location you'd like that's nearby—within reason."

"Jones, you choose," Lane said. "North knows me too well. Anywhere I can think of, he might have already bugged."

North barked out another burst of laughter.

"The rooftop," I said.

"It's windy and cold," Lane said. "And..."

"You never would have suggested it? Then it's perfect."

North thought for a moment before nodding. "If you can find your way up there, I don't see why not. Oh, and Lane," he added, all levity from his voice gone as he spoke the name. "Convince her. I don't want to destroy her life."

Destroy my life? What an odd way to phrase a threat.

North handed me the stack of documents in exchange for my cell phone, and walked behind us on our way to the elevator. He punched the button going up to the top floor, then waved goodbye as the doors closed behind us.

In the short ride to the hotel's top floor, I thought Lane and I might share a quick kiss to take the edge off of the stressful situation. Instead, he took the plastic-covered pages from me and held them up to the light.

"Nice to see you, too," I mumbled to myself.

"One second," he replied distractedly, running his fingers along the edges of the plastic. "Unless technology has progressed exponentially in the last few years, there's no way these are bugged."

He handed them back to me, and I tucked them gingerly into my shoulder bag, careful not to bend them.

After getting off the elevator on the top floor, which dropped us in front of the hotel's restaurant, Lane scanned our surroundings.

"This way," he said, leading us to a service door. A red slash on a sign indicated people weren't to enter, but the door wasn't locked. We climbed the last flight of stairs leading to the roof of the hotel.

A burst of cold air hit me as we opened the metal door. It was apparent why the door below had been unlocked. Dozens of cigarette butts lined the space next to the door.

Though the roof was flat, it was covered with chimneys and other obstructions. Lane took a few minutes to circle the roof. I didn't know if he was making sure we were alone or looking for surveillance devices.

Standing near the ledge, I could see for miles across an overcast Paris. The city was full of so much life and so much history. A living history I was now part of. I was so entranced by the sweeping views of the snaking Seine river with its stone bridges, the modern buildings mixed with ancient ones, and the famous Eiffel Tower rising lower into the heavens than I'd imagined, that I was surprised by Lane's presence back at my side.

I was even more surprised when he pulled me into a kiss that I felt through my whole body. My shoulder bag nearly fell to the ground as he swept me into his arms. The scent of his aftershave and the feel of his strong lips took me back to where we'd left off all those months ago. My lips welcomed his, and I felt myself lost in this moment I'd fantasized about for all these months.

But at the same time, I felt a small tinge of uncertainty stir within me. The last man I'd kissed had been Sanjay, under circumstances that had never been resolved. He was drugged, and he didn't remember kissing me. Before that accidental kiss the previous summer, I never imagined I could have romantic feelings for my best friend. I knew I loved Sanjay, but I was almost certain it was in the same way I loved my brother.

As Lane continued kissing me, all thoughts of Sanjay faded away. I was vaguely aware there was something else I should have been thinking about, but at that moment I didn't care. It was Lane who pulled away, snapping me back to reality.

"I believe we have twenty three minutes," he said, "before North joins us."

"I can barely believe we're here together on this rooftop." A cold burst of wind blew my bob of black hair around my face. It was colder than it was when I'd arrived. Being ten flights from the ground made a difference. "You're all right?"

"Better now."

"That's not what I meant, you know. I mean you, life—everything that's been going on the last five months! I didn't know what to think."

"I hoped the Ganesha figurine would put your mind at ease."

"You mean the statue that barely fit through the door." I couldn't suppress a grin. "He's perfect."

Lane cleared his throat. "I wish we had more time to catch up, but North—"

"I know, I know. Scratch that. I *don't* know. What exactly is going on?"

"Since we don't have much time, before you look at these documents, you need to understand something." He was no longer smiling. "North is a very dangerous man—"

"Then why don't we use a phone in the restaurant below us to call the police? God, unless he's got spies everywhere...Why don't we find a fire escape and climb down?"

"Let me finish. North isn't dangerous in the way you'd expect. He doesn't hurt people—not physically. He's much more clever than that. He ruins people's lives."

"What do you mean, *he ruins people's lives?*"

"Exactly that." Lane swallowed hard. "I know one man who's living out his days in a Moroccan prison because North tipped off the authorities. North was displeased with the man's perceived disloyalty, so he planted extra evidence to be sure he'd be convicted. Another one of our associates had every single one of his hidden bank accounts disappear and his identity erased—aside from a few damning pieces of false evidence left for his wife to see. You need to trust me that the police can't do anything. No, I should clarify that statement. The police can't do anything to help *us*. They might very well arrest me if I don't do as North asks, based on 'evidence' North charitably provides."

"Wait," I said slowly, the implication sinking in. "You're going to be an indentured servant thief for the rest of your life?"

"Of course not." He ran his hands through his hair, visibly frustrated. "This is a one-time deal. If I do one last job for him, he'll leave us both alone."

"What could he possibly do to ruin my life? I'm not a criminal, and I don't have a family to embarrass."

"If you look at the papers he handed you, you'll see what he'll do to you if I don't cooperate."

Pulling the stack of papers from my bag, I noticed that there was a stapled set of typewritten papers separate from the historical documents inside protective sleeves. It was these papers that made up the bulk of the stack North had given me.

A gust of wind threatened to steal the papers from my grasp, so I led us to a nook that provided some shelter. I sat down and looked over the peculiar assortment for a minute, confused. They were copies of the front pages of research papers I'd written, but my name wasn't on them. Not only that, the dates and sources were all wrong. In addition, notes about other people's work in my handwriting, only I didn't recall writing those notes. Taken together, the collection appeared to be my work, but attributed to other people long before I'd written it.

"This doesn't make any sense," I said. "This makes it look like I've plagiarized everything I've ever written."

"It could be worse," Lane said. "North created a trail that makes it look like you're a plagiarist, not a criminal. You won't have criminal proceedings against you, but you'll lose your position at the university. And you'll lose any credibility to be a historian anywhere."

"This will ruin my life," I said, speaking the words slowly as my confusion turned to discomfort, and above all—panic. He couldn't be serious, could he? If North hadn't created such an elaborate ruse to get me to Paris, I wouldn't have believed it. But now? Lane sensed my fear. He took my hand in his.

"With one word from North," Lane said, "your life as you know it will be over."

CHAPTER 6

"If you cooperate," I said, "how do you know he'll do what he promises and forget about these faked papers?"

"He gave his word."

I laughed bitterly. "Because of his posh British accent, you think he'll keep his word? That's a pretty stupid reason to think—"

"I'm not even sure it's his real accent."

I groaned.

"But that's not why I trust him," Lane continued. "He's a gentleman who always keeps his word."

"A guy who laughs the moment before he says he's going to destroy our lives is a *gentleman*?"

"Keeping his word is how he's amassed so much power in this business over the years. He's always done so. Always. He's both respected and feared. In a world where you don't always know what to expect, North is a constant. It's rather refreshing." He cleared his throat. "At least I used to think so. If a member of his crew holds up their end, they get paid regardless of whether the job is a success—"

"Back up," I said. "Who *is* this guy?"

"Though he's a forger and thief, his greatest skill is being a con man. It allows him to be powerful behind the scenes without getting his hands dirty, and to pull all of this off. He doesn't get involved with the most dangerous parts of a job."

"That's where people like you come in."

"Exactly. My mentor, John, always knew better. He warned me against working with him, but I was young and cocky. North is incredibly well-connected in the world of art theft. And incredibly good at convincing people to do things. He makes you feel like you're the one making the decision, when really you're doing exactly what he wants."

"Coercing you doesn't feel like that."

"He doesn't usually resort to such coercive measures. Normally he can get things done without involving outsiders." Lane paused. He closed his eyes and shook his head. "He found me through a mutual acquaintance. I met with him a little over a week ago, as a courtesy, to avoid any ill will. If I'd just done as he asked, he wouldn't have had to resort to this. He wouldn't have involved you."

"But you aren't a thief anymore."

Lane opened his eyes and looked at me as if he was looking through me. "I can't escape it. I thought I could, but—" He shook his head and broke off, looking out at the ancient city for a few moments, lost in his own thoughts.

"Nobody is sure exactly where North is from," he continued, "but he claims to be English. He appeared on the scene before I was in the game, and has continued to be a force. Unlike a lot of other thieves, he has *vision*. Not only grand ideas, but he thinks so many steps ahead of anyone I've ever known. Think having two contingency plans is good? He'll have five. But he plans so well that he rarely has to use them. Before people are contacted, the whole job is figured out with exacting precision. He knows who he wants for every single part of the plan. That's why it's so important for him to be good at convincing people to go along with what he wants them to do. He needs the exact team of people he's envisioned in place. He's smart. He knows the best way to get cooperation is to be fair and generous."

"By paying well and following through on his word."

"Only as a last resort does he use coercion. But he never uses violence."

"What is this, a Cary Grant movie?"

"He doesn't *need to* use violence, Jaya. He doesn't have to. I doubt it's for moral reasons. It's simply what makes most sense. Violence is messy. You can instill fear much more effectively through other means. Especially if you want people to continue to work with you. People were always in control of their destinies with him. But I was never really part of his network."

"I remember what you told me in Scotland." I thought back to that night in the moonlight in front of the Dunnottar Castle ruins. It felt like it was last week, not nearly six months ago. "How you started stealing to get back at your father, his rich friends, and their whole way of life."

"And everything they stood for. I never wanted to steal anything that would hurt people who didn't deserve it."

"But somehow you got caught up with North?"

"If you're any good, it's hard not to."

"And you're good," I said, my head spinning. "That's why he needs you now."

I stood up hastily, pressing the papers into Lane's hands and sucking in the cold air as I hurried to the edge of the roof. I needed to be reminded of reality. Watching tiny people going about their daily lives below reminded me that Paris was a city like any other. And like the Eiffel Tower's iconic iron peak, Notre Dame Cathedral's gargoyle-covered spires were smaller than I'd imagined. Paris was simultaneously exactly and nothing like I thought it would be. The scariest thing, I realized, was that standing high above Paris with Lane, I felt more alive than I had in months.

"Jaya, I—"

"I know we don't have much time. Let me look at the documents North asked me to authenticate."

Lane knew me well enough not to argue or try to placate me. He followed me back to our rooftop nook that shielded us from the wind, and I turned to the plastic-covered historical documents.

There were only two pages, both handwritten letters. The bottom of one was missing—ripped off. If that was North's doing, I would wring his neck.

Looking more closely, though, my anger was quickly forgotten.

The substance of the letters demanded my attention. Dated in 1793, these were letters written home by an Englishman named Trenton Smith, a clerk from the British East India Company stationed in Pondicherry, India.

I didn't recognize the name, but the date placed the letters shortly after the British retook control of the territory from the French. Control of Pondicherry ping-ponged back and forth between the British and the French for centuries, changing hands seven times between 1700 and 1954.

"How does he *get* things like this?" I asked, glancing up at Lane.

He shrugged. "North is creative. I'll give him that much credit. A lot of things he acquires legitimately, through auctions or estate sales, when he sees value in things that others miss. And a lot of other ways, too. I heard he recently acquired a hoard stolen during WWII by the Nazis."

Looking at the weather-worn letters written centuries ago, I was in my element. For a few moments, the world around me dropped away. I felt myself smiling as my fingers traced the narrow, uneven handwriting of the man telling his brother of his adventures in the southern Indian territory.

Trenton Smith was homesick. He wrote of the mechanical automatons that were all the rage back at home, and how he'd heard they were catching on in India, too, in the form of tiger and elephant automatons, some of them made of gold. I looked again at the date, 1793. He couldn't be referring to Tipu's Tiger, could he? It was around that time that the tiger automaton was commissioned by Tipu Sultan, AKA The Tiger of Mysore. His wooden automaton was famous for its macabre display of a Bengal tiger mauling an Englishman, so it made sense Trenton Smith would know of it. But as far as I knew, nobody outside Tipu's court had seen the automaton until the sultan was defeated by the British in 1799 and they divided up his treasures. How could Smith have heard of Tipu's Tiger in 1793?

Tipu was a captivating figure in part because of his fierce

hatred of the British, which caused him to form an alliance with the French to drive the British out of Mysore. I'd included him in my first lecture of the semester as an example of the complex relationships local Indian rulers had with foreign powers. In one of Tipu's characteristically colorful acts, he hired a French engineer to build his legendary wooden automaton of a tiger eating not only a man, but a man identifiable as an Englishman. With the turn of a hand crank, the tiger roared and the Englishman moved his arm in an ill-fated attempt to shield his neck from the sharp teeth of the tiger.

Shortly before the end of the torn letter, Smith began to tell his brother of the alcohol and opium available. Perhaps it wasn't North who ripped up the bottom half of the letter, after all. It might have been destroyed by a prudish family member who wanted to save only the better memories of their young relative. That would also explain his delusions of automatons made of gold. I'd never heard of such a thing existing.

Why had North wanted me to look at these? Was it a test? Or was there something else in these pages beyond the stories?

"Would these be valuable?" Lane asked, reading my face.

"To me, yes." I forced myself to pull my eyes from the letters. "To be studied as a historical document. But for monetary value? I can't imagine it would be worth more than a few thousand dollars, if that."

"I wonder if he's testing you," Lane said, "to see if you'll tell him the truth about a document relating to your expertise that he's already had appraised."

"That's what I was thinking. But in case he really needs to know if these letters are authentic, I'm certainly not going to be the one to tell him so."

"Have I mentioned how much I missed you?"

The sound of a squeaking door pulled the smile from his face.

"Thank you," an English voice said. "That's exactly what I needed to know."

A feeling of dread washed over me as North appeared in our

line of sight. Lane swore under his breath, and a smile spread across North's face.

"How did you do it?" Lane asked. "You didn't get close enough to Jaya to slip a surveillance bug into her bag. I'd have noticed."

"I didn't have to. Jaya already had the bug with her."

My mouth went dry.

"You're a smart one," North said, studying my face. "You've figured out what I'm talking about now, haven't you?"

"The invitation," I whispered, reaching into my bag and pulling out the envelope. The envelope with lining so thick it could easily disguise a small piece of electronic equipment.

I'd had the surveillance bug on me this whole time.

CHAPTER 7

"I'm afraid this particular model doesn't have much range," North said, "so I wasn't able to hear your reaction to my masterpiece when you received it in San Francisco. But here at the hotel, that's quite another story."

Lane's shoulders shook as he took shallow breaths. His jaw was clenched so tightly that I was worried he'd leap up and throttle North.

"It's quite brisk up here," North continued. "I took the liberty of getting us a private table in the restaurant below, so we can continue our conversation under more civilized surroundings. The view won't be as nice, but I'd rather you two not freeze to death before you help me with my little job."

By the time we were seated in a private room of the restaurant, Lane had regained control of himself. I think. At least his shoulders were no longer shaking.

North rested his elbows on the table. "Thank you, Jaya, for completing my little test with such precision. I had to be sure I'd judged your intelligence and your moral compass correctly, as well as your relationship with Lane. Aren't you hungry? The food here is quite good." He picked up a piece of bread from the center of the table and dipped it in olive oil and vinegar. "Mmm. The French know a thing or two about cooking, don't they?"

I stared at him, at a loss for words. I couldn't imagine eating, but I took a long drink of water. My mouth still felt dry, but somehow I managed to form a coherent sentence. "These other documents—the ones that make it look like I plagiarized all of my work. These weren't part of the test, too, were they?"

"Unfortunately not," North said. "Lane here will assure you I'm quite serious about using them. It wouldn't do to have all that evidence of your plagiarism surface at your university, would it?"

"I haven't plagiarized anything in my life," I said. "Nobody will believe they're real."

"Won't they?" North said with a warm smile that under other circumstances I would have described as charming. "Being a historian, you're a scholar of human nature. You have to put yourself into the minds of all those people in the past to figure out their stories. Think about your own. You've had quite a good run these last couple of years. *Too good*, some might say. You can't *really* be as good as people think you are, can you?"

"I'll be able to prove these are fake," I said, but my voice was less forceful now. He'd planted a seed of doubt in my mind that was already beginning to grow. He was right about human nature. People would jump at the chance to think the worst of someone who'd received public acclaim.

"Maybe you'll be able to dig yourself out eventually," North conceded with a wave of his hand, "but the damage will have been done. The shadow will follow you around forever. But I hope it won't come to that. All Lane has to do is one little favor for me, and we won't give these documents another thought."

"You don't have to do this, Lane," I said. "I'll figure something out."

"He's not bluffing, Jones. He'll destroy your life in addition to mine."

"Oh yes, Miss Jones," North said. "Don't forget that I'll destroy Lane's life, too, if he doesn't go along with this little job."

"It's little?" I asked, wondering how I could even be contemplating what would merit a "little" theft.

"To someone like The Chameleon," North said.

Lane groaned. "That's *not* my name."

"They called you *The Chameleon*?" I felt ill.

"No," Lane said emphatically.

"I tried," North said. "I really did. But it didn't stick. Lane protested too much."

"It makes me sound like a comic book character."

"But you have to admit it would be perfect if you *were* a comic book character." North chuckled. "How many languages do you speak fluently?"

Lane glared at him.

"Seven, isn't it?" I said.

He shifted his glare to me.

"Chameleon or not," I said, "you can't just *steal* something for him."

"It's the only way."

"This isn't very gentlemanly of you, North," I said. "And Lane led me to believe you were a gentleman."

"Lane owes me a favor. I'm simply choosing how he repays it."

Lane refused to meet my gaze.

"What is it he wants you to steal?" I asked.

North raised his hand. "Pick me! I can answer that question. It's simple. I'm not telling him what it is yet."

"Wait, *what*? You can't expect him to agree without—"

"This is Lane's decision, Jaya."

I stared at Lane, watching his impassive face. "But how are you supposed to prepare? If, hypothetically, you were to do it."

"North told me the *place* I'm supposed to steal from."

"Which is?"

"The world's most famous museum. The Louvre."

CHAPTER 8

"You're joking," I said. "Please tell me you're joking. He wants you to steal something from the *Louvre*? As in the huge, famous, highly-secured museum in the heart of Paris?"

"It's not *that* secure," North said calmly.

I gaped at him. "I can't believe I'm having this conversation."

"There have been many successful thefts at the Louvre, as well as other museums like it, over the years."

"Lane is *not* attempting to steal something from the Louvre."

"Don't underestimate him, Jaya," Lane said.

"I know we haven't seen each other in a while, but that doesn't mean I want you to be carted off by the police in the dead of night."

"That's not how it's done. Nighttime is a terrible idea for the Louvre."

I choked on my water.

"In 1998," Lane continued, "a Corot painting was stolen from the Louvre in broad daylight, during opening hours. It was during the one day of the month when the Louvre has free admission. It was the perfect backdrop to pull it off. With so many thousands of people in the museum, after the painting was removed from the wall, it was chaos."

"Oh, I remember that one," North said. "The entrances were blocked, and thousands of guests herded into the main entrance, under the great pyramid."

"Armed guards were called in," Lane said, picking up the story, "with the intent to search everyone. But it didn't work. They were going to have a riot on their hands. With thousands of tourists, many of whom had flights to catch that day, they had to let people go. In the mix, the thief got away, too."

"You two can't do this," I said. "You can't!"

"It's only art, Jaya," Lane said. "It's not as important as your life."

"Perhaps this will help you feel better," North said. "I've assured Lane that the piece in question isn't anything he'd object to."

"What's that supposed to mean?"

"I know all about this moral compass of his. And from what I overheard, I know you're already well aware of Lane's scruples. Lane has always had the silly little idea that stealing from rich men who keep their treasures hidden from the world is morally excusable, even honorable, whereas stealing from the people is not. Except when it inconveniences him. But this isn't Sherwood Forest. It's the real world. Things are less...black and white."

North broke off as Lane coughed.

"Forgive me," North said. "You only *used to think* such things were honorable. Now you're straight as an arrow, or so you say."

"Can't you two stop being so convoluted and tell me what you're trying to say?"

"He gave me his word," Lane said, "that the object in question is nothing of cultural significance. It's nothing the museum will even miss."

"How is that possible?"

"Like we told you, he won't tell me what it is until I agree to do the job."

"Once you're not able to back out."

"Yes, but—"

"But he's a *gentleman*, so he can't possibly be trying to trick you."

"I'm mortally offended," North said. "I'm a true gentleman."

"Then you won't stop me when I stand up and walk out of here."

"If you're planning on calling the police," North said, "don't bother. I took the liberty of creating a record of your arrests here in France for drunkenness due to psychological problems. Tsk tsk, you've been quite a naughty young woman. One message from me, and the file will be made public record."

"I've never even been to France before!"

"Computers don't lie, my dear." He smiled innocently. "Or do they?"

"I thought you said you needed our agreement," I said.

"I was attempting to be nice," North said with a devilish grin. "But I never work without a contingency plan."

"Save it," Lane said. "I told you I'm in."

"Very good," North said. "You realize I'll want to keep an eye on your girlfriend until the job is completed."

"I expected as much."

"I'm a prisoner?" I asked, feeling my throat tighten.

"Not at all, dear girl," North said. "I've added a monitoring device to your mobile phone." He pushed my phone across the table. "I wouldn't want you to be without a phone in the big city. But remember, someone will be listening. It would be easiest for everyone if you were to stay with Lane. If not, I've made arrangements for someone to accompany you. I've reserved that spacious hotel room for you for the entire week." He turned to Lane. "It's not exactly your style, I know, but that hovel of yours in the thirteenth arrondissement just won't do."

Lane coughed. He recovered quickly, but he was visibly shaken.

"Didn't know I knew about that place, old boy?" North said. "Give me some credit. I do my homework. Now if you two don't want to order any food, shall we adjourn to your hotel room?"

As soon as we reached the hotel room, the creepy man from the airport appeared. In his muscular arms, he carried two high-end pieces of luggage. He dropped the small bags by the door and departed.

Lane reached instinctively into his jacket pocket, but nothing was there. He must have been looking for a packet of cigarettes. Not good. That meant North's knowing where he was living had stressed him out more than anything that had transpired that day.

"I hope you'll find the clothes I picked out for you acceptable," North said. "If you desire anything else, I can send Dante back to get more items."

"I'm sure it's fine." Lane's voice quivered almost imperceptibly, but I heard it. It was unnerving to see someone so noticeably shaken.

"Right," North said, slapping his hands together. "I'll let you two kids get comfortable. Well, not *too* comfortable. I'd be terribly embarrassed if I accidentally saw more than I meant to. Oh, but I should mention that of course I didn't put cameras in the bathroom. Audio, though, so don't get any ideas. And don't even think about bringing anything besides yourselves and your clothing into the bathroom. Jaya, you're to leave any makeup bags here in the main room and use the mirror above the bureau. I think that covers it. I'm next door, so don't hesitate to give me a shout if you need anything."

I stared at him, openmouthed. Did he really think I was going to write secret messages to Lane in lipstick on the mirror? That wasn't actually the worst idea... "Wait," I said, "we're supposed to stay here while Lane plans this heist?"

"You're free to go wherever you wish," North said. "Someone will be there with you. Discreetly, of course."

"Of course."

"I wouldn't want to ruin any romantic dinners out in this most romantic of cities. Please feel free to explore. You seem like a lovely girl. I can see why Lane fell for you. When I thought of this way to get you to Paris, I really did hope you would enjoy the city. My research into you unearthed the fact that you had never been here."

"We're supposed to go to romantic dinners with one of your henchmen at the next table?" I said. My instincts were screaming at me, but unfortunately my instincts were yelling at each other, too.

Part of me wanted to run away and never look back, but the other part knew I would never abandon Lane and throw away my own life.

"*Henchmen?*" North looked from me to Lane. "You've kept her quite sheltered, haven't you?"

Lane gave a casual shrug, but he couldn't stop nervously fiddling with his hands. Where was the confident man I knew?

"Make the best of your time in Paris, Jaya," North continued. "I have a feeling Lane will be busy planning the acquisition with our associates for most of his time here."

"The *acquisition*," I grumbled, shaking my head. "*Associates.*"

"From the expression on Lane's face," North said, "I think you'll be ordering room service tonight rather than dining out. Feel free to order whatever you'd like. It's on me. Now that I have your unconditional agreement, I'll have the details of the acquisition delivered this evening."

With that, he slipped out.

As soon as he was gone, Lane's body language transformed. I wouldn't say he was exactly happy, but he was no longer as shaken. He caught my eye and gave me a barely noticeable wink. He was up to something. I only wished I knew what it was.

CHAPTER 9

"I need to think," Lane said. "I think best in the shower."

Of all the things I expected him to say, that wasn't in the top one thousand.

"Why don't you order some room service while I take a shower?" Not waiting for an answer, he left his glasses on a side table and picked up the weekend bag. What was he up to?

Now that North was gone, my stomach told me room service wasn't a bad idea. I was ravenous. I picked up the phone and ordered half the menu. Well, perhaps it was only a third of the menu. Smoked salmon canapés, Niçoise salad, Black Angus steak, a cheese platter, a piece of chocolate truffle cake, and a side of what I thought was probably green beans even though the translation had gone very, very wrong.

After hanging up the phone, I saw my room service order for what it was: an attempt to avoid being alone with my thoughts. For the first time since arriving in France earlier that day, I was alone. Sort of. The knowledge that I was being spied upon continued to freak me out.

I couldn't believe how much my life had changed in the space of one day. My stable life was gone. It had disappeared the moment I stepped onto that airplane.

That wasn't entirely true. I'd said goodbye to my life the previous summer, when I'd chosen a treasure hunt over finishing a research paper, and when I'd let myself get involved with Lane even when I knew what he'd been before turning his life around.

Yet *neither* of those things—my treasure hunting or my involvement with Lane—explained why North had brought me to France. Why couldn't he threaten me from afar? Not only that, but he didn't need *me* at all. Lane was the one he needed to convince to go through with this ridiculous plan. Wouldn't it have been easier for North to get Lane to do this job without me trying to convince him otherwise?

Listening to the sound of Lane moving around in the bathroom made me smile. The two of us together, I knew we'd figure it out.

The smile fell from my face. That was my answer to why North lured me to Paris. He needed to see what Lane's true feelings were, and whether he cared enough about me to go through with a risky plan if it meant preventing my life from being destroyed.

I closed my eyes and lay back on the couch, pulling a plush pillow over my face, as if that would make my troubles disappear. We'd played right into his hands. North now knew with absolute certainty that he could use me to coerce Lane, no matter how dangerous the request. If only we'd realized North's intentions sooner, we could have acted accordingly. But it was too late for that now.

It wasn't, however, too late to fight. We couldn't do so overtly, but as surely as I knew Lane was coming up with a plan, the gears in my mind were spinning, too. I wasn't going to sit back and let Lane steal from the Louvre to protect me. I didn't know what I was going to do, but I was going to get us out of this mess.

I tossed the pillow aside and sat up, grabbing my phone. I knew North was monitoring my communications, but there had to be something I could do that wouldn't arouse suspicion.

When Lane emerged from the shower fifteen minutes later, I hadn't come up with any great ideas. All I'd done was respond to emails from Tamarind, Sanjay, and my brother, telling them I'd arrived safely in Paris and that all was well. My father hadn't emailed, because I hadn't told him what I was doing. It was best that way.

Lane was fully dressed except for bare feet and no glasses. He rubbed a hand towel over his wet hair. His hair was perhaps an inch shorter than when I first met him, but it still hung long over his ears and his distinctive cheek bones. A white t-shirt clung to his damp body. He caught me looking at him and returned my look of longing. Damn those cameras.

"Food should be here shortly," I said.

"Why don't you go freshen up?" he suggested.

"I look that bad after the flight, huh?"

A series of emotions flashed across his face. "You look beautiful as always, Jones. I only meant that I know it's a long flight."

I grabbed my backpack, then remembered North's warning about not taking anything big into the bathroom. I removed a change of clothes, wondering how much longer I could live like this without going crazy.

As soon as I closed the bathroom door, I saw why Lane had feigned the need to take a shower. Written painstakingly on thin toilet paper was a note. The pen broke through the flimsy tissue in several places. It was a wonder he had time to step into the shower at all after constructing this note. I started the shower and read what he'd written.

Jones, don't worry. North didn't find my apartment. He found a place I keep as an open secret, for situations like this. I reacted as I did because I wanted him to <u>think</u> he had the upper hand and let his guard down.

Only write messages here if urgent. Otherwise an unnecessary risk. If you leave a note to say something North shouldn't hear, say the name Emma Peel in conversation. Then I'll know to come look for it.

When out, assume our tail can hear everything we say.

Flush this note once done reading.

The tissue pulled apart at my touch as I read the words. No wonder North hadn't thought this could be a way to communicate. I wished Lane had thought of a code word that would be easier to work into conversation than the name of the female spy from a 1960s British TV show, but I supposed the obscurity was the point. The code word would need to be something that wouldn't come up in normal conversation, yet it couldn't be so obscure it would arouse suspicion. In that sense, a character who made our present situation seem glamourous was a wonderful choice. *Emma Peel* was the perfect code word, and I never would have thought of anything like it. I was no good at being a spy.

I flushed the toilet twice to make sure the black ink of the marker didn't leave a trace in the porcelain toilet bowl. As I watched it circle down the drain, I felt both invigorated and let down. Lane wanted to fight the situation right along with me, but he hadn't come up with a concrete plan either.

When I stepped out of the luxurious bathroom after a quick shower that did nothing to calm my nerves, a huge spread of food sat on a table near the couch, and Lane was pouring two glasses of a smoky Scotch from the selection of full-size bottles at the mini bar.

"You remembered," I said.

"How could I forget?" He set the bottle down and looked across the room service cart at me. "I missed you. I almost got in touch. So many times."

"But you didn't, because of this."

He handed me a glass. "In spite of everything, it's good to see you. More than I can say."

"Me too."

We toasted with pathetic attempts at smiles.

"At least we can make the best of it," Lane said. "I see you've got a head start." He eyed the vast expanse of food.

"I was hungry. I didn't know what I felt like."

"Mmm hmmm," Lane murmured, taking a sip of the Scotch.

"I hate this," I said. "Talking to you like this, with that man listening."

Lane sighed, and when he spoke, the awkward stiltedness of the previous few minutes was gone. "You're right. This is stupid. I don't think North is listening. *Someone* is listening for him, to tell him about it if there's something he should know about. So we shouldn't have the most intimate of conversations, but keeping that in mind, try to forget the fact that the room is bugged. I wouldn't recommend karaoke either."

"You can't sing?"

"The opposite," he said, his eyes twinkling. "I'm so good I'm afraid North's eavesdropping associate would have no choice but to call a talent scout if he heard me sing. We don't want that kind of distraction."

With the awkwardness lifted, I felt I could finally appease my grumbling stomach. I popped a salmon canapé into my mouth.

As soon as I'd done so, a knock sounded at the door. Without looking at me, Lane walked to the door to open it, his bare feet leaving faint impressions in the lush carpet. Standing in the doorway was a man I hadn't seen before. Though I couldn't hear his voice, his perfectly pressed black slacks, razor sharp black jacket, and designer shoes suggested he was French. It wasn't only the clothes. It was the way he held himself. If North dressed in this man's clothing, he wouldn't give the same impression. But if Lane donned the same clothing, that would be another story. Picking up on subtle cultural differences and blending in was perhaps his greatest skill.

Lane didn't greet the Frenchman warmly, but gave a curt nod of recognition. They exchanged a few words, and the man handed Lane a small envelope before departing.

Lane's face darkened as he read the contents. "It's the information about the item I'm supposed to steal."

CHAPTER 10

"What does he want you to steal?" I asked, my eyes fixed on the innocuous envelope. After learning the invitation I'd received the previous week had been secretly bugged, I didn't think I'd ever look at a piece of mail the same way again.

Lane shoved two pieces of paper back inside the envelope. "The less you know, the better."

"You're not going to tell me? I'm the reason you're in this mess!"

"No, you're not, Jaya. I got into this all by myself. I'm only sorry I dragged you into it with me. I'm serious. The less you know, the better."

"You have to tell me."

"Things are a bit more...*challenging* than I anticipated." He downed the last of his drink.

I followed suit. This was not the time to savor good Scotch. I was going for its medicinal effect as a reliever of shock. "Nothing good can come of you keeping things from me," I said. "Let me help."

For a moment it looked as if he was going to object—but then he grinned at me. It was the first real happiness I'd seen that day.

"God, I missed you," he said. He took my empty glass and enveloped me in a hug. Though he looked calm on the outside, before he let me go I felt how quickly his heart was beating.

"Tell me what you're supposed to do," I said.

"I'll do better than that. Grab your shoes."

"Where are we going?"

"To the Louvre."

"It's almost eight o'clock at night. And we've barely touched our food."

"It's open twice a week in the evening."

"You're not going to—"

"No, I'm not going to steal anything tonight. I haven't visited lately. I want to get the lay of the land."

The phone on the side table rang. Lane picked it up. He listened for a moment then held the phone to his chest.

"Would you like to walk or have a car pick us up?" he asked.

"If this weren't super-creepy," I said, "I could get used to this."

"You want the car?"

"How far is it?"

"Twenty minutes on foot. Maybe half an hour."

"I've been sitting for over ten hours. Let's walk."

The waterfront walk was beautiful. It was a chilly evening, but the night sky was clear. The moon even cooperated, providing a romantic, moonlit walk along the Seine. I glanced over my shoulder. The stylishly-dressed Frenchman who'd brought Lane the envelope was a few yards behind us, ruining the mood. I tucked up the collar of my coat and nearly tripped on a cobblestone. Lane took my hand to steady me.

"How come you've never been to Paris before?" he asked.

"Why does everyone keep asking me that?"

We walked in silence for several minutes, hand in hand. It was past evening rush hour, and cars whizzed past us only sporadically. Lane pulled me away from the river and we crossed the street.

"This is the start of the Louvre complex," he said.

"Really?" I paused in front of the thick stone walls, surprised at Lane's statement. The sprawling, connected buildings in front of us looked more like a royal estate in the countryside, not a museum in the center of Paris.

"Wait until we get to the courtyard."

As we stepped through a stone arch, the famous pyramid I'd seen in pictures came into view. The modern steel and glass structure emerged from the ground and gave light to the subterranean ticket lobby. Smaller pyramids flanked the big one. It was after sunset and the courtyard was bathed in light from the buildings and old fashioned streetlights.

Before reaching the indoor ticket booths, there was a security checkpoint visitors had to pass through to enter the museum. Beyond the security station and the lobby's ticket booths were four different entrances to choose from, each leading to a different wing. We checked our coats, then Lane led the way to the Richelieu wing, our shadow following.

"Can we stop by the painting with the haunted chandelier?" a voice from behind us asked in a faint French accent.

Lane turned and raised an eyebrow.

"We all know I'm here," the man said. "I might as well have the opportunity to see this painting I like."

"Sure," Lane said, stifling a laugh. "Why not? I want to go through the whole museum anyway. We're tourists, after all."

I found myself straggling behind the two men as Lane led us through several rooms full of priceless paintings and sculptures. Beautiful, powerful works of art I'd seen in textbooks or online, all right here in front of me. There were also plenty of plainer objects that must have had fascinating histories attached to them. We paused briefly as we passed through a section of antique desks that were far from ornate. Were they desks of famous painters? I began reading the placard next to a particularly ordinary desk that had once been used for decorating illuminated manuscripts. Before I could learn more, Lane said we had to keep moving. I tried to keep up, but as we moved through another section, I fell behind.

"Jaya," Lane said. "What are you doing?"

"That's Winged Victory," I said, gaping in front of the headless sculpture. It was bigger than I'd imagined it would be.

"*Regardez*," North's associate said. But he wasn't pointing at the sculpture. He was making shadow puppets on the wall that mimicked the wings of the masterpiece.

"We'll be coming back," Lane said, rolling his eyes at both of us. "The museum is only open for another hour tonight."

I trotted after the two men. When we reached a grand room of oil paintings depicting gruesome mythological scenes, they slowed down, stopping in front of a small Expressionist painting dwarfed by the larger pieces in the room.

"Where are all the people?" I asked. "I thought the Louvre was a crowded museum."

"It usually is," our handler said. "But not as much in the evening."

"He's right," Lane said. "At eleven o'clock in the morning you don't want to be here. It's wall-to-wall people, including tour groups who stop moving in the most inconvenient places to listen to their guides."

"*That's* when you want me to look at the art I want to see?"

"Marius, I don't suppose you'd let Jaya look around on her own? No? I didn't think so. Sorry, Jones."

So that was his name. Under the circumstances, it had seemed strange to enquire.

"*Merde*," Marius muttered.

"I was only joking," Lane said. "Where's your usual sense of humor?"

"Not that." Marius tilted his head toward a man who was approaching us.

"Hugo?" Lane said.

A wide-eyed, spectacled man walked toward us. When he came within a few yards of us, he nearly dropped the fedora he held in his hands.

"*Je suis désolé*," the newcomer said, his eyes darting between the three of us.

"Hugo," Marius said, his voice clipped. "What do you think you're—"

"I did not see you there, Marius." The man's voice shook, and his stance indicated he might turn and run at any moment. If this was one of Lane's "associates," he was clearly in the wrong business.

"Hugo must have confused the dates his services are required," Marius said, shaking his head and keeping his eyes on Hugo. "There's to be no discussion of future assignments until North has completed this current job."

"I merely wished to visit an old friend," Hugo said, holding up his hands in a placating gesture. "There is no misunderstanding."

Lane was the only one of the three men who appeared calm. "It's good to see you, my friend." He shook Hugo's hand. The juxtaposition between them was striking. Though they both had fair hair and looked around the same age, Hugo wasn't much taller than I was, and he might have been even skinnier. I wondered if he was the little guy they used to fit through tiny windows.

"This is Jaya," Lane continued, ignoring a sharp glare from Marius. "Jaya, Hugo."

"*Enchanté*," Hugo said. He gave me a warm smile and shook my hand. Unlike Lane's other associates, I liked Hugo immediately. It's a funny thing how people make snap judgments about one another. As surely as I'd known I didn't want to go with the unpleasant man at the airport who North had sent to pick me up, I knew if this had been the right time and place, I'd want to be friends with Hugo. It wasn't only because he was a fellow tiny person. It was the genuine warmth in his eyes.

I felt all eyes on me and Hugo, including those in the Old Masters portraits surrounding us. Silence hung in the nearly empty gallery.

Hugo broke the silence. "*Je suis désolé, mes amis.* I should not have come."

"How did you find us?" Lane asked.

"You changed your phone and email, my friend," Hugo said. "This is the third time I've visited to the Louvre this week. I knew you would come."

Marius responded to Hugo in French. Three days of intensive

French lessons weren't enough to understand their terse words, but the intonation made it clear Marius was angry. Hugo spoke a few words in French, before switching back to English as he turned to me.

"I have decided to retire, you see," Hugo said. "I merely wished to see my old friend Lane before I did."

Marius crossed his arms. "Go ahead. Say your farewells."

"You'll be leaving Paris?" Lane asked.

"Perhaps," Hugo said, glancing nervously at Marius before turning back to Lane. "I love my flat on Rue Sainte-Croix de la Bretonnerie. I would miss the way the light falls on my statue of Michelangelo's *Angel* in the window if I were to leave." He had to be talking about a replica, didn't he? "But when one wishes to cut ties..." He shrugged, causing his wire-rimmed glasses to slip down his slight nose.

"I plan to leave Paris very soon," Lane said. "Otherwise I'd suggest we meet in a few days. But as things are—"

"Of course, of course."

While Hugo and Lane spoke for several minutes, with Marius watching them, I looked around at the paintings in the room. Lane had led us through much of the museum, but he hadn't told me what it was he was supposed to steal. I turned back to the men. They hadn't moved from their spot in front of the tiny Expressionist painting. Was there a reason they lingered in front of that particular painting?

"Don't go far," Marius called after me as I stepped away from them to look more closely at the masterful art encircling us.

Why were Lane and Hugo going through the charade of saying stilted farewells with Marius looking on? I froze. Marius wasn't only watching. He was *listening*. Hugo had gone through a lot of effort to find Lane, and he'd been so nervous when he realized Marius was there. There was something Hugo wanted to tell Lane. And with us under surveillance, he had no way to tell him.

CHAPTER 11

After our unsettling encounter with Hugo, the mood shifted for the remaining time at the museum. Lane, Marius, and I walked silently through the nearly empty rooms, the sound of my heels clicking on the marble floors echoing around us.

When we left, a car was waiting for us on the street outside the courtyard. Dante, the driver from the airport who'd also dropped off Lane's bag of clothes, was behind the wheel. The black SUV was larger than most of the cars on the streets of Paris, but I was glad for the space as Lane, Marius, and I climbed into the back seat. Marius sat in the middle. In spite of the cold, I wished we were walking.

"It was one of the paintings in the room where Hugo found us," I said, "wasn't it?"

Marius shot Lane a pointed look.

"North didn't say anything about keeping secrets from me," I said.

Marius sighed. "You two interrupted my dinner for this excursion. I know a superb place not far—"

"We're not hungry," Lane said.

"I wasn't asking for your input," Marius said.

"I, for one, am starving," I said. "I *still* haven't eaten."

"As the lady says," Marius said. "Dante, change of plans. Take us to my favorite bistro."

Dante nodded from the driver's seat. He changed course abruptly, causing me to knock into Marius as he made a u-turn onto a bridge.

A few minutes later, Dante dropped us off at a hole-in-the-wall restaurant in an alley barely big enough for a single car to slip through. Stepping out of the SUV, we were greeted by the sound of a pumping drum beat from a nightclub next door. As soon as we stepped through the ivy-lined doorway of the narrow restaurant, the thumping sound fell away. Small candle-lit tables lined the brick walls, a formally-dressed waiter effortlessly maneuvering through the aisle with a tray of wine and bread.

A pretty hostess greeted Marius warmly with air-kisses next to his cheeks, and led us to the farthest table in the half-full bistro. A rainbow of wax drippings covered the wine bottle that served as a candle holder. The candle flickered as we sat down.

"Listen," I said, "I'm already in, so why not let me help?"

"First," Marius said, "we order food and wine. I realize you're an American, but this is a civilized country."

Over a bottle of Burgundy and plates of stroganoff, Marius regaled us with stories from the novel he was writing, a humorous tale of the life of a charming French thief. "It is based on my life, you see," he said. "Therefore I must write under an assumed name, since it will become a bestseller."

"Won't the publisher need to know your true identity?" Lane said. "Seems awfully risky."

Marius frowned at him. "What is the American expression? You are a *buzz kill*?"

"What about this particular job?" I said, getting the conversation back on track. "Will it go in your book?"

Marius shrugged.

"You were right about the painting you asked about, Jaya," Lane said. "That's the item that's involved."

After the briefest hesitation, Marius nodded for Lane to continue.

"We'll be taking it," Lane said, "and then putting it back."

"You mean you're taking it and replacing it with a forgery?" I asked, feeling my cheeks flushing with anger. How could Lane think that giving a forgery to the Louvre was acceptable?

Lane shook his head. "We're not stealing the painting. We just need to borrow it."

"But they'll notice it's gone," I said.

"Will they?" Marius asked, smiling as he cut his food into delicate bites.

I stared at them. "You're after something hidden behind the painting's canvas. That's it, isn't it?"

"Jaya," Lane said, "please don't insist upon knowing all the details."

"Exactly," Marius said. "That's enough talk about business. Now about my book—"

The awkwardness of knowing your room is bugged doesn't fade. At least not within a day. I slept far away from Lane that night, and it took me ages to fall asleep.

In the morning, I found a note in plain sight.

Had to go out to get some things together. Marius is with me. Dante will go with you if you want to go anywhere.

Did Lane really think I was going to go sightseeing while he was off planning a heist? A heist that *wasn't* a heist. Dammit, I hated that I was such a sound sleeper.

I grabbed my cell phone and checked for email and text messages. Which, of course, I now knew North was reading as well. I threw the phone onto the couch.

I flipped on the TV, expecting to find everything in French. Besides news channels in multiple languages, it was.

A strange feeling snuck up on me as I stared at the television, hitting me with full force. I was homesick.

It was a strange sensation, and not one I was used to experiencing. I'm used to feeling like I don't fit in. My dad is an American who went to India to find himself, and he stayed on after he met my mom. I spent the first seven years of my life in Goa. After my mom died, my dad moved my brother and me to Berkeley. I'm used to being asked "where I'm from" in both places I'm from.

Lane had grown up overseas after spending the early part of his childhood in the Midwest. That experience of being uprooted at a young age and never quite fitting in is one of the things we had in common. But this situation was different. I was in a country and a situation that were both truly foreign to me. I didn't speak the language, I was being coerced into going along with a frightful plan, and my sort-of boyfriend was out in Paris without me, planning the art heist we'd been forced to go along with. I'd say I had a right to feel homesick.

I found my phone between the couch cushions and pulled up Sanjay's number. An illustrated poster from one of his "Hindi Houdini" magic tours popped up on the screen. I felt immediately better looking at the silhouette of Sanjay in a bowler hat, his arms raised as he conjured a fierce Kathakali dancer. The illustration was in the classic style of the magic posters of the early 1900s, where magicians like Thurston and Kellar were drawn with apparitions of ghosts and devils swirling around them.

I stopped myself before hitting the button to call Sanjay. Not just because it was the middle of the night in San Francisco, but because I couldn't tell him anything that was going on.

Then it hit me. Even though I couldn't get help through conventional means without being found out, I knew how to communicate with Sanjay in an unconventional way. Sanjay had taught me how to read minds when I helped him with a magic show. It wasn't actually reading minds, but that was the trick. It was knowing how to communicate with your accomplice in a secret way that the audience didn't understand. This time, instead of the crowd of a theater, North was my audience.

Since North would be reading everything I typed onto my phone, I could use that to my advantage. My plan wasn't to ask Sanjay to call the police. I could have done that myself, but unfortunately Lane was right that it would be a terrible idea. My idea in contacting Sanjay was to find out if I could communicate with him like this, in case there was an opportunity in which sending a coded message would help.

Sanjay had a magician friend in France, so I decided that's what I'd ask him about. The email I composed used the principles of the mind reading trick, in which we could either use coded words that meant other words, or signal different letters of the alphabet, for more complex messages. I had to do the latter in this case.

I constructed a short email telling him on the surface that the France trip was a bust—but that underneath was asking the question of what his magician friend's name was, and if he'd be someone I should be interested in visiting while in France.

The trickier part was thinking of how to signal to Sanjay that he should read the email as a coded message in the first place.

I lay back on the brocade couch and stared at the ceiling, pretending to be frustrated that I couldn't email with my friend openly—which was easy, since I wasn't pretending. I couldn't see any surveillance cameras, which made them all the more creepy. North's tiny cameras could be anywhere.

Focus, Jaya. The last time Sanjay and I had done the mind-reading illusion together was at the Folsom Street Theatre. I hoped that would be a big enough signal. I sat up and finished the email, smiling as I typed the last line: "I hope your current show is going as well as our show at the Folsom Street Theatre." The show had been a disaster, and he knew I would never say anything otherwise.

Sanjay loved puzzles, so he would easily believe that if I was bored, I would make the effort of writing him emails in code, just because.

While I waited to hear back from him, I ordered room service: a full French breakfast of coffee, croissants, bread, jam, butter. When it arrived, I was disappointed by how small each of the items was, but then I took a bite of a croissant. I don't know what they put in the croissants in France, but the sensation of them melting in my mouth stimulated my senses almost enough to make me forget how apprehensive I was.

By the time I'd polished off the last fluffy croissant dipped in black cherry jam, Sanjay had already emailed me back.

Sorry everything blows. Anyway, sadly this illusion eludes new assistant. Really, everyone needs a usable distraction. (How hard is that? That's the whole point of a magician's assistant! Do I ask too much???) Nevermind about new trick.

Endearingly,
Sanjay

I smiled to myself. There was no way Sanjay would have written such an awkward email if it wasn't a code. Bad grammar, using the word "trick" to describe one of his illusions, and a clunky sign-off. The parenthetical part of the message was his real voice, so I knew to omit that part of the message when I decoded it.

I wished I could have written out the message on a notepad to more easily decode it, but the cameras were watching. I read the email slowly, reading it for what it truly meant.

Sorry
everything
blows.
Anyway,
sadly
this
illusion
eludes
new-assistant.
Really,
everyone
needs
a
usable
distraction.
Nevermind
about
new
trick.

Endearingly,
Sanjay

Sébastien Renaud. Nantes.

The name of a man and a city in France. The code had worked. I now had a way to communicate with the outside world that only I knew about.

CHAPTER 12

I was simultaneously giddy and disappointed. My code had worked! Maybe being a magician was cooler than I thought.

But...my efforts hadn't led to anything I could use. I didn't have anything to ask Sanjay in code that would help me out of the situation I was stuck in.

Even if I could convey to Sanjay the gravity of the situation, what could he do? If he sent the police, that would be an even bigger disaster than the mess I was already in. North and his associates had distanced themselves from the crime, leaving Lane to take the fall. And even if Sanjay's French friend could help me in some way, he wasn't in Paris.

What I needed was a run to help me think. I usually went for a run in Golden Gate Park nearly every day, and I'd packed my running shoes. I wondered if my shadow would be able to keep up with me. I could probably lose him, but I'd already established that was a bad idea.

I flung myself back down on the couch—and immediately shot up again. I had too much adrenaline coursing through me to sit still. I went to the side table where the hotel had provided bountiful information about Paris. Locating a map of the city, I looked in the street index. Finding the street I was after, I smiled to myself. Normally I would have found it frustrating to find my way in a new city where the names of streets changed every few blocks, but in this situation, it was a stroke of luck. The street I was after was only three blocks long.

I closed the map and thought about m_ by my success at conversing with Sanjay in \\ something with more immediate results.

Creepy Dante was the man assigned to wa\\ hotel. He didn't seem to be the brightest of mei _ght Lane was the bigger risk. Sometimes it wa\\ _e to be underestimated.

"Dante!" I called out to the ceiling. "I'd like to go out!"

Less than a minute later, the hotel room door opened and an unsmiling Dante walked in.

"I'd like to go on a walk," I said.

I wouldn't have been surprised if he grunted his answer, but he simply nodded.

The weather forecast predicted it might snow, so we bundled in coats before setting out for a walk under the stormy sky. I flipped up the collar of my thick black coat as the doorman held the door open for us.

"I heard that Rue Sainte-Croix de la Bretonnerie is beautiful," I said. "Do you know how to get there?"

"In the Marais," he said, his breath visible in the crisp air. "That's a long walk from here."

I realized I hadn't heard him speak before. He spoke with an Italian accent. More importantly, his voice was strong. That gave me pause. Perhaps I'd misjudged Dante. I'd assumed he was hired for his brawn rather than intellect, but perhaps he was simply the silent type. If so, dare I risk the real reason for my walk to Rue Sainte-Croix de la Bretonnerie?

"Good," I said, after only a moment's hesitation. "I need some exercise."

He eyed me with disdain as he pulled gloves on. "Let's take a taxi."

"What's the point of a walk if it's not a walk?" I said.

He muttered something under his breath that I guessed to be an Italian swear word, then glanced right and left. "This way."

Even under gray skies and the strangest of situations, Paris

...y breath away with its beauty. No wonder nobody could believe I'd never previously visited the city. Modern shops and apartments were housed in stunning old buildings, many of which I'm sure had been there for centuries.

I wondered if it was my heightened alertness that brought out an added appreciation to the details of my surroundings. The threat of danger created a more acute experience of living. I wasn't merely walking down a street lined with cafes full of people drinking coffee, smoking, and speaking various languages under heat lamps. Instead, I breathed in the scents of the swirling cigarette smoke from a group of Spaniards drinking espresso, the fragrant ham-and-cheese baguettes toasting under the watchful eye of a café's chef, and the subtle perfumes of French women walking purposefully down the street in stiletto heels higher than my own. I noticed routes I could use to escape, if the need should occur, down a narrow alley bracketed by colorful apartment buildings, across a nearly-hidden courtyard with shadows cast by arches and barren trees, and through a heavy gate for delivery vehicles that stood ajar.

The thirty-minute walk helped me relax—until I saw a sign indicating we had entered the Marais neighborhood. The purpose of this visit wasn't to see a pretty street, as I'd told Dante. I was fairly confident Hugo had wanted to tell Lane something he wasn't able to while Marius was there. He mentioned the street he lived on, as well as a piece of art in the window. It had struck me as an odd thing to say at the time—but not if he wanted Lane to find him.

There was no way for Lane to seek out Hugo while he was with Marius, but I was hoping the details of the museum conversation hadn't reached Dante. So far, that seemed to be the case. Dante hadn't raised an objection when I mentioned the street name.

"Americans," Dante mumbled, looking around at the apartment buildings on Rue Sainte-Croix de la Bretonnerie that must have been over a hundred years old. "If you want *real* history, you should visit Rome."

We walked slowly down the street, which was lined with shops on the ground floor and apartments above. If Hugo had indeed been trying to tell us where he lived, his window must be visible from the street. Dante startled me by grabbing my arm. I tensed. Had it finally dawned on him what I was doing? He shook his head, and pointed resolutely at a ladder propped against a building, steering me away from it, so neither of us would walk underneath it. It was difficult to conceal a smile.

Two blocks in, I stopped abruptly. A statue with angel wings was silhouetted in a second floor window. It was Michelangelo's *Angel* statue, and I was relieved to see it was a reproduction. I'm not an expert on art, but it was much too small to be real. This had to be Hugo's apartment.

"Must you walk so slowly?" Dante asked, rubbing his gloved hands together. I was full of too much adrenaline to mind the cold.

"Since we're here," I said, "I thought we might visit Hugo. He seemed like such an interesting man when I met him yesterday."

His brown eyes narrowed as realization dawned on him. "Hugo?"

"That's who told me this was a beautiful street worth visiting," I said, hoping my voice wasn't shaking along with my pounding heart.

Dante shrugged. "As long as he has the heat on in his apartment."

A thick blue door to the apartments was nestled in between a small general market and a pastry shop. Dante rang Hugo's buzzer in front of the building, then scowled at me as we waited. "He's not home."

"Try again."

Dante did as I asked, then shook his head. "We take a taxi back."

He started walking in the direction of a larger street, presumably to find that taxi. I stood still. I'd come this far. I couldn't give up so easily. I spotted a green trash bin on wheels underneath an awning of the next building over. I ran up to it.

"Hey!" Dante called out, running after me.

"I'm not going anywhere," I said as I pulled the heavy trash bin underneath Hugo's window. "I want to get a better look inside. Maybe his buzzer is broken." Hugo had said he'd be home, hadn't he? Unless I'd read too much into his words... "Help me up onto this trash can."

"Americans," Dante grumbled again, but did as I asked without question, steadying me as my heel sank into the plastic.

Balancing on the trash bin several feet off the ground didn't lift me high enough to see directly into the window—but the little I saw made me lose my balance.

Dante grunted as I fell into his arms. As I struggled to stand up, I dislodged the contents of his coat pocket. A piece of chocolate wrapped in wax paper, several euros in large denominations, and colorful receipts from a tailor in Paris and an artisan chocolatier in Saint-Malo all fluttered to the sidewalk.

"We need to call the police," I said, not trying to disguise my shaking voice.

Dante grabbed my forearms forcefully, a coldness in his eyes that scared me more than what I'd just seen. "No police. Why do you want them?"

"The angel's wing," I whispered. "It's covered in blood."

CHAPTER 13

Dante wouldn't let me call the police.

He hoisted himself onto the trash can to see for himself. The lid sagged under his weight, and crumpled newspapers poked out from the strained edges. A nearby proprietor yelled at him. The incomprehensible words Dante said back to him caused the man to retreat into his shop.

He hopped down and grabbed my arm, pulling me along until we'd turned down two side streets and reached a more crowded main drag. I tripped several times, and would have fallen if Dante hadn't maintained his firm grip on me. I barely saw the street in front of me. All I could think about was what must have transpired to leave the swath of blood on the statue. Was Hugo lying dead on the floor beyond my field of view?

"Stay there," Dante said, shoving me against a recessed nook next to an apartment complex door.

The tiny cars on the busy street and well-dressed people on the bustling sidewalk seemed to go past me in slow motion. I watched Dante pull out his phone and bark angry French words. I heard my name and Hugo's, but didn't understand much else. He glared at me as he clicked off the phone.

"We wait here," Dante said, motioning to one of Paris's ubiquitous cafes only a few yards away.

Mutely, I let Dante take my arm and guide me to a small table under a heat lamp. Should I scream and have Dante arrested? That way I could call the police. What if Hugo wasn't dead, but dying?

I opened my mouth, but no sound came out. It gave me a

moment to think. North said he'd created a file on me for drunk and disorderly conduct in France. Could he really do that? Even if I risked going to the police, would they believe me?

"Drink," Dante said, holding a glass of wine under my nose.

"What if he's—"

"We aren't monsters." Dante shook his head sadly, and I saw the first trace of humanity in him I'd noticed. "North will go to the apartment. If Hugo is injured, he'll help."

The change in Dante's tone was so unexpected that I found myself believing him. A moment later, he went back to glaring at me. He continued to glare at me for the next fifteen minutes, until North stepped out of a taxi. Instead of sitting down with us, he motioned for us to join him in the taxi.

I thought North would be angry about my trying to talk with Hugo, but I was wrong. His face showed concern, but I saw no trace of anger as I eased into the seat next to him. "He wasn't there," North said quietly. He was no longer enjoying himself. The laugh lines on his face were now lines of misery. Was he upset to learn that something had happened to Hugo? Or did he regret what he'd have to do to me after I'd attempted to contact Hugo?

We rode back to the hotel in silence, my spirit broken.

When we opened the door of the hotel room, Lane rushed across the room. "You're okay?"

"Physically. But what's—"

He pulled me into his arms, cradling my head in his hand and pulling me close to his chest. "I'm so sorry, Jones."

I broke away. "You know what's going on?"

"North called me from Hugo's apartment to tell me Hugo was *missing*. He wanted to know if I had any idea what had happened to him."

"He *is* missing," North said. "Jaya's imagination is a bit overactive."

"I know what I saw," I said.

"I'm not denying there was blood on that statue of his. But not enough to suggest severe bodily harm. My guess is that someone roughed him up, and he fled. Not everyone in our business is as civilized as I." North paused and whispered into Dante's ear, sending his lackey scurrying away, then walked straight to the bar and opened a bottle of Scotch. He poured himself three fingers of whisky.

"I could use one of those."

North gave me a weak smile. "Quite." He splashed amber liquid into a glass. Before he handed the glass to me, he appraised my wind-swept hair. "Explain to me," he said slowly, "how you came to be at Hugo's apartment."

"Does it matter?" Lane cut in.

"I'll be the judge of that."

My heart thudded in my chest. "When we met at the Louvre, he seemed like such a nice man." I forced myself to stand casually, not wringing my hands together as my instincts pushed me to do. "I'm homesick. Lane was off preparing, and I was lonely." I shrugged. "Since Hugo told us where he was living—"

"He did?" North cut in.

"You can ask Marius if you don't believe her," Lane said.

North pursed his lips together. He took a long drink from his glass, then sighed heavily. "I don't want anything bad to happen to Hugo any more than you do."

Lane snorted.

"You think I would harm him?"

"If you needed to."

I sank down into the chaise lounge in front of the window, wishing it would swallow me up and transport me anywhere else. As I listened to the men fight, I watched as a light snow began to fall. The snowflakes weren't yet sticking to the ground, but they fluttered by the window in a scattered blur that seemed to understand my thoughts. The image of the beautiful Angel sculpture smeared with blood was an image for nightmares. I took a large gulp of the whisky, swallowing nearly half of what was in the glass. If it hadn't been so smooth, I would have coughed. Instead, smoky warmth filled my throat.

"There's nothing to suggest he's anything more than roughed up," North said.

"Then why isn't he answering his phone?"

"You of all people know the smartest thing to do when someone is after you is to turn off your phone."

"Hugo wouldn't get involved with that sort of people," Lane said. "His religious conscience wouldn't stand for it."

"Religious conscience?" I asked.

"He used to be a priest," Lane said. He moved to pour himself a drink. "He's a religious iconography expert, which comes in handy with artwork. That's how he got involved with North."

A priest? I took another gulp of whisky.

"He couldn't stand the gulf between rich and poor," Lane continued. "He felt he couldn't do enough to save the world in a small parish. He was a radical trapped behind a collar, so he quit."

"What, to join your little Robin Hood gang?" I asked.

"I didn't say he was *good* at being a priest."

I groaned and drank more whisky.

"I don't know what else he was involved in," North said, "but *that* must have been what led to his disappearance. I've always been respectful of the people I work with."

"How is what you're doing to Lane respectful?" I asked. The whisky was loosening my tongue more than was wise. Lane gave me a sharp look and took the nearly empty glass from my hand. I didn't stop him.

"This situation is different," North said. "I never coerced Hugo. There had to be a good reason for him to cross someone." He spoke as if he was trying to convince himself as much as me and Lane.

North didn't look like he was faking his emotions, but I knew I shouldn't believe what I saw. He was a con man. It's what he did.

"The job goes on as planned," North said, regaining his composure.

"We can't—" Lane began.

"We don't need Hugo. He had nothing to do with this job."

"That's not what I meant," Lane said. "I need more time."

"Too bad you don't have it."

"You want this to work, don't you?"

"The job," North said, enunciating the words, "goes on as planned. *Tomorrow.*"

Lane downed the last of his drink. His hand clutched the glass so firmly I wouldn't have been surprised to see it shatter. "I don't have a choice, do I?"

North cleared this throat. "Marius and Dante are at your disposal."

"I've never understood why you've favored Dante over Hugo for so long," Lane said.

"You *know* why."

"That was a long time ago—"

North cleared his throat. "I need to attend to some things. In case anything untoward *has* befallen Hugo, I want to make sure his family is safe and taken care of."

"He has a family?" I asked.

"A sister. He supports her. Whatever is going on, I'll make sure she's well cared for."

I sank onto the couch.

"Can we have some privacy?" Lane asked sharply. "You'll still be able to hear whatever we say. But you can see she's upset. Your being here isn't helping anyone."

Without another word, North departed.

Lane sat down on the couch next to me. He pulled me toward him and kissed the top of my head. "Are you going to be all right, Jones?"

I nodded.

"After this awful day," he said, "I wish there was an episode of *The Avengers* on TV. I could go for some Emma Peel to relax." He stood up and went into the bathroom.

As we'd planned, that meant he was leaving me a note. With

everything going on, I didn't want it to appear suspicious for me to go into the bathroom right after Lane returned. But if I was crying, I'd need to wash my face. I forced myself to cry. It wasn't difficult.

When Lane emerged a minute later, my face was blotchy. "I need to wash my face." I pushed past Lane on my way to the bathroom.

This tissue note was broken in so many places it was difficult to read.

No more notes after you flush this. It's not worth the risk. I misjudged North.

This job just got a whole lot more dangerous. Hugo might be dead—murdered by North.

CHAPTER 14

I grabbed the edge of the porcelain sink and took several deep breaths. This wasn't how this was supposed to go. Nothing important was supposed to be stolen. And nobody was supposed to get hurt.

Hugo was either roughed up and on the run, or dead. North wasn't supposed to use violence. Even if Hugo gave North a reason to kill him, wouldn't North have destroyed his life instead? Unless...What if Hugo didn't *care* about his life being destroyed? Then North wouldn't have a hold over him. Hugo wanted to tell something to Lane. That's why he had to be stopped.

I gripped the sink even more firmly, trying to convince myself that my life wasn't spinning out of control. Right now it felt like the room itself was spinning. I'd always thought that was such a silly expression, but at that moment I couldn't deny the unsteadiness of my legs and how the walls felt like they were coming closer and stifling me.

I splashed water on my face and flushed the toilet paper note. I watched it spinning down the drain along with my life.

Once I'd gotten a hold of myself, I returned to the room. I found Lane pacing, looking like he was going to punch a hole through the wall.

"I need to get out of here," Lane said. "Want to go on a walk?"

"It's snowing."

"Not too badly yet, but we can catch a cab if you want. I need to look at one more thing at the museum today."

"Let's walk. I think the fresh air will be good for me."

As we walked to the Louvre, Lane bummed a cigarette off Marius. Not a good sign. He only smoked when he was stressed and needed to think. I doubted Marius would notice such a detail, so it wasn't for show. Lane wasn't faking that he was rattled.

Marius nearly lost us when he stopped to cup his hands and light another cigarette for himself, but he knew where we were going, so he easily caught up. Our shadow was only a formality at this point anyway. It was the mental coercion that was holding us to the plan. If Lane wanted to flee, I had no doubt that he would have managed for us to be on the other side of the world by now.

In spite of the light snow, the inner courtyard of the Louvre was packed with two lines that snaked slowly toward the entrance. Pre-paid tickets allowed us to wait in the shorter line, which still took over ten minutes. A little snow wasn't deterring Saturday afternoon tourists.

I pulled off my wet coat as we rode the escalator down into the lobby. The inside of the Louvre was even more packed than the outside lines suggested. At the sight of the heavy crowd, Lane's shoulders relaxed.

"This is more like it," he said. "Let's go."

We maneuvered through the crowds, Marius close beside us. Methodically, Lane led us through the four wings of the museum. We passed by priceless paintings, sculptures, and artifacts, but I couldn't focus on any of them.

"You don't have to keep things from me," I snapped as we entered the last wing. "Remember you two already told me which painting was important."

Lane's eyes drew together in confusion. "You think I'm leading you around to confuse you? Patience, Jones."

"If you haven't noticed, I don't have any left."

Marius laughed. "She's great, eh?"

Lane glanced at his watch. "Almost done."

After we'd walked through the last room in the top floor of the Sully wing, Lane led us back to the main lobby, where we'd be able to exit through the glass pyramid.

We caught a taxi back to the hotel, and Marius left us alone in our room. Lane sat down at the desk and opened a laptop computer.

"Let me help," I said.

"I'm glad to see you're willing to throw yourself into this project as wholeheartedly as you do everything else," he said. "But in this case, we're covered. It's a three-man job to borrow the painting. One technology man to circumvent security, one actor to play the role of a museum guard, and one generalist to supply a painting-size box."

"It can't be that easy. What are you going to do with the painting?"

"North was telling the truth. It's not morally objectionable."

"Then why won't you tell me what it is you're doing?"

Lane closed the computer and walked up to me, taking my hands in his. "The reason I'm doing this," he said slowly, "is so he won't ruin both of our lives. The more involved you are, the harder it will be for you to step away once this is over."

"You think I'll decide I want a life of crime?"

"By getting you mixed up with these men, I've already pulled you into this world more than I ever wanted to. Lives have a way of getting away from us when we're not looking. I want to keep you away from this as much as I can. Will you let me do that?"

"Would it make any difference if I said no?"

"Don't say no."

Lane was up for most of the night preparing. Between my apprehension and my curiosity, I don't know how I managed to fall asleep, but I managed to sleep for a few hours. When I woke up before dawn, Lane was standing at the window. He turned when he heard me sit up.

"I'm glad you're up," he said. "I have to go out to finish preparing."

"Did you get any sleep?"

He ran a hand through his hair and looked back out the window. "The important thing is that it's not snowing."

"Why is that important?"

A knock sounded on the door to the hotel room. Marius popped his head in without bothering to wait.

"We'll be back soon," Lane said to me.

There was no way I was getting back to sleep, so I got up and took a shower. Even in the opulent hotel, the Parisian shower was small and only half shielded by a glass door. The hot water didn't help me relax.

As I dressed in the last of my clean clothes, I heard a voice in the hotel room, and found North waiting for me on the sofa. Dressed in a tailored gray suit, he was speaking on a cell phone with the newspaper spread out in front of him. When he saw me, he gave me a friendly nod. I couldn't imagine him killing someone, but looks can be deceiving.

I had to get my feelings under control. I couldn't show fear. I couldn't. Not if I wanted to get out of this.

While North finished his phone conversation, I gathered my dirty laundry. "I need some laundry done," I said as soon as he hung up, dropping my clothes in a pile at North's feet.

"Good morning to you, too."

"How can you sit there so calmly like that? Shouldn't you be helping? At the very least, aren't you nervous?"

"I wouldn't be very good at what I do if I got nervous, would I? And who says I'm not helping?" He walked over to the room's phone and called the front desk. After hanging up, he said, "You'll have your clothes in a few hours. Care to join me for breakfast?"

"Is that a question?"

"I'm trying to be polite. But you're right, I've already ordered."

My wet hair dripped onto my neck. I rubbed the water droplets away with my hand.

"Better dry your hair," he said. "It's cold out there today."

I slammed the bathroom door before picking up the hotel hair dryer. I watched my black hair swirl around my face in the mirror. *Jaya Anand Jones, what are you doing here?* By the time I was done a few minutes later, my laundry had been picked up and our breakfast delivered.

I took a mug of coffee and sat in the chaise lounge window seat, watching the dark sky brighten with the sunrise.

"I thought you liked pastries," he said.

"How can you eat right now?"

"Lane knows what he's doing."

"I know. But this is *the Louvre.*"

North's forehead creased as he looked at me. "You really don't know, do you?"

"Know *what*? You two haven't told me what's going on today, remember?"

"He's done it before."

"I know what he used to be."

"I'm not talking about what he's done in general," North said.

This was getting tiresome. He wanted me to bite, to beg for more information, but I was done playing along. Lane was doing what North wanted. I didn't have to be polite to his blackmailer. I took another sip of coffee and turned back to the window.

"Lane Peters," North continued, his voice barely above a whisper, "has robbed the Louvre before."

CHAPTER 15

I coughed as my coffee went down the wrong pipe, then I stood and faced North. "That's not possible," I said, in between coughs. "He would have told me."

"Would he?"

"I don't know why you're doing this—"

"I'm sorry," North said. "I don't mean to mock you. I thought you'd feel *better* knowing he's pulled this off before."

In spite of the high ceiling, I felt claustrophobic in the hotel suite. Had I misjudged Lane? I knew he was once a thief, but everything at the Louvre was of cultural and historical significance. It wasn't the type of thing he would have done.

Unless I didn't know him at all.

Lane said North was a man of his word. But that was before Hugo's suspicious disappearance cast doubt on North's word. Had North killed Hugo to keep him from telling Lane something? Could he have been killed by someone else?

"How," I said in between deep breaths, "could you possibly think that would make me feel better?"

"I'm sorry about all this, you know. I wish it hadn't come to this."

"You could call it off."

"I'm afraid I can't do that."

"You're calling the shots. You can do whatever you want."

He looked at me with a curious smile. "You really are quite innocent, my girl. Forces are in motion that I'm powerless to stop."

"Difficult is different from impossible."

"Ha! The more time I spend with you, the more I see why he likes you. How did you get mixed up with him?"

"You already know the answer to that."

"True. But I thought it would be nice to hear it from you. God knows we could both use the distraction."

"In that case, I'd rather hear more about you. How did you get into this life of being a master criminal?"

"Such an active imagination you have. I'm simply an art dealer with humble beginnings."

I stared at him, from his perfect hair down to his fashionable wingtips. "You really are, aren't you?"

"Why yes." He flashed me a charming smile. "I knew you were a smart one. Not smart enough to stay clear of Lane, though."

"I'd like some time to myself."

North frowned. "Look, I really am sorry—"

"Please."

With a silent nod, North respected my wishes and left. In some ways, that was worse. Confused about what to think of both Lane and North, I didn't know where to direct my anger. I had no idea who I could trust.

I didn't have much time alone with my own thoughts. By the time I'd sucked down a second cup of coffee, Lane burst through the door, followed by North, Marius, and Dante.

"I'm telling you," Lane was saying, "he's not answering *any* of his numbers. We have to call this off."

"Not an option," North said.

"What's going on?" I demanded.

"I was afraid something like this would happen," North said. "Lane has been out of the game for long enough that his contacts aren't the most up-to-date. One of them decided not to participate."

"So you're postponing things?" I asked, wondering if I was

relieved or scared. How long would I have to stay a prisoner in Paris?

"No," North said. "Everything goes on as planned. All this means is that we go with a back-up plan."

"I don't *have* a back-up plan," Lane said. "You didn't leave me enough time—"

"Who said you were the one with the back-up?"

"If you didn't need me in the first place—"

"Oh, we needed you," North said. "You're the one who came up with the plan, and you're the one who's going to pull it off. It's your *people* who are replaceable."

"It's Sig," Lane said tentatively, "who's fallen off the grid."

"The generalist." North drummed his fingers together. "Jaya, it's your lucky day."

A heavy feeling told me it was quite the opposite.

"What are you saying?" Lane asked.

"All Sig had to do was deliver the box. It's essential, but by far the least skilled job. It requires no special training. It only needs someone who functions well under stress. After learning about her exploits in Scotland and India, I'd say we have our third man to help you: Jaya."

Lane stared at him. Were his neck muscles bulging? "Are you crazy? Absolutely not."

"She wanted to help from the start," North pointed out.

"I'm right here," I said.

North grinned. "What do you say, Jaya?"

My thudding heart gave way to a serene calmness. "I'm your back-up plan," I repeated softly.

"Yes," North said at the same time Lane said, "No."

"This means you need me to pull this off," I stated.

"Why can't it be Marius?" Lane asked.

North shook his head. "No. It can't be Marius or Dante. Jaya will come through."

"I will," I said. "But only after you give me half an hour alone with Lane—at a location with nobody listening."

"I hardly think—"

"If I'm wrong that you need me..." I let my voice trail off.

North's nostrils flared. "Very well. A few minutes can't hurt. You've got ten. You know what I'll do to you both if you don't come through for me."

The air froze my cheeks as we walked along the Eiffel Tower promenade. It was too cold to stay still. The sky remained clear, but the wind reminded me it was winter. I pulled my hat down over my ears and tugged my coat more tightly around me.

Glancing over my shoulder, I saw Marius and Dante fifty yards behind us.

"Sorry this had to be outside," Lane said, wrapping his own jacket more closely around him. "But it's the best way to be sure they can't hear us. Are you all right? What's so urgent we needed to talk before we're free of North forever in a few hours?"

"Why didn't you tell me?" I asked.

His eyes narrowed behind his glasses. "Tell you what?"

"That you've done this before—stolen from *the Louvre* before?

Lane stopped short. "*That's* what this is about?"

"Stealing priceless art from a cultural institution isn't what I thought—" I couldn't continue. I looked down at the ground, feeling foolish for convincing myself Lane was what I wanted him to be.

Lane groaned. "I knew my youthful cockiness would come back to bite me."

My attention snapped back to his face. "So you admit it?"

"No, that's not what I mean. I was good at what I did, and it's true I did some stupid, stupid things when I was young. But I never stole anything of cultural significance. Not on purpose, at least. Jewelry primarily, and sometimes art, but from private collections. You know all that. But several years ago..."

"What?"

"There was a theft from the Louvre that was *attributed* to me." He watched my expression carefully as he spoke.

I squinted at him in the cold, bright sunlight, the silhouette of the Eiffel Tower behind him.

"I never," he continued, "set the record straight. At the time, it was good for my reputation to let people think I'd pulled off something like that. By the time I thought better of it, it was too late."

"Wait. That means North has confidence in your ability to steal from the Louvre that's based on a lie."

"I can do this, Jones." His breath was visible in the cold air between us. "I didn't want you to be involved, but the role you have to play isn't big. Technically, you're not even doing anything illegal."

"Besides conspiring," I pointed out.

"Well, there's that. But it doesn't matter. I'll give you a disguise so you won't look like you, and there won't be any way for any of this to be traced to you. I'll make sure of that. Only—"

"Only *what*?"

"Nothing."

"You can't start saying something like that and then—"

"I was wondering," Lane said, "whether North planned all along for you to be involved. Then he'll have a hold over you, like he does with me. But it's a stupid thought. That's not his style."

"After what happened to Hugo, how can we trust North? Are you sure we should go through with this at all?"

"We don't have *any* good choices." Lane shook his head. "I've learned to trust my instincts. North sticks to his word. It's not a matter of trust. If he didn't, his reputation would be destroyed. He'd be ruined. If North killed him, Hugo must have given him no choice."

"How can you say that?"

"I'm not excusing what North might have done. I'm saying why our situation is different. Hugo had more of a conflicted conscience than anyone I've ever worked with. If he decided to take North down—"

"Then any gentleman's agreement would go out the window."

"I think Hugo was trying to do exactly that. He was trying to tell me something at the museum. You picked up on it, too. That's why you went to see him, wasn't it?"

I nodded, my face numb from the cold.

"I couldn't ask you about it while North was there, but that was dumb, Jaya."

"I'm the only reason we found the blood—" The words caught in my throat.

"It doesn't change what we do today. Today, we get out of the Louvre without handcuffs, and free from the threat of North destroying our lives. Once we've lived up to our end of the bargain, then we can see if we can find out the truth about what happened to Hugo. All right?"

My attention shifted to two approaching figures. Marius and Dante strode toward us, their coats billowing in the wind. "They're coming for us, Lane."

CHAPTER 16

Two hours until show time.

My part in the plan was easy. That didn't stop my whole body from tingling as Lane applied my disguise, or my foot from tapping nervously as I watched Lane speaking on his cell phone to his— *our*—conspirators.

I was to deliver a folded cardboard box to a man carrying a painting. The box would be tucked inside a shopping bag with other purchases, so as not to arouse suspicion. It was the timing that was important. I had to wait until he walked by an appointed spot, then drop the bag where he could pick it up. It was easy—in theory.

If things went right, there was no need for me to be in disguise. It was only a precaution, Lane said. Why not be careful?

While Lane transformed my appearance with a skillful hand, the impact of what I was doing caught up with me. I was supposed to be saving history, not destroying it. Stealing from the Louvre was the exact opposite of what I'd dedicated my life to do. Lane had promised the painting would be returned, but still refused to reveal the details of the plan beyond what I needed to know to play my part. There was no time left to argue. I trusted him. That had to be enough. It had to be.

I expected to get a wig, and perhaps a pillow wrapped around my waist. But the ways in which Lane altered my looks were much more subtle. My disguise was more of a non-disguise. My hair that usually fell at my shoulders was pulled into a bun, and a white scarf wrapped around my hairline. Tooth caps shifted the shape of my mouth and affected my speech. Lane put three pairs of glasses on my face before settling on pink cat-eye frames. He sat back and nodded as he appraised me.

"That's it?" I asked.

"The simple route is almost always the best one," Lane said as he handed me the final touch: bright pink lipstick.

"Lipstick? You think this garish shade of pink will make a difference?"

"Trust me."

I applied the lipstick, then walked over to a mirror. My pink lips parted in surprise. Though not much had been done, I was a different person.

Lane came up behind me and held up a fluffy white cashmere sweater and pink jeans. "Put these on, and your transformation will be complete. You'll be the anti-Jaya."

That almost got a smile out of me. I only wear subtle, dark colors. After growing up with my hippie father who believed tie-dye was meant for every possible fabric from clothing to curtains to bedspreads, I'd had a lifetime's worth of bright clothing by the time I left home at sixteen.

My gaze stayed fixed on the mirror, looking between the stranger in front of me whose reflection mirrored my own, and the strange man behind me who looked nothing like the real Lane Peters.

Like my own transformation, Lane's had been subtle, yet he was a completely different person. His dark blond wavy hair was now slicked back, a subtle reddish tint showing under the lights. Blue contact lenses covered his hazel eyes, replacing his glasses. Freckles dotted his nose and cheeks. A fitted set of teeth, covering his own, changed both the shape of his mouth and did more to lessen the impact of his angular cheek bones than I would have thought possible.

"Where's everyone else?" I asked, turning around from the mirror and taking the white and pink clothes from Lane. "Don't we have to go soon?"

"Everyone is arriving separately."

"You and I aren't going together?"

Lane shook his head. "Just remember, in a little over an hour, this will be over."

When I was done changing into the cute, fluffy clothing, Lane was gone, North there in his place, holding two coats and a shopping bag from the department store Le Bon Marché.

"Very nice," he said, looking me up and down. "Lane would have been superb in Hollywood." He shook his head. "If only he'd had different mentors."

"Why aren't you ready?" I asked.

"Whatever are you talking about?" He held up the coats and bag in his hands. "The pink coat is yours, as you may have gathered."

"But you look like yourself."

He blinked at me. "I'm merely a respectable art dealer visiting the Louvre. I have no part to play in whatever madness is about to take place at the museum."

I grumbled and grabbed the pink coat.

Riding the elevator down into the lobby of the Louvre, I felt like I was descending into the belly of the beast. Throngs of tourists swarmed over every inch of the lobby. My chest tightened. This was a very bad idea. What was I thinking, going along with this?

"Thirty minutes," North said, shrugging out of his coat. "You have time to join me for coffee."

"I don't want any."

"Don't you want to see what's going on?" He held up his phone. On the screen was a video. The camera bounced around from person to person, going in and out of focus. I caught a glimpse of one of the sculptures I'd seen on my earlier tour of the museum. This was a video feed from inside the museum.

"Lane," I whispered, watching the jerky movements of the video feed. It wasn't the type of view I'd expect from a hand-held camera. From the height of the camera, I wondered if it was a cell phone sticking out of Lane's shirt pocket.

"A lapel pin camera," North said. "Now, let me get you that coffee."

The museum had several cafés. North selected the most central location, the Pyramid Cafeteria on the first floor, overlooking the lobby on the ground floor. Only a handful of tables were placed in the outer areas of the cafeteria, which gave a better view of the crowds. The self-service tables were full when we arrived. North strode confidently up to a family at one of the tables. Not just any table, but the one at the end that both had the best view and the most privacy as it was only next to one other table.

The family sitting at the table consisted of a frazzled man, a gaunt woman who sat with perfect posture, and two sullen children, one of whom was pleading with his father. I couldn't tell what he was saying, because it was in German, but I had the distinct impression that the museum was not a hit.

With a wide smile, North shook the man's hand, and a few moments later they were all laughing together. North handed something to the dad in the family and they happily stood up and left. North motioned me over to the table.

"What did you say to them?"

"I happened to have extra all-expenses pre-paid passes to Disneyland Paris that I couldn't use because my kids came down with the flu. They looked like *such* a nice family."

"What would you have done if the table you wanted didn't have a family?"

"I also have box seats to an opera matinee, and also—"

"I get the picture."

"I'm always prepared."

Dante brought us coffees and pastries, then departed. North propped the phone up on the table. Based on our vantage point, the two of us could see the screen, but nobody else could. I looked up and saw another reason he liked this particular table. It wasn't close to any surveillance cameras.

My heart beat faster. Even though I'd barely slept, I didn't think I could stomach any coffee. The next thing I saw on the video screen nearly made me knock over the tray of coffee on the table.

The hands of the person with the lapel camera came into view. *It wasn't Lane.* "Who are we watching?"

"Oh, *I see,*" North said with a flash of annoyance.

"I don't see."

"Look at the cuffs of the jacket. Really, I thought you had an eye for detail."

"It's a museum uniform," I said. The thief—whoever he was—was pretending to be a guard or a docent. Or maybe he really was one? Could he have been bribed? It must be one of the men who were part of the plan. But where was Lane?

"I don't understand what I'm seeing," I said, my heart pounding in my throat.

"My *goodness.*" North's eyes sparkled.

"What?"

"You think it's exciting." North's annoyance from the moment before was replaced with a wide grin. His nose scrunched with amusement.

"That's not how I would describe what I'm feeling."

"I can see your pupils expanding, and how quickly you're breathing. That's adrenaline. *Excitement.* I knew you'd be perfect."

"Anyone ever tell you you're kind of creepy?"

"Only in a charming way." North tapped the edge of the phone screen showing a clock. "It's time." He handed me the Bon Marché bag with the flattened cardboard box tucked in between two winter sweaters.

With sweating hands, I picked up the bag and stepped into the crowd.

CHAPTER 17

I followed the instructions perfectly. I didn't dare lose my concentration.

As I made my way through the dense crowds, I was overcome by the most unexpected feeling. My hand that gripped the shopping bag stopped sweating. The claustrophobia I felt while sitting with North was replaced by a powerful sense of control. The multilingual chatter died away as I focused single-mindedly on my goal.

As I walked through the Sully wing to the room where the heist would go down, I watched my surroundings through the pink glasses, feeling as if the clear glass had given me x-ray vision. The paintings on the walls were more vibrant than I remembered, and the sculptures more formidable. Though I was shorter than most of the people surrounding me, I felt taller today. More powerful. My shoulders squared, I strode into the room where I'd be taking action in five minutes.

Several docents and guards milled around with the museum guests. I had no way of knowing which one was part of the plan, until he acted.

"*Bonjour,*" a voice said in my ear. "*Jolie peinture.*"

I jumped. A muscular blond man gave me a wide smile that revealed exceptionally bright white teeth. For a fraction of a second I wondered if Lane had donned a completely different disguise, but I quickly saw I was mistaken.

I shook my head. "*Je ne parle pas français.*"

"An American!" he said with an accent that told me he was from Australia, or perhaps New Zealand. "Even better. I'm David. I ditched my tour group. Too boring. Want to look at the art in a completely superficial way with me?"

"Sorry, I'm busy," I said, my nerves from ten minutes before returning full force. "Meeting up with someone." I turned to walk away.

"I'm wounded," David said, his hands grasped over his heart.

I spun on my heel and faced him. This was *not* part of the plan. I glanced around at the people in museum uniforms. None of them were near the painting yet. "Look, my boyfriend is meeting me any minute. He's, um, the jealous type."

He flexed his muscles, his smile never wavering. "Don't you worry, I can handle myself."

I kept my eyes on the painting. A nondescript museum guard made his way around a boisterous Italian tour group and walked up to the painting, stopping directly in front of it. My concentration instantly sharpened. This was it. It was time for me to act.

"Come on," my suitor continued. "I'm a fun guy. And unlike the guy you're waiting for, I'd never leave you alone in this crazy place."

I smiled and batted my eyelashes at him, throwing myself into the part. "All right. Let me get rid of him first. I'll meet you in front of the Richelieu Cafe in ten minutes."

"That's more like it." He winked at me.

"I see him!" I said in a loud stage whisper. "Go!" I shoved him away, keeping my eyes locked on the fake guard in front of the painting that was going to be "borrowed."

I watched as the guard's hands reached out and touched the frame of the painting. I held my breath, expecting a shout from a real guard or the piercing shriek of an alarm. Nothing happened.

Jostled by a passing Japanese tour group, I lost sight of my accomplice and the painting, but when I looked up, *the painting was gone.*

A moment later, I caught sight of the fake guard. With a stoic face and a casual strut, he walked in my direction with the painting firmly grasped in both hands. Rather than tackling him, as I would have expected, the sea of people parted. Visitors' expressions showed various degrees of confusion or surprise, but not horror. They gave him wide berth.

I didn't have time to think about how on earth he'd managed to remove the painting. It was my signal to leave the fancy orange shopping bag at the room's south entrance. I dropped the bag, and after one last glance at the painting in his hands, I forced myself to walk out of the room, not looking back.

The buzz of the crowds filled my ears as I made a beeline to the lobby. Why wasn't something happening? Or maybe it was. If a security alarm sounded, I wouldn't necessarily hear it. The museum was large—the size of eleven football fields, I'd read.

When I reached the cafe above the lobby, North was sitting in the same spot where I'd left him.

"This is better than the movies," he said, his eyes not leaving the phone screen. "Come look."

Shown on the video feed, the thief didn't run. That would have been a giveaway. People in front of him weren't going to question the person they believed to be a museum employee simply doing his job. Who were they to judge when was an appropriate time to remove a painting? A few of them cast dirty looks in his direction, though. Looking more closely, I saw the reason for the scowls. The thief wasn't walking—he was *dancing*.

"What's he doing?" I asked with a sinking feeling. "And why is he still carrying the painting? Does that mean he didn't find the box I left for him? Or he didn't have time to locate whatever is hidden in the painting?"

"All in good time. Ah! Here we are."

On the video screen, we watched as a real guard spotted him. The guard's mouth opened, almost in slow motion. Or maybe that was merely my memory of it.

That's when the thief ran.

"Something's gone wrong." I sprang from the chair. This was exactly what I'd been afraid of. Lane hadn't had enough time to prepare.

"Sit down," North hissed. "Any moment now—"

I ignored North, and ran to the railing overlooking the lobby below. The video feed had showed the thief heading back towards the lobby. If he didn't get caught, I would see him within minutes. As I scanned the crowd, North joined me next to the railing.

"Where's Lane?" I asked. "Shouldn't he be stepping in now that something has gone wrong?"

"What makes you think something has gone wrong?"

"Look." I pointed all around us. From each of the wings, people streamed into the lobby more quickly than they should have, tripping over each other. "The alarm has been raised. They must be directing guests into the main lobby."

North held up his phone, watching the video. The thief was in one room, then another. Dodging people. A spot of orange flashed across the screen. It was the shopping bag I'd left for him. If he had it, why wasn't he using the box inside?

"Brilliant," North whispered.

A shout echoed in the lobby below. It was followed by several more. Something was happening. I don't know what I expected—a deafening alarm blaring or metal bars clamping down around each wing—but none of that happened.

Instead, a dozen military-looking men ran down the small, circular staircase in the middle of the lobby across from the escalators most museum attendees used. Another set of men, and one woman, fussed around the main entrance doors. There was no message over an intercom, but people began to notice that something was going on.

The video image on the phone screen was now fuzzy. It was clear for a second or two, then went fuzzy again. I realized what was happening. The camera kept bumping into other people. The blur wasn't an error, but rather the image of the camera pressing up against other people's clothing. The thief was no longer running. *He was being carried along in the crowd.* It was so crowded that the thief appeared to have lost the museum guard who had spotted him.

Tourists shouted questions. Children shouted with glee. Museum staff shouted instructions—at least I assumed that's what they were doing. They didn't have bullhorns, and the snippets I heard from the closest wing were in French.

"Isn't this fun?" North asked. "You can see a whole swath of humanity right here in front of you. People from every continent, speaking dozens of languages, all brought together for their appreciation of art and history."

"Where's Lane?"

"I anticipate he'll be along shortly."

North smiled as he looked into the chaos surrounding us. The escalators stopped moving. The armed guards prevented people from climbing the unmoving escalator to reach the exit. The loudest voices wafted up to us. *"Stop shoving!" "I told you this was a bad day to come to the museum!" "Harold, is that man carrying a painting?"*

"There," North said, tucking his phone into his pocket, "by the entrance to the Sully wing."

My throat ached as I realized what was happening. He was going to get caught. I was sure of it. Then, the most curious thing happened.

The thief smiled as he made eye contact with the guards. He gave a little wave. It was a wave goodbye—right before he dove into an especially thick section of the crowd.

People were shoulder-to-shoulder throughout most of the lobby now, so the maneuver wasn't difficult. One moment the thief was there, and then he was gone.

"Where did he go?" I scanned the crowd, but the man had disappeared as effectively as if he'd jumped into a black hole. If this hadn't been the Louvre, I would have sworn he'd gone down a trap door like in one of Sanjay's magic tricks.

Seconds later, half a dozen guards reached the spot where the man had vanished. Four of them pushed people back while two of them looked at what was left in the spot.

I almost expected to see the man lying dead on the ground

after swallowing a cyanide pill. But this wasn't a spy movie. There was no dead man on the ground.

There was no man at all.

The guards pushed people back far enough that there was now at least a fifteen foot radius. Enough space for me to see from above what was happening.

On the floor was a navy blue jacket that looked like that of a museum guard. Next to it was a narrow cardboard box with a purple peace sign spray-painted on the surface, and a can of spray paint.

One of the military-looking men reached into the box. He pulled out the painting. With a stoic face, he turned it over, inspecting it for damage. He nodded to one of his compatriots, unable to suppress a smile.

If the painting was undamaged, did that mean the thief hadn't been able to remove whatever it was they needed to borrow the painting for? I was glad he'd escaped, but wondered if North would think Lane and I hadn't lived up to our obligations.

"What an interesting piece of performance art!" North said, raising his voice loudly enough to be heard by everyone around us. "Look, everyone, it's a political statement!"

Murmurs of assent echoed through the crowd. *"Did you see the performance below?" "Wait 'til the kids hear about this!" "Damn hippies."*

"That," North whispered in my ear, "is what I call a brilliant diversion."

CHAPTER 18

"A diversion," I murmured. The painting wasn't important at all. It was merely a diversion.

"A nice one," North said. "Lane is good."

"But won't they realize something else was—"

"Let's get going," North said, putting his arm on my shoulder to guide me through the crowd.

I pulled away. "There's no rush. It doesn't look like they're letting anyone out."

"They will soon."

"Won't they want to find the guy?"

"Oh, they'll look for a short time. But soon enough they'll realize the futility of the situation. They won't find him."

"But he wasn't disguised."

"Wasn't he?" His eyes twinkled as he paused and turned to me. "Tell me, what did he look like? Average height? Average brown hair? Not too old, but not too young? Half the men in this museum fit that description. And the painting wasn't damaged—that was the purpose of the box you provided—so there was no harm done."

"But—"

"Such impatience." He glanced at the time on his phone. "Come on. We're due to meet Lane. If he's done his part—"

"*If?*"

"Regardless, I'd like to be near one of the exits as soon as they start letting people out."

We maneuvered through the crowd. Agitated people from

every continent looked around in confusion. *"But I have a flight to catch!" "I'm an American! I have rights!" "You can't keep us here without telling us what's going on! Honey, do something!"*

"As you can tell," North said with a giddy smile, "they're going to have a riot on their hands if they keep us too long."

It took longer than North expected for the authorities to open the doors. But as he predicted, they gave up before they identified their suspect. At least it looked that way. The authorities weren't telling us anything.

From where we stood nearly underneath the pyramid, I could see a large crowd gathered outside in the courtyard. Visitors weren't being let in, but people were now being let out. Dozens of armed guards ushered people toward the exits, no doubt trying to prevent a stampede. North hooked his elbow around mine so we didn't lose each other in the throng.

In my heels, it was possible for me to see at least a little bit of what was going on. Even so, I was lifted off the ground by the force of the crowd, which perfectly matched how I felt. Whatever control I thought I had was all an illusion. My feet touched the ground after only a few seconds, and North kept a firm hold on my elbow and pulled me from underneath the pyramid into the courtyard.

"Dear girl, you look like you've seen a ghost. Let's get you some sustenance."

Fifteen minutes later, we sat in the corner of a bistro that looked small from the outside but stretched back the depth of eight tables. We sat at the farthest table from the front, facing the door. In my dazed state I couldn't remember ordering anything, but North must have requested both wine and espresso, because an elegantly-attired waiter set both in front of me.

"I do appreciate a woman who knows what she wants."

"I ordered this?"

His eyes crinkled as he took a sip of wine. "You don't remember?"

"Does this mean I'm in shock?"

He laughed. "It's almost over now. You can relax."

"Hugo is missing, possibly dead. And Lane isn't here yet. I don't call that being over."

The smile left North's lips. "I'm truly sorry about Hugo." He paused to take a long drink of wine, almost finishing the glass. He picked up the bottle and poured himself some more.

"Shouldn't we be meeting Lane by now?"

"This is where he's meeting us."

"In public?"

"I'm glad to know you're not going to be competition for my business. With the look of excitement in your eyes back at the museum, I wasn't so sure. But you've got a lot to learn about how things work. Doing business in public is the best way for us legitimate art dealers to ensure that nobody gets the wrong idea about us."

I was distracted by the sight of a tall man wearing a newsboy cap who had just walked into the restaurant. The hat had a large brim that obscured part of his face, but that didn't stop me from recognizing Lane. He wasn't disguising how he carried himself. That was all I needed to know it was him.

He took off the hat and headed straight for us. "It's good to see you, Jones," he said, sitting down next to me and slipping his hand into mine. His body was alert and relaxed at the same time, as if a great weight had been lifted but his adrenaline was still running strong.

"I trust there were no problems," North said.

"None at all." Lane took a flat object, roughly the size of his hand, from his shirt pocket. Even though we were handing it over to North, I was pleased to see Lane had placed the historical piece into a clear protective sleeve.

North snatched it from his hand and tucked it into his own pocket, but not before I caught a glimpse of the item. It was a piece of parchment paper, with a few words of faded calligraphy and a painting of two animals intertwined with a man. The painting sparked a sense of recognition, but I didn't have time for it to register.

Lane cocked his head to the side, looking uncertainly at North. "That illuminated manuscript page *is* what you expected, isn't it?"

"Of course," North said. "I simply thought you'd show a bit of common sense. That's why I provided the envelope."

That was odd. North had said the exact opposite only moments before. Lane must have found the request unexpected, too. He handed over a small envelope.

"It's a bit late for that now." North watched me for a moment before breaking into a smile. "Well, no harm done."

"Won't they be looking for it from whatever exhibit you stole that from?" I asked.

"Nobody," Lane said, "will realize it's missing."

"Because of the diversion? That bought you time, but surely they'll notice soon enough."

North laughed. "Not really. You see, nobody knows this exists."

CHAPTER 19

"What do you mean nobody knows it exists?" I whispered.

"Speak normally," North said. "It's much less suspicious."

"He's right," Lane said without lowering his voice. He continued speaking as a waiter set a wine glass in front of him. "We're all old friends here." He poured himself a splash of wine and raised his glass. "A toast to old friends about to say a fond farewell."

"Fine," I said. "I'm not toasting, but if I speak normally, will someone answer my question?"

"I can tell you this, my dear," North said. "This page is the missing piece of an illuminated manuscript that's been in my client's family for years. The man who's paying me for this will be very, very happy. This missing page has been a life-long obsession of his."

I stared at the imperfections on the thick wooden table in front of me, a combination of incidental scratches from years of use and purposefully carved initials. The worn table must have been decades old, but that was nothing compared to the age of the hand-painted piece of parchment I'd been a part of stealing. What did it mean to steal a piece of history if nobody knew about it?

"You found it where the information indicated?" North asked.

"I did," Lane said. "Did you like the artist's contribution on the other side of the museum?"

"That was a lovely touch."

"He's really a performance artist?" I asked. "Not one of your associates?"

"That was the beauty of the plan," Lane said. "He's an artist who likes to subvert the system by showing how patriarchal art obscures larger political problems. I knew of his work, so I thought he'd be up for the challenge. The difficult part was finding him, because his identity is a closely-guarded secret."

"That's one of the things Lane was busy with," North added.

"He has no connection to me," Lane said. "If he'd been caught, he'd still have created a diversion, and since his intention had never been to steal the painting, he wouldn't have gotten much jail time."

"How thoughtful of you." I said sarcastically.

"He's done things like this before," Lane said. "He'll take credit for this one, too. I merely provided his next opportunity."

"While you were in another wing."

Lane nodded. "It was important that the crowds be heavy for the plan to work—for both of us. That's why things had to move forward today, on the most crowded day of the month. It worked perfectly. As soon as the guards and docents started leading people to the main lobby from the wing I was in, I began planting seeds of alarm within the crowd. People began pushing and shoving to get out. In the commotion, I 'accidentally' fell against a desk. What nobody else knew was that there was a secret panel in that particular desk."

"The information I acquired told of the secret panel," North said, "as well as the steps needed to unlock it. My client will be overjoyed. He's a rich collector nearing the end of his life, and he desperately wanted the page for sentimental reasons because of his family's history. The precarious nature of his health meant there was some urgency in acquiring it for him. When I learned that the desk had been inconveniently acquired by the Louvre some years ago, that complicated things, but I still had to act quickly. I knew the perfect man for the job."

Instead of looking at North with disgust, Lane was almost giddy. "It worked like a charm. While I pretended to right myself after being pushed into the desk, I was able to press the right combination of spots along the side of the desk and liberate the parchment from its hiding spot."

"You two are having far too much fun with this," I said.

Lane cleared his throat. "Let's go, Jaya."

"Why the rush?" North asked. "You two don't want to stay to join me for lunch? This place has an excellent pot-au-feu."

"We're done here? My obligation is fulfilled?"

"With flying colors." North patted his lips with a napkin and gave Lane a nod. "Nice doing business with you. I know we no longer see eye to eye about this line of work, but I hope it's a small consolation that I'm being paid enough for this parchment that I'll be taking a long holiday." Turning to me, he said, "Though it was lovely meeting you, I trust we won't meet again."

I should have been relieved, but I was too busy puzzling over why the brief glance at the illuminated manuscript page had sparked a sense of recognition.

Lane stood to depart, pulling me up with him. My hand felt so natural in his that I'd forgotten they were intertwined.

North, ever the gentleman, rose along with us. "I'll see to it," he said, "that those documents of yours don't make it into the wrong hands."

The documents North had showed me.

North's words took all the wind out of me. I swayed, and Lane steadied his grip on my hand. I squeezed back. I needed all the strength I could get.

"Sorry," I said. "I'm not cut out for this line of work." I desperately hoped North believed me. That he hadn't just figured out that I knew what he was up to. That I knew, now, that this wasn't the end.

It was only the beginning.

CHAPTER 20

Lane led us to a taxi. It must have been cold, because snowflakes stuck to my clothing, but I don't remember anything about the walk.

North's last remarks were niggling at the back of my mind. I wasn't crazy, was I? Those papers were the key to the importance of the stolen parchment. Not the fake documents with evidence of plagiarism, but the East India Company man's letters North showed me "as a test." I went over everything that had happened since I arrived in Paris. As much as I didn't want to believe it, it all fit.

"Now that your adrenaline is wearing off," Lane said, misinterpreting my spaced-out silence, "the shock is kicking in. But it'll soon pass. Don't worry."

"Lane, we need to talk about—"

Lane held a finger to his lips. "Soon," he said, giving me a pointed look. Were we still being monitored?

The taxi dropped us off at the hotel. As he had on our way out, Lane spoke loudly in an English accent about our friends who we were visiting at the hotel. If anything went wrong and we'd been identified at the museum, we didn't want to be traced.

Once we reached the room, Lane again held up his finger. He quickly discarded his disguise and gathered up his belongings, asking me to do the same. I put on a change of clothes that had been laundered by the hotel, then shoved the rest of my clothing and my shoulder bag into my backpack. Within the space of five minutes, we looked like ourselves again and had packed our possessions. Lane left a big tip on a side table, and I took one last look at my prison before hoisting my backpack onto my shoulders.

I trotted to keep up with Lane as we swept through the hotel lobby. "I really need to—"

"We'll have plenty of time to chat on the train," Lane said, cutting me off. "The metro is nearby, so that's the easiest way to get there."

The train?

The metro station, only a block away, was crowded. It was mid-afternoon on a Sunday, but I had a feeling Paris was always bustling. Though the entrance had been close to our hotel, we maneuvered our way through what felt like several city blocks underground, including several sets of stairs.

Lane led us to a platform where we boarded a crowded car. I desperately needed to tell Lane of my suspicions, but not while we might still be under surveillance. I sighed and followed along.

We walked out of the metro station and straight into a fast food restaurant. A fast food restaurant? I had no idea such things existed in Paris. Lane handed me a small stack of clothes from his bag, and motioned for me to give him my backpack.

"Why—?"

"One second," he said as he scribbled a few words onto a piece of paper. He handed it to me.

"*Go to the women's restroom and put this on,*" the note read. "*I'll meet you back in this exact spot in five minutes.*"

With that, he was gone.

In a stall of the women's restroom, I opened the bag he'd handed me. It consisted of a dark green raincoat in my size, a flattened black cloche hat, and thick tortoiseshell glasses that looked nothing like the pink cat-eye glasses I'd worn at the Louvre. I tucked my hair under the stylish hat. I didn't look half bad. I did, however, look like a completely different person—again. I wondered where he'd gotten these new items.

I stared at the woman in the mirror, almost unrecognizable. Another woman said something to me in French, and I realized I was blocking the sink. I moved and she kept speaking in French. Maybe I could pass as French in this attire. I smiled at her and departed, my old self gone, a different person in her place.

I did a double-take when I saw the man standing where Lane had told me to meet him. He looked nothing like Lane. There's something intangible that makes a person who they are. It's amazing how small alterations change someone's whole appearance. In Lane's case, it didn't even have to do with clothes. Instead of the tall, confident man in jeans, a dress shirt, and sexy glasses that he really did need, I stood in front of a mousy, stooped man with bad hair and small eyes. His jeans sagged and the sleeves of his shirt were awkwardly rolled, giving him a disheveled appearance. He hadn't changed a single item of his clothing, except to remove his glasses, yet the seemingly-insignificant alterations had transformed the whole man.

"Shall we?" His hesitant voice matched the mousy appearance. He held up my backpack. The movement of his arm was different than usual. He was playing a role. But when he caught my eye, the look he gave me was all Lane Peters. The emotional intensity he conveyed in that moment was nearly crushing—a mix of sorrow for what was going on and happiness that I was there with him.

"There aren't any surveillance devices in our bags," he added in a quieter voice as we walked out the door. I gaped at him and he shrugged. "I'd be stupid to trust North completely."

"About that," I said. "We need to talk."

"Can it wait until we get to the airport?"

I stopped walking, causing a man behind us on the sidewalk to shake his head and mutter about tourists as he darted around us. "I thought we were going to the train station."

"I said that for the benefit of North, in case he was listening."

"Why are we going to the airport?"

His face fell. "We need to get you home, Jones."

"You don't understand. This—"

"I'll look into Hugo's disappearance. Once all this is over, maybe we can—"

"You're not listening to me!"

Several people on the sidewalk glanced our way.

"This isn't the place—"

"There's *never* a good time and place," I said, feeling icy snowflakes fall onto my face. "But you have to listen to me. I know what North is doing. It *wasn't* only the illuminated manuscript page that he was after. North lied to us. He's after something much bigger than a single piece of parchment from an illuminated manuscript."

CHAPTER 21

"You're sure?" Lane asked.

I hesitated. "Pretty sure."

Lane swore and looked up at the descending snow. Easy for him to do. He was the one no longer wearing glasses. My own vision was obscured by droplets of melting snowflakes on my fake lenses. I shivered under the light rain coat that wasn't meant for snow.

"This isn't just a hunch because you don't trust North?" he asked.

"I wish that were the case. But it all fits. It all points to—"

"Let's get off the street and go somewhere we can talk privately."

"Hiding in one of these cafes?" Within my field of view were three sidewalk cafes, two of which had set up plastic tarps and heat lamps to accommodate the French pastime of simultaneously smoking, drinking (either coffee or wine), and people-watching. Even in the light snow, the tiny tables with chairs that faced outward were half filled.

"That's not what I had in mind."

"Then where *are* we going?"

The brief smile in Lane's face took some of the chill out of my bones. "A place that three days ago I thought I'd never be able to show you."

*   *   *

Twenty minutes later, we emerged from a metro stop and walked down three side streets before Lane stopped in front of a run-of-the-mill Parisian apartment building—by which I mean beautiful architectural details surrounded each narrow window in the five story Baroque building, and a brass lion's head greeted us at the front door. At home in San Francisco, the building would have been a historic landmark.

In the time we spent on the crowded metro, I was able to solidify my thoughts about what North was up to. I was more certain than ever that the hidden parchment meant something very different from what North had told us.

"Home sweet home," Lane said as we climbed a narrow, twisting flight of stairs. Was it my imagination, or had he said it with an English accent?

"You're living here?"

"For the moment." It wasn't my imagination. He'd taken on a British accent. He was also still walking in the stooped manner he'd assumed when we changed clothes before hopping on the metro. I wasn't sure who Lane was putting on the show for, but I was tired of thinking.

With two separate keys, Lane unlocked a narrow door on the first landing. I stepped into an apartment that must have been 200 square feet, at most. It made me think of the small hotel room at The Fog & Thistle in Scotland. Lane and I had known each other for less than a week when we'd been forced to share that microscopic room with a sloping ceiling. Through a door that Lane would have to stoop to walk through lay a bathroom, the only separate room in the apartment. A small cut-out held a kitchenette with a fridge tucked under the counter, two stove-top burners, and a sink with a removable stainless steel cover so it could serve as added counter space in the tiny area. The largest pieces of furniture were a couch that looked like it doubled as a bed and a reclaimed wooden dining table with two chairs tucked underneath. Bookshelves and art lined nearly every square inch of wall space. Philosophy, art history, and mystery fiction filled the shelves, their spines cracked from repeated reading. Above the shelves hung reproductions of paintings from India and photographs of temple art in Cambodia. I wished I'd been there under other circumstances, and that I didn't have to tell him what we had to do.

"It's beautiful," I said. As I spoke, an item on the largest bookshelf caught my attention. I lifted the small pewter frame. Inside the woven ivy design was a photograph of me. Lane had taken it in Scotland.

"What can I say?" Lane said, taking the picture of me from my hands and straightening up to his usual way of carrying himself. "I can't resist beautiful things."

Unsure of how to respond under our bizarre and urgent circumstances, I turned away. I dropped my bag on the hardwood floor, kicked off my shoes, and peeled out of my wet coat.

"My safe house North found was a decoy," Lane said. "This is the real one. I never meant to live here for a long period of time, but...Life gets in the way of life sometimes."

"I know. God, I know."

"I wish...I wish a lot of things, Jones. But right now, you need to tell me what you mean that the parchment isn't North's end game. This apartment is safe. We can talk here." Seeing me shiver, he turned the dial on a rusty radiator.

Standing so close to Lane, I hardly remembered what I was supposed to be thinking about. I took a step back and tucked my hair behind my ears. Even before he said so, I knew this apartment was safe. It had only one window, which was made of frosted glass. The glass was so thick I couldn't tell if it faced an inner courtyard or the busy street from which we'd entered.

"I don't know where to start," I said, "so I'll start at the beginning, before you 'liberated' that parchment from its hiding place. The East India Company letters North showed me *weren't* just a test. He really did want my expert opinion as to whether the documents were authentic."

Lane shook his head. "That doesn't sound like North. Not if the letters would clue you in to something he was doing."

"He would," I said, "if he knew there was no way I could put it together with the theft he wanted you to do for him. Remember, one of the letters had been ripped in half. He didn't want me to see it in its entirety."

"But you saw something?"

"Nothing I realized was important at the time. He was careful to remove any references that would alert me to what he was doing with them. But—" I shook my head.

"What?"

"He set things up perfectly! I wasn't thinking. I'd just stepped off a transcontinental flight, walked back into your life, was absorbing the fact that I was being blackmailed or coerced or whatever it was, and didn't have much time...I did what any historian would do at first. I started with the author, date, and location—who, when, and where. These letters were written by a man working for the British East India Company who was in Pondicherry in 1793, when Britain had recently regained control of the city and the French East India Company was dissolving. The French were miserable colonizers compared to the British."

"What does that have to do with the parchment I got out of the desk?"

"I'm getting there. Local Indian rulers got in the middle of the two European powers, backing different nationalities for political reasons. Tipu Sultan in nearby Mysore had the support of the French in his battles against the English. Tipu, who was both a military leader and a scholar, was a hugely important ruler during the 18th century. He had a vast estate of riches that were divided up after his defeat, including the famous Tipu's Tiger automaton that's now at the Victoria & Albert museum in London."

"I'm not following."

"You're not supposed to. That's why North thought it was fine for you to steal the manuscript page, because you never would have made the connection. Indian rulers often presented lavish gifts—

treasures—to their European allies. In addition, when the British or French won a battle, they claimed Indian treasures as the spoils of war. That's how men like Robert Clive accumulated so much wealth."

"Clive of India," Lane said, "whose gold coins sank on an East Indiaman ship before it reached England. But weren't more of his stolen Indian treasures auctioned off for close to ten million dollars at Christie's a few years ago?"

"At least that much," I said. "Because they were once owned by such an important historical figure. He was instrumental in securing the British East India Company's stronghold in India through his military moves against England's rival for colonial control: the French. He was successful because of his brave leadership in battle—which was actually reckless, youthful bluffing that happened to turn out for the best because the French never believed he could be so stupid...but I'm getting off topic." I warmed my hands over the radiator. When I looked up, Lane was smiling at me.

"I love it when you get carried away," he said, unable to hide a smile.

"You're not taking this seriously enough!"

"You're shivering. I think you caught a chill outside. I'll make tea."

"How can you think about tea at a time like this?"

"You haven't told me what I need to take seriously." He filled an iron tea kettle with tap water and lit a gas burner with a match. "A letter from a homesick Englishman is hardly reason enough to think there's more going on. And I know a thing or two about illuminated manuscripts. This page wouldn't be particularly valuable, aside from the way North mentioned. You've been through a lot these last few days. I know it's difficult to believe it's over."

"The illuminated manuscript page," I said, trying to keep my voice even and not yell, "is what made the pieces fit together. Did you look carefully at the painting?"

"Animals with a person. That's pretty common in illuminated manuscripts."

"But this is a man wrapped in the trunk of an elephant, with a tiger circling at the elephant's feet. Two animals more commonly associated with India than with France. And *two* references to those animals in two days. It's related to the letters North showed me. It's too big a coincidence. This has to be about something stolen from India that North is on the trail of."

Lane stared at me, the color draining from his face, then shook his head. "You've over-thinking this, Jaya. It could be as simple as this fellow with a tiger obsession learned about the hiding place of a unique illustration, so the letter was the piece of information that told North where to find the parchment. That's why North wanted you to give your expert opinion about whether the letters were real. You could be right that there's a connection, but it's one that's easily explained."

"I wish it was that simple, but it doesn't follow. Why would a *single page* of a larger volume be hidden inside the desk from a scriptorium, unless there was some larger significance? North had a pretty weak explanation for all the effort that went into finding it. We're missing something. I wish I'd had a chance to take a closer look at the parchment, but it was clear North didn't want me to see it."

"I think," Lane said, "I can help with that."

"Don't tell me you have a photographic memory and can draw it perfectly."

"Even better." He reached into his pocket and held up a piece of electronic equipment smaller than his thumb.

"A miniature camera?"

"This is why I gave North's video feed to the performance artist. I knew North would be amused, and therefore not care that I disobeyed him in this case. His weakness is that he has too much fun with his role. I knew he wouldn't question my handing off the video camera, since he'd be getting a more entertaining show." As he spoke, he extracted a miniature memory card from the camera, plugged it into a laptop, and tapped a few keys. "The real reason I wanted to ditch that streaming video was to take a better look at what I was stealing. It was a precaution in case I'd been misled about the value of what I'd taken and needed to get it back."

He placed the laptop in front of me on the dining table that also seemed to serve as a desk, turning the computer so I could see the screen. A photograph of the illuminated manuscript page filled the screen. Though the colorful painting must have been more recent, the parchment itself looked like it could have been close to a thousand years old. The writing was so faded it was barely visible. I looked at it more closely.

"I'm going to need something stronger than tea," I said, staring at the elephant, tiger, and their victim. My mouth was dry and it was difficult to speak. "This piece of parchment is a *clue*. A clue that leads to the real treasure North is after."

CHAPTER 22

"Look at the writing," I said. "Next to the painting, there's only a single sentence of writing. It's *a message*, not a page from a book."

Lane stared at the image, then promptly kicked over an empty trashcan. It bounced off a bookshelf and skidded across the hardwood floor. "I should have seen the signals."

"You couldn't have known," I said. "That was the point."

"I appreciate you trying to make me feel better, but I screwed up."

"Not for the reason you think. It's only my background that made it possible for me to make the connection. That's exactly why I was never supposed to see this. Did you see how North reacted when you handed him the parchment but it wasn't stuffed into an envelope as he requested? He was flustered. That's when he told us far too much information about his 'eccentric' client. It felt forced. Why the hard sell? The job was already done."

"But I should have seen the problems with North's behavior. I told you how he's used to getting his way through his generous agreements. Bringing unwilling participants into this was out of character for him, especially bringing an outsider—you—into this. I was on such a high from pulling off the job without a hitch that I wasn't thinking."

"Well then, let's start thinking now."

"If I'd stopped to think sooner, maybe Hugo—"

"You can't blame yourself. We don't even know what happened to him."

The kettle whistled and Lane stood up to make the tea, while I stared at the photograph. Though the paper was worn with age and the calligraphic writing faded, the painting of a tiger standing on top of a man was vibrant.

"How's your Ecclesiastical Latin?" Lane asked, coming up behind me and handing me a mug.

"Mediocre at best. *Cementarium claustri ad cryptam.* Why isn't this written in French? And don't you have anything stronger than tea in this place?"

"Take a sip."

I complied, finding the black tea generously spiked with brandy.

"Illuminated manuscripts from the 12th century were written in Latin," Lane said.

"This can't be that old."

"It certainly is."

"But the painting—"

"That painting," Lane said, "was added *later.* You can tell because of the pigments, and also the subject matter, as you pointed out. But why would the text and paintings be from different centuries?"

"*Cryptam* sounds like a crypt," I said, turning back to writing. "I wish I could ask Tamarind for help. She'd love a mystery involving a crypt. Oh! Can I get in touch with her now?"

Lane shook his head. "Not a chance. If you're right that North is still looking for something related to this information, he'll be keeping tabs on us. When you gave me your bag, I disabled your phone. North has no way to trace us now. And don't even think about sending her an email from this computer, unless it's to say how lovely Paris is."

"Doesn't turning off our phones raise his suspicion?"

Lane shook his head. "He knows I'd be careful." He pulled open a kitchen drawer, revealing four cell phones of the same model but in different colors. He selected the black one for himself and handed me the red one. "Don't get in touch with anyone you know, but we can communicate with each other."

Pushing the gravity of the situation from my mind, I turned my attention back to the Latin. "*Cementarium claustri ad cryptam,*" I read.

Lane slid his fingers across the cell phone. "Translated, it approximates 'stonemasons of cloisters to crypt.'"

"Stonemasons who built cloisters and a crypt," I repeated. "It's all so medieval."

Lane gulped the last of his spiked tea. "Hugo," he whispered. "That's why he was involved. Now that we know it involves a church with cloisters and a crypt—"

"Because Hugo was a priest?"

"His expertise was religious iconography. He *knew* this job involved something of larger significance. That's why he sought me out! I'm the reason he's probably dead."

Lane stood and filled his mug with brandy, sans tea.

"You didn't kill him."

"Didn't I? He risked his life to try to speak with me. If the bigger treasure North is after involves something a monastic community felt the need to protect, that explains why it's a big enough deal—" He broke off and downed his brandy. He slammed the empty mug down, then squatted and rummaged through a drawer underneath the one with the cell phones. From the very back, behind batteries, flashlights, scratch paper, and several odd electronic devices I didn't recognize, he pulled out a mangled box of cigarettes and a crystal ashtray.

"You think Hugo was involved in *this* job?" I asked while Lane lit a cigarette and inhaled deeply.

"It would explain how Hugo found me at the Louvre. North isn't in the habit of revealing details about jobs that a member of his crew isn't involved in. We know now that we can't take North at his word. God, this must be a huge treasure if it's enough for North to ruin his reputation over. What have I gotten you into? We need to get you on a flight home."

"What are you talking about? We just figured out—"

"You held up your part of the bargain," Lane said. "I'm willing to trade a tiny piece of art history that nobody will miss for your happiness and safety. But this theft is a bigger deal than I thought it was."

"Which is exactly why I can't go home. I don't even know why I'm sitting here talking with you when I should be going to the police. It made sense at first to protect ourselves by going through with North's plan, but this has gotten way out of hand."

Lane crossed his arms over his chest and stared at me. "You want to go to the police after we robbed the Louvre?"

I slouched in my seat. "Point taken."

"Even if we could get the police to believe us, what could we tell them? We haven't figured out what any of this means. We don't yet know what North is after—some sort of treasure that made its way from India to a crypt in France? And Hugo is a grown man who can do as he pleases. His disappearance wouldn't be taken seriously as a missing person."

"What about the blood I saw? Surely that suggests foul play."

"I'm sure it's been wiped clean by now."

I groaned. "I wish I knew what to do. I feel like I'm being pulled deeper under water with every step I take. I'm stuck, and I don't know how to get myself out."

Lane left his cigarette at the edge of the ash tray and kneeled down in front of me. Taking my hands in his, he said, "Let me save you from the quicksand, Jones. I risked stealing from the Louvre so that you'd be safe. Please, let me handle this."

My chest constricted and I found it difficult to breathe. "What are you going to do?"

He sighed and stood up, retrieving his cigarette and taking one last drag before stubbing it out. "Whatever I have to do. I need to find out what happened to Hugo and what North is really trying to steal. I can't let him get away with this."

"You don't even know what *this* is. You need me to figure it out."

"I can—"

"You can do what? When we first met, you were the one who

convinced me of the importance of turning to an expert when it comes to piecing together history. I turned to you for help. Now you need me." How could I go back to my apartment, my office, my life teaching history classes, all the while knowing I'd been complicit in losing an important piece of history to a murderer?

"I'm not getting on a plane," I said. "I was part of the theft. It's on my hands, too. I was stupid to agree to one small item being stolen, but it's forgivable under the circumstances. What's unforgivable is letting a historic treasure fall into North's hands and not finding out what happened to Hugo."

"Is there anything I can do to make you get on a flight home?"

"Yes," I said. "We can stop North, get justice for Hugo, and find the treasure."

CHAPTER 23

"Let's go over what we know," I said.

Lane rested his elbows on the table, put his head in his hands, and yawned.

"I'm boring you with all this talk about jumping into action?"

"You may have noticed I didn't get to sleep last night, and the night before I only caught a few hours. I've been running on adrenaline."

"I wish you had time to sleep, but we don't have that luxury."

Lane raised a sleepy eyebrow at me. "What am I missing?"

"We know time is of the essence—"

"We do?" He snapped up.

"Yes," I said, "we do. North made a mistake in his plan to get me here. If he wanted to be sure I'd come, he would have waited until I was on spring break. Instead, he had to risk that I'd come right away. It was a *risk*, and now I've seen firsthand that he doesn't like risk."

"That's good. That's very good. But it's still not much."

"I know. But since North is acting differently from his usual MO, we need to figure out why. Tell me what you know about North. Everything."

"I told you the basics already, when I was trying to convince you to take the threat seriously."

"I know not to underestimate him. But what about personal details. How did you meet him?"

"In a way, through John."

"Your mentor."

"It's probably not the most accurate description of our relationship, since he always worked alone, but since he took me under his wing, that's the easiest way to describe it. John was one of the few people I knew who told me to stay away from North. I was skeptical of the advice, because I'd heard that North was a man of his word. He was also a man of vision, something I found compelling at that time in my life. It was when I wanted to hurt people I thought deserved it. North took advantage of my motivation. He used it. That's what he does. He's smart, so he can manipulate people to get what he wants. I did one job with him, because it was stealing from a rich baron who'd acquired his wealth through questionable means, and also happened to beat his wife."

"You robbed a wife-beating baron of some art. That doesn't sound so bad." I cringed as I spoke the words.

"John was right. North only told me what I wanted to hear. He never *lied*—he left out the full truth through omission. I decided to work alone from then on."

It was odd hearing more about things Lane had done in his life before he went straight and converted from an art thief to an art historian.

"North is universally known in the business," Lane continued, "and also in the legitimate art world, as Henry North."

As Lane spoke, I used the laptop to look up Henry North. "It says he's a wealthy art dealer. Exactly like he told me. How boring."

"And a great cover."

"Is that his real name?"

"I highly doubt it. But he covered his tracks well. It looks like a real identity."

"Dante and Marius are real names, too? Everyone on this museum job?"

"As real as you can consider the names they've gone by for years. Which reminds me..." He took the laptop from me. As he typed, a smile lit up his face. "Perfect."

"What's perfect?"

He turned the screen toward me. It was a news service article in an English-language newspaper. "Performance Art in Poor Taste at the Louvre," the headline read, next to a photo of thousands of people crowded into the lobby of the Louvre, underneath the great pyramid. "Paris, France," I read out loud. "At eleven o'clock this morning, a performance artist known as Chaos singlehandedly wreaked havoc at the world's most famous museum, the Louvre. Chaos, whose real identity is unknown, dressed as a museum docent and brazenly removed a painting in front of hundreds of people, before running through the museum and leaving the unharmed painting inside a box with a political message—" I broke off and skimmed the rest of the story. "It goes on to say guards circled him and foiled his plans to leave the museum with the painting. How can they say that? That's not what really happened."

Lane shrugged. "It's sort of true. You'd prefer they report the truth?"

"Of course not." I handed the computer back to Lane. "It's still unsettling."

"It's similar to what happened when the Corot painting was stolen in 1998. The press reported that the museum had searched all the guests before letting people out, but they hadn't."

"How could they—"

"Let's get back on point," Lane said. "North isn't as far ahead of us as he thinks he is. Like only knowing about my hideout that's an open secret. Not this place."

"Is that where you got this camera and added disguise from?" I asked. "I thought he was having you watched the whole time up until the heist."

"When Marius and I needed a food break, I suggested grabbing a bite at a restaurant around the corner from that place. When I excused myself to go to the bathroom, he didn't find it necessary to follow. Which is what I expected. He's very proper in many ways. I was back within three minutes, with the bag tucked under the back of my shirt."

"What if he had followed you to the bathroom?"

"I didn't leave it up to chance. Not *too much* chance. I weighed the risk, like I always do. Marius was eating his favorite dish, which the waiter brought out moments before, so it was highly unlikely he'd follow me. But if I'd known what North was capable of, I wouldn't have taken the risk." Lane ran his hands through his hair, then picked up a pen and twirled it between his fingers. "There's something we're missing."

"There's *a lot* we're missing. Such as the fact that the parchment doesn't say where the cloister is, or what's hidden in the crypt. But right now, you need sleep. You look like you're about to fall over. Take a nap. I'll research while you get some rest."

"You might be right that I need some sleep to think straight. Remember, no contacting anyone about the illuminated manuscript page. Communications with people you know, like Tamarind, might be monitored. And communications with experts, even anonymously, might alert North that someone is looking into it when they shouldn't be." His eyelids drooped.

"Come on," I said, leading a bleary-eyed Lane to the couch. "Where do you keep the blankets around here?"

"Closet," he murmured, already lying down.

I found a narrow closet next to the front door, disguised by a hanging mirror. I brought back a plaid wool blanket, but I needn't have bothered. He was already asleep. At least I thought so. But as I placed the blanket over him, his lips moved.

"Did you say something?" I whispered.

"The desk," he said, opening his eyes. "Don't forget about the desk. It may tell us something." He told me the name of the desk at the Louvre, so I could look it up. "Any more questions for now?"

"Since you're awake," I said, "There's a question I've been dying to ask. How did you choose the painting for the diversion?"

"You mean because it risked getting damaged?" He grinned. "I've always hated that painting."

CHAPTER 24

While Lane slept, I got to work. I made myself another cup of tea, then sat down at the table with the laptop. Before I tackled research, there was something more important I had to do.

I needed to get back in touch with Sanjay sometime soon, lest he call the National Guard—or whatever the French equivalent was. The last time I was abroad and didn't call him for more than a day, he hopped on a flight to India. To be fair, in that case he believed he had evidence that a treasure I was tracking down was also being sought by a killer. But Sanjay had always been one to overreact. I hoped that because he was currently in the midst of preparing for a magic tour, he wouldn't have time to consider doing anything drastic, but I wanted to be sure.

With Lane's word of warning, I knew my email couldn't contain any information about what was going on. I logged onto my email on the laptop and sent him a brief messge telling him that France wasn't a bust after all, as I'd written to him shortly after arriving, and that I was going to enjoy a few days relaxing before flying home.

I was about to log off and get to work when I saw an email from Tamarind.

J,
Why aren't you posting photos of Paris?
Things are boring here. Thanks for asking. What's with the radio silence?

Most importantly, why did you let Naveen take over your classes while you're gone??? He changed your syllabus—the nerve of that man!!!!!!!

Scratch that. It's true about Naveen, but that's not the most important thing. How's Paris??? Send photos! You should do this thing where you pose in front of the Eiffel Tower making it look like your finger is on top of it.

T

I shouldn't have opened the email. I couldn't worry about Naveen or my students. I sent her a quick reply saying I had a spotty internet connection but that all was well.

I forced myself to push all thoughts of Naveen Krishnan from my mind. Whatever was going on at home could wait. I glanced at Lane, sleeping like the dead on the couch.

I closed the laptop and found a paper notebook and pen in the junk drawer where Lane had salvaged his cigarettes. Making myself a list, I came up with four main avenues of research to pursue:

First, the clue itself. *Cementarium claustri ad cryptam.* Stonemasons, cloisters, and a crypt. Without more to go on, the words didn't tell us anything. I had to set aside that piece of the puzzle for now.

Second, the Indian elephant and tiger motif in both a French illuminated manuscript and in a letter written by a clerk from the East India Company. How were the two connected? We wouldn't be able to get the parchment painting dated, so that was a dead end. And Indian rulers loved pageantry, so there were far too many riches involving tigers and elephants to narrow it down that way.

Third, the East India Company's connections to the religious community in France. Before seeing this parchment, I hadn't known there was such a connection. The letters North had might help connect the dots, but I had no way to see them. I've never fooled myself into believing I have anything close to a photographic memory, but when I focus on something, I give it my all. I remembered the date in the letter from the Englishman: 1793. But

North had been careful not to show me anything too revealing.

Lastly, the desk at the Louvre where the parchment had been hidden. This was my best lead, because the parchment was deliberately placed inside the desk's secret hiding place.

I knew close to nothing about the history of furniture, but from Lane I knew it was a high wooden desk with an angled top that was once used by monks in a scriptorium. The Louvre maintained a comprehensive website of its art, and I quickly found the desk in question. The information didn't specify the provenance, but it was a desk once used by Benedictine monks circa 1100, before the Louvre acquired it during the French Revolution.

Switching browser tabs to look up where monks might have had such a desk, I saw that I'd forgotten to log out of my email. A new message was waiting for me. Sanjay had written back already. It was only around 6 o'clock in the morning in San Francisco. Did he ever sleep?

This illusion is killing me. Up all night again. I need a break. Why don't you send me a mentalist puzzle for a break?

I froze. If North was still monitoring my email, this was bad. Why had I thought it was a good idea for me to write to Sanjay in code from Paris? Of course, I knew the reason. At the time, I didn't realize the lengths North was willing to go to.

I tried to breathe. Was this what hyperventilating felt like?

I read the email again. Sanjay didn't actually say the word "code." Nor did he say anything about our previous coded communication in which he'd directed me to Sébastien Renaud. I was overreacting.

But my mini freak-out gave me an idea. If I was right that the message on the piece of parchment was there to provide a clue, then there was no point in it being so obscure. It had to tell us something specific. Otherwise it wouldn't have been worth hiding. I pulled up the image of the parchment of faded calligraphy and zoomed in.

I looked first at the painting. I didn't know much about the artists who painted illuminated manuscripts, but to me it didn't look like the animals and the man wrapped in the elephant's trunk were the work of a skilled artist. The animals were recognizable, but that's about all that could be said for them. As for the poor fellow being squeezed by the elephant's trunk, his open mouth indicated agony, but there weren't any identifiable details to suggest he was a specific historical figure.

Scrolling down to the text, I was struck by the differences between the inks Lane had pointed out. Where the animals remained vibrant, the Latin lettering had almost completely faded into the paper. I adjusted the contrast to get a better look.

"There's another word," I whispered to myself.

At the beginning of the string of words was additional lettering we'd missed because it was so faded it was nearly invisible.

Sequere. Follow.

These were *directions* from the cloisters. "*Follow* stonemasons of cloisters to crypt."

I'd solved it! Oh. Damn. Once I thought about my breakthrough for more than two seconds, it was clear I hadn't solved a thing. Which stonemasons? Where was this cloister and crypt? How did a treasure end up there? Was it truly an Indian treasure as the painting suggested? I'd been wildly speculating when I told Lane I was sure the piece of parchment led to a bigger treasure. My head spun with everything we didn't know.

I took a swig of tea, which had gone cold. I'd forgotten about it in the last hour spent delving into research. I stood up from the table and stretched. I was itching to go for a run to clear my head, but it didn't seem wise to leave the apartment. Instead, I turned to the bookshelves in search of a break. A few cheesy adventure novels by H. Rider Haggard, like *King Solomon's Mines*, were nestled in the corner of one shelf. I devoured those books as a guilty pleasure, but I'd never mentioned it to Lane. Several Jorge Luis Borges books lined one shelf. He hadn't told me he read Borges, too. I picked up a dog-eared book.

"After you mentioned Borges on the train to Aberdeen last

year," Lane's voice said from behind me, "I thought I should give him a try."

"I didn't mean to wake you."

"You cried out a minute ago."

"I did?"

"I thought you might have made a breakthrough." He tossed the blanket aside and got up. "As exhausted as I am, I couldn't get back to sleep. Probably for the best anyway, since I've got these contact lenses on."

"I thought for a second that I'd figured something out, but it doesn't tell us anything. I'm afraid I may be leading us on a wild goose chase."

"Metaphors and philosophy," Lane said, looking at the book in my hand. "It's interesting you enjoy these books. I thought you liked things to be more straightforward. Finding the truth in history and teaching it to college students, not getting caught up in messy, unanswerable questions."

How did he know me so well in such a short space of time? "You're right, but Borges' motif of the labyrinth is about as straightforward as you can get. It's winding, but unlike a maze that leads off in too many different directions and includes dead ends, a labyrinth leads you exactly where you need to go."

"Which one do you think we're trapped in right now, Jones?"

"I wish I knew."

CHAPTER 25

"What did you find out while I slept?" Lane asked.

I handed him my list and told him that I'd placed the 12th century desk from a Benedictine monk scriptorium acquired by the Louvre during the French Revolution. "I must have inadvertently exclaimed aloud when I saw this additional faded word telling us to follow the stonemasons."

"Not bad for an hour's worth of work."

"Weren't you listening? We don't know anything! I don't even know if you were right to listen to me. Maybe I'm crazy."

"You're not crazy."

"You know what I am? *Hungry.* I didn't realize it until just now, but I'm starving. I don't think I've eaten all day."

"I don't think it would be good for us to go out to eat together."

"I figured as much. Do you have any canned food in this miniature kitchen?"

"Hey, don't knock the kitchen. It's where I'm going to cook us dinner when I get back from the market."

Lane turned to grab a canvas shopping tote from a hook on the back of the door with one hand while he ran his other hand through his hair. When he turned toward me again, he was a different man. He was the stooped, disheveled man who rode the metro and walked up the stairs while speaking in a British accent. *Chameleon,* indeed. No wonder North liked the moniker.

"Who *are* you?"

"Right now?" The voice was hesitant, almost scared. "I'm an

unassuming Englishman originally from the small town of Nether Wallop."

I laughed. "Knowing English village names, I bet that's a real place."

"Most assuredly."

"And what's your name?"

"I'm far too shy to get to know the neighbors, so they don't know my name, only that I'm a quiet neighbor."

"You're spooky, is what you are."

"I say, the quiet gentleman from Nether Wallop isn't spooky. *Odd*, perhaps, but *spooky* is going a bit far." With a wide-eyed expression of false outrage, he grabbed the door handle.

"Hang on. Aren't French shops closed on Sundays?"

"Not in modern day Paris. Unless there's a strike. Which, to be fair, is a frequent occurrence in this country. But the nearby market does close early, so I'd better get going if we want to eat."

Breaking character, he grinned and blew me a kiss on his way out the door.

I rested my back against the door and closed my eyes. *What are you doing here, Jaya Jones?* Instead of thinking about buying a plane ticket home or figuring out the treasure North was after, all I could think about was Lane shopping for fresh food from a Paris market—as long as there wasn't a strike.

My eyes popped open. The French had *always* had a tradition of protesting, going all the way back to the French Revolution. It was the same timing as both the letters North showed me and the Louvre's acquisition of the desk. The 1790s. The illustration had been painted on the old parchment by monks and hidden inside a French scriptorium desk at the same time Trenton Smith had written home to England from India—about the same treasure.

I flung open the apartment door and ran onto the landing overlooking the staircase leading down. The twisting stairs were empty. Lane was already gone.

I ran back to the apartment and opened the computer. There was one incredibly important religious site with cloisters and a crypt that I knew had come under siege and had its belongings seized during the French Revolution. And it was right next to Saint-Malo, the town where Dante had purchased chocolates.

Mont Saint-Michel.

One of the most iconic sites in France, Mont Saint-Michel was constructed on an island off the coast of Normandy. It had been a monastery, a scriptorium, and a prison. Because of its strategic location surrounded by dangerous tides and quicksand, it had been a relatively secure fortress during periods of history that were anything but secure.

I began to research in earnest to fill in the details about the Mont. I could barely contain my excitement as I read about the hilly island off the northern coast of France in Normandy that was transformed into Mont Saint-Michel after a local bishop had a dream in the year 708. Saint Michael appeared to the bishop in his dream and asked him to build a monastery. It was a difficult process, building on a rocky hill rising out of the ocean, but several miracles were attributed to making the seemingly impossible construction a success.

Looking at pictures of the castle-like Mont, it was easy to see why it had spiritual significance. The island had an ethereal look to it, rising out of the fog and surrounded by the ocean during high tide, but allowing people to pass during low tide. To this day, people died in the waters surrounding the Mont, either by getting caught unawares in the dangerous tides that seemed to come out of nowhere, or by stepping into quicksand that was deceptively the same color as solid sand. I shivered at the thought. The Mont tricked people, painting a perfect picture of calm tides and pristine sand, yet both were an illusion. Danger lurked just beneath the surface.

The monastery attracted many monks who wanted a place of solitude, and it also became a major destination for Christian pilgrims. Over the years, the significance of the site grew, and the abbey grew in size accordingly. More and more rooms were built over the centuries, and ramparts were constructed surrounding the

Mont to protect it from invaders. The island monastery and village held fast through different rulers, wars, and periodic mudslides and fires. Through it all, the monks continued their work of serving God through prayer—and creating illuminated manuscripts.

Why wasn't Lane back with those groceries yet? The more I read, the more sure I became that this was what we were looking for.

Buildings on the Mont were frequently damaged through both natural and man-made disasters, and they were rebuilt with current architectural techniques, leading to a hodgepodge of styles that combined thick Romanesque walls with ornate Gothic arches. With that history, there were plenty of opportunities for treasures to be hidden within its walls.

Even now, the site was often in a state of disrepair and in need of renovation. In fact, a huge renovation project was currently underway. Much of the Mont was currently surrounded by scaffolding. The majority of the renovations were scheduled to be completed the following month.

That was it: *our ticking clock.*

The renovations were why North had to act now—and why we did, too.

CHAPTER 26

When Lane walked through the door twenty minutes later, vegetable greens poked over the top of the shopping bag and he carried two cups of coffee in his hands. I took both cups of coffee from his hands, set them down, and threw my arms around his neck.

"If I'd known the reaction that good French coffee would evoke, I would have gone earlier. You should appreciate how difficult it is to find somewhere that offers coffee 'to go' in Paris."

"I've got it," I said, letting him go and bounding on the balls of my feet. "I know where North is going and why there's a ticking clock that made him rush into this."

"Slow down. I don't think you need this coffee after all."

I filled Lane in on what I'd pieced together.

"You said Dante had a lot of things in his pockets," Lane said. "A lot more than chocolates from Saint-Malo."

"Yes, but—"

"And I'm sure there are other religious sites that were sacked during the French Revolution."

"But not one that's so old and sprawling, is known for its famous illuminated manuscripts, and that's currently undergoing a major renovation wrapping up next month. There are tons of workmen and scaffolding around right now. Once the renovations are complete, it will be nearly impossible to do any secret digging for a hidden treasure. This ticking clock explains all of North's odd behavior that's out of character. He had no choice but to act more recklessly than usual."

"You could be right," Lane said, but he didn't look convinced. "It's only a couple hours drive. Worth checking out."

"How are we going to rent a car? I thought you wanted to stay under the radar?"

Lane left the bag of groceries in the kitchen, then disappeared into the hall closet and returned with a UK passport. It was his face on the ID, but the name was "Al Monkshood, Jr."

"You're not serious," I said. "What kind of alias is that?" I handed the passport back to him and sank onto the couch with my coffee. I took a sip, happy he'd remembered exactly the way I like it, thick with sugar.

"There's history to the name," he said.

"But it's not your name!" I felt my stomach tighten. "Is it?"

"You know my name."

"Do I?"

"What's that supposed to mean?"

"You can't be serious about using a fake passport. I thought all that was behind you."

"It is. But this situation—"

"You never got rid of your old fake IDs." My voice trembled as I spoke, the truth sinking in. "You never planned on getting rid of them."

I was so rattled by what I'd realized that I thought my head might pop. It was one thing to have thought he wasn't completely honest with me about his past. This was his future. A future I had been stupid enough to think I might be a part of. We knew each other so well in some ways, but in other ways, we hadn't begun to scratch the surface.

"It's coming in handy, if you hadn't noticed," he snapped. I'd hit a nerve. A nerve that was there because he hadn't fully committed to giving up his old life.

"You never planned on giving this up, did you?" My voice was flat. I wasn't scared. I wasn't angry. I was hurt. I'd been betrayed.

At every turn, I tried to trust him. I wanted so much to believe him. But how could I? It wasn't just the fake IDs. There were also the multiple hidden apartments.

Lane swallowed hard. "This isn't the time for this conversation, Jaya."

"If you use that fake ID," I said. "I'm out."

"Good. That's what I wanted all along. You *should* be out."

"Don't be stupid. I'm the one who figured out what's going on!"

"We don't know what's going on yet. You know I wish you could stay with me. I wish, more than anything, that there was a way to have you in my life that wasn't like this. You know that. But I don't want you to be a part of *this*. I never did."

"You can't do this alone."

"I'll manage."

"We do this together. But we do it above board."

"After robbing the Louvre, isn't that a little late?"

"That was different," I insisted. "We were being coerced. From this point on, do this right."

The rational part of my brain told me I shouldn't trust him. And yet, I was overwhelmed by the feeling that I trusted him completely. I didn't blindly trust Lane to give up who he was, but I believed his motives were good in all the ways that mattered.

"We can do things without the fake ID," Lane said, "but you've given me another chance to think about your involvement in this. I don't want North seeking retribution against you, after everything we did to protect you in the first place. If he knows you're coming after him, all bets are off."

"I've been thinking about that, too. What if we can find the treasure and catch North, all without him realizing it's us who did it?"

"How do you propose we pull that off?"

"The same way North is pulling it off. If we're right about what he's doing, his men are disguised as workmen who are working on the renovations to the Mont."

Lane shook his head. "Even if we put on the best disguises, North would know us."

"Not if he doesn't see us," I said. "He doesn't know we're onto him. We can spy on them, then make sure their work happens to be discovered by the proper authorities, tipped off by an anonymous good Samaritan who saw what they were doing. If we do this right, there's no way he'll know it's us."

Lane studied my face for a moment before speaking. "That might just work."

"There's one more thing." My voice quivered, but I had to ask. "Show me your passport. Your *real* one. You've never let me see it. If you want me to trust you, you need to trust me completely."

Lane's face flushed red, but he nodded. "Here goes nothing. If you don't walk out the door after you see it, I know you'll stick with me through anything."

He retrieved a passport from a hidden compartment of his bag. "This," he said, "is the real Lane C. Peters." He handed me a U.S. passport.

"*Lancelot?*"

"You can see why I prefer Lane."

"*Caravaggio?*"

"I completely understand if you no longer want to be under the same roof as me."

"Lancelot Caravaggio Peters," I said. "It's a bit fanciful for your father, isn't it? From everything you've told me about him—"

"It was my mother who named me. She was bored from my father being away at work so much. She retreated into art and literature. I bet you can guess who two of her favorites were. She didn't think too much about the significance of either one. At least I hope not. And I doubt my father even noticed what she'd named me until it was too late to change the birth certificate. So here I am."

For dinner, Lane made bowls of mushroom risotto, and an arugula salad with beets, shaved radish, and a tangy vinaigrette.

"How did you make this in that tiny little kitchen?" I knew I'd been concentrating on additional research, but I hadn't thought I'd missed so much.

"A chef never reveals his secrets."

"I thought that was magicians."

He shrugged. "Same difference."

"God, this is good," I said through a mouthful.

"I cheated. Risotto is one of those dishes that sounds complicated, but really all it needs is patience. With only two burners, it's a good choice. I boiled the beets for the salad on the other one."

"Thank you, Lancelot."

"If you ever call me that again, I'll slip a sleeping pill into your risotto and put you on the next flight home to California."

CHAPTER 27

Over dinner, we caught up on our lives over the past five months. Lane had been bouncing around from place to place as he contemplated his options, using Paris as a home base. It was after two a.m. before we got back to our plan of action. First thing in the morning, we could head to the Mont to see if we were right. I wanted to leave right away, but Lane pointed out that my insistence on taking public transportation hindered our options. The plan wasn't to confront North. Instead, we would see what was going on and then call in an anonymous tip once North's men were close to finding whatever it was they were after, leaving the authorities to take it from there.

Lane looked as if he was going to pass out, so we agreed we should get a few hours sleep. At sunrise, we donned disguises from Lane's closet, primarily consisting of hats and scarves, which would look natural given the cold weather.

After packing a few additional items of clothing into a small daypack of Lane's, in case we ended up staying the night, we took the metro to the Gare Montparnasse train station. From there, we could catch a train to Rennes, then board a bus to Mont Saint-Michel. Lane wasn't kidding that renting a car would've been much easier. Still, my resolve didn't waver—not until we'd been subjected to stale croissants on the train.

We now stood waiting on a cold, rainy sidewalk with twenty rowdy Australians who were also waiting for the bus to Mont Saint-Michel. I wished it could at least have been snowing instead of sleeting, because then I wouldn't have been both cold and wet. Lane gave me a pointed look that clearly said "I told you so," but he remained silent.

The bus driver spoke highly accented broken English as he pointed out interesting sights visible from the bus windows, and even some invisible points of interest, such as when we passed from one region of France to the next. The regions had friendly rivalries, and the bus driver was a Breton who poked fun at the Normans. The border between the two regions was determined by the placement of a river which had changed course years ago, effectively moving Mont Saint-Michel from Brittany to Normandy.

Only thirty people called the Mont their home, the driver informed us. It was a tourist destination, with thousands of tourists flocking to the site each day. Even most of the locals who worked on the Mont lived in nearby villages on the mainland and took a shuttle bus to reach their shop, restaurant, or tourist site. No vehicles were allowed inside the gates except for small delivery vans. Mont Saint-Michel was very much like it was when pilgrims walked hundreds of miles on foot to reach it.

"Shopkeepers," the talkative driver said, "are in the same spot they were over a thousand years ago. Only instead of selling you a religious trinket, today they sell you a plastic *gargouille*. You understand? A gargoyle, *en anglais*. You are pilgrims, all of you. When you arrive, you will walk on the same street as your ancestors. You will visit the same restaurants, the same shops. Impressive, no?"

When the bus deposited us in front of a Tourist Information Center in a small town a couple of kilometers outside of Mont Saint-Michel, the rain had stopped. Stepping off the bus, I breathed in the salty air of the nearby ocean. But although I could smell it as well as if I were hovering above it, I couldn't see either the ocean or Mont Saint-Michel. Seeing my confusion, Lane pointed. There was yet another form of public transportation we had to take. A shuttle bus to the Mont.

"You've got to be kidding me," I mumbled.

"Rethinking the car option?" Lane asked.

"Shut up."

He kissed my forehead underneath the wool hat that covered my hair to make me less recognizable, and we followed the herd onto the bus.

Looking out the window of the shuttle bus, my grumpiness drained away, just like the receding tide alongside the causeway leading to the Mont. Looming in front of us, the castle's ramparts rose from the rock formation. The jagged rock sprang forth from the ocean on the lonely stretch of coastline. Fierce storm clouds were gathering in the distance beyond the majestic spire.

I was so in awe of the sight that Lane had to nudge me to get off the bus, once we'd stopped a few dozen yards from the entrance to the Mont. I nearly tripped, unable to pull my eyes from the fortress.

Even before we entered the Mont, it was clear that massive renovations were underway. A footbridge of flat wooden planks covered rough ground and formed a walkway guiding people to the front entrance gate. Ubiquitous scaffolding caused tourists to frame their photographs creatively, lest they be reminded it was the early 21st century, not the romantic Middle Ages they'd come to see. I felt like a character in a video game as I zigzagged around dozens of modern-day pilgrims who stopped in the narrow path without warning whenever they saw what looked like a good shot to photograph their family.

In spite of the attempts to turn the island into a gaudy tourist attraction, Mont Saint-Michel refused to be cheapened. Gaudy wax museums telling the brutal history of the Mont and shopkeepers selling t-shirts with silkscreen silhouettes of the abbey couldn't diminish the power of the structure that had been carved out of solid rock over 1,000 years before. Like the scaffolding, the shops and attractions were momentary distractions quickly forgotten as soon as you looked up.

Lane had been right to suggest I put on my running sneakers so I could maneuver around tourists on the steep cobblestone streets. But not for the reason he thought. It wasn't that I couldn't handle the uneven paving in my heels. It was the fact that the city planning of the Mont was created for a single purpose: to lead pilgrims toward the monastery and its abbey. The Mont had but one main road, a narrow cobblestone street that snaked upward toward the entrance of the abbey. With the architectural wonders that lay above us, I couldn't be bothered to look at the ground. Inside the gates, a drawbridge led the way into the monument. I craned my neck to see the ramparts and towers that loomed above.

"You've got the awestruck tourist role down to a T," Lane whispered in my ear.

"I'm not kidding around," I said. "I couldn't stop staring if I tried." Now that we were here at the Mont, it felt like a travesty that we were there to foil a plot rather than explore the living history of the French fortress.

"Remember the plan."

"We ask a guide about stonemasons, then go through to the cloisters and the crypts of the abbey. And if that doesn't tell us what we need to know, we trace the walkways of the Mont for additional instances of scaffolding, to make sure we've covered all the possibilities."

"The whole island shouldn't take more than half the day." Lane paused and steered me away from a family with a stroller that had stopped in front of a souvenir shop. "This place is even smaller than I thought it would be."

"Says the tall person. I feel so strange in my running shoes when I'm not on a run." I wriggled my toes, feeling the uneven surface below my feet. I might as well have been naked and barefoot with how vulnerable they made me feel. There's power in height. Sure, there's power in other things, too. But when you're not even five feet tall, stepping into three-inch heels is like taking an elixir to feel powerful.

"I know I should start paying attention," I said, "but it's just so hard to concentrate—hey, is that a gargoyle up there? It's so weathered and covered in moss that I can barely tell."

"Your scarf is slipping."

"It's not as cold today. Not yet, at least." I glanced past the gargoyle toward the stormy sky.

"I can see too much of your face. Not that I'm complaining, but I'd hate to see what happens if anyone else notices."

I wound the long scarf around my neck one more time, covering my nose. The gray woolen scarf smelled vaguely of an unexpected mix of sandalwood, tarragon, and smoke.

"I can see too much of your face, too," I said. "You're smiling. You're enjoying this place, too."

"It's impossible not to."

The main road, no wider than a path, led directly to the abbey. After fifteen minutes climbing upward, during which I'd nearly forgotten about our quest, we found ourselves at the base of a steep set of stone stairs that led to the abbey's entrance.

We bought entry tickets and asked about an English-language guide. We found a friendly young woman who was going to be giving a tour shortly, but had a few minutes to answer our questions.

"Let me show you the 'jobbers mark' stones!" The perkiest French woman I'd ever encountered led us into the abbey's front courtyard. "Stonemasons and their workers were often paid by the stone. In many sections of *Le Mont,* you will find their inscriptions." She pointed at a section beneath our feet with various symbols.

From the courtyard high on the Mont, the wind was stronger than it had been on the narrow street shielded by tall buildings. I was glad for my scratchy hat and scarf. I took a few steps to the edge to enjoy the view of the barren sandy beach that surrounded us. The powerful tides had painted deep swirls in the sand. Looking over the thick stone ledge, with the wind whipping around me, the sand below seemed miles away.

"What about the stonemasons who built the cloisters and crypts?" Lane asked the guide.

"Yes, most of Mont Saint-Michel is made of stone."

"We wondered," he said, "if there are records of the stonemasons who built the cloisters and the crypt."

"You mean crypts."

"There are *multiple* crypts?" I said, turning back from the view.

"Oh yes. There are many crypts. Three are on the tour."

"And the men who built them?" Lane asked.

"Their individual names are not recorded," the guide answered with a smile.

"There's no information about them?" I asked.

"Only an image of the likeness of two of the masons, in the cloisters."

"There are paintings in the cloisters?" I said, surprised.

"Not paintings. A carving. Stone carvers who carved themselves in stone." She beamed at me. "Though it was not looked favorably upon, they wanted to be remembered."

"Are there any rumors about the stonemasons building any secret rooms?" I asked. "Perhaps underneath one of the crypts?"

She must have been used to people asking her strange questions, because her smile didn't falter. "There are enough mysteries at the Mont without secret rooms. If you come on the tour, you will learn about Aubert's message from Saint-Michael, and the miracles..." She prattled on for the next two minutes, until her tour was scheduled to begin.

"Are you sure you don't want to join the group tour?" she asked.

Lane thanked her in French and tipped her generously, before grabbing my hand and running into the abbey. I understood the urgency. With the type of exploring we'd be doing, we wanted to stay ahead of the tour groups.

In the cloisters, we found the carving of the stonemasons. It was easy to find, because it was one of the few carvings that hadn't been worn beyond recognition.

The weather-worn stone faces of two men who'd lived nearly a millennium ago looked down at us.

"These stonemasons don't appear to be telling us how to follow them," I said.

Lane snapped a picture with his phone. "North is the one with more information. Let's go see if he's already set up scaffolding in any of the crypts."

Over the next few hours, we walked over ancient stones and through the hodgepodge of architectural styles used over the centuries. The result of the varied building methods was harmonious splendor.

"I can't think straight," I said. "This place is a maze."

"Labyrinth," Lane said with a wink.

"I get the feeling I got this all wrong. You're right. I've got an overactive imagination. Hugo ran off of his own free will after being roughed-up by an associate of his less civilized than North, Dante could have visited Saint-Malo because he loved that chocolate shop, the illuminated manuscript page really was North's endgame, and we're free and clear of him forever. Let's still check out the rest of the island, but I doubt we'll find anything. Then we can take a break for a meal."

"That, my dear Jones, is the best idea I've heard all day."

After leaving the abbey, we followed the ramparts, which ran along the outskirts of the Mont. Off the main drag, we had the medieval path to ourselves. Faint French folk music wafted up from one of the nearby restaurants.

"M'lady," Lane said with a bow. "May I have this dance?"

"What accent is that?"

"Czech. I rarely get to use it."

"I like it."

"Does that mean you'll dance with me?"

High above the quicksand below, Lane spun me around the wide walkway of the ramparts. The rest of the world fell away, and I forgot about the madness that had brought us to that spot. For a few minutes, at least, I wasn't a college professor who'd made some questionable choices. I was a princess dancing inside ancient castle walls.

I was pretty sure Lane was leading me in a waltz, though it required some creativity to make it work with the guitar on the nearby restaurant's speakers as our background music.

With my eyes locked on Lane's, I tripped on a cobblestone and we slid gently against the stone parapet.

"I'd be steadier in my heels."

"Ha. It's this bulky clothing. Not the best for dancing."

"You think I'd have an easier time in a ball gown?"

"Good point."

"I'm starving," I declared. "Didn't I read that omelets are the specialty here?"

"I'm only surprised it took you so long to suggest it."

The fluffy omelet set in front of me twenty minutes later wasn't quite as large as the leather backpack I'd brought with me, but it was at least as big as my messenger bag I'd left at home. That didn't deter me. I polished off every last bite, along with three espressos.

"You better be willing to drink that quickly," Lane said after I ordered my third espresso. "If we leave shortly, we can probably catch the last bus of the day to the train station."

"Speak for yourself. Before I leave, I want to find a local historian, in case they can tell us more than the guide. There's bound to be one."

I polished off my coffee, and we left to visit the abbey once more.

The ticket-taker didn't speak much English, so Lane conversed with her in French for a few minutes. As they spoke, creases formed on his forehead. He thanked her and motioned for me to follow him outside.

"What's the matter?" I asked.

"Massi Bruel is the man to see," he said.

"What's the matter with that?"

"He's an elderly man in his late eighties, and rarely has visitors. She said he'd be so pleased to have more people to talk with about the history of this place."

"Even better," I said. "He'll probably have more time than the guide to talk about rumors nobody thinks are worth mentioning."

"That's not the problem," Lane said. "The problem is that we weren't the first people asking after him this week."

CHAPTER 28

I sank down onto a cold stone step at the top of the abbey's grand staircase. "It could be a coincidence."

Lane shook his head. "It was a charming Englishman. Who does that sound like?"

I swore. "That means I was right about everything after all."

"It sounds like it. I was hoping you were wrong, too."

"Thanks."

"We don't know for sure. Let's find Massi. I got directions."

In silence, we climbed to what must have been the most remote part of the small island, behind the abbey, and came to what looked like a guard post. I hesitated before knocking on the door, unsure about what I was hoping for. I wasn't sure if my hands were shaking from the excitement of knowing I might be standing close to a lost treasure from French India, or from the disappointment that I was being pulled deeper into the mire.

I took a deep breath and knocked on the door.

There must be something to French life, because the man who opened the door seconds later was remarkably vigorous for someone in his eighties. Though his skin was weathered enough to look like he'd spent multiple lifetimes in the sun, he moved gracefully. The dark olive tone of his skin suggested he was North African, yet his eyes were the lightest of blue. He looked past us, but I realized he wasn't looking at anything at all. His blue eyes were cloudy. He was blind.

Lane introduced us in French, but I understood a reference to my being a historian and his inquiry as to whether Massi spoke English.

"You give me an excuse to practice," he said with a gap-toothed smile. "*Mrahba,*" he added, shaking our hands and inviting us in for tea, happy to speak about history. We'd decided not to ask him about the other people who had been to visit him recently, lest we cause him to be suspicious. Instead, I wanted to see what Massi knew about rumored hidden treasures. I've learned that true history is often buried deep within local lore. The challenge is pulling out the truths that are hidden under layers of embellishments.

"A fellow traveler and historian," Massi said after I told him how I ended up a history professor in California, across the world from where I was born in India. "You of all people understand the importance of history."

"That's why I love to learn the history of the places I visit."

Massi insisted on serving us tea as he told us the history of the Mont, which had passed down to him. Lane held me back when I tried to help Massi with the tea, and I saw that he was right. With an expert hand, Massi steeped the traditional Maghrebi mint tea in a stainless steel pot. He poured it theatrically, from high above glass teacups filled with crushed mint leaves. I took a sip of the strong, sweet tea, wondering what secrets Massi held in his tower cottage.

Originally from Algeria, Massi explained that he'd lived on the Mont for many decades, ever since immigrating to France. He settled in this particular area because he wanted to raise sheep, and he'd heard that the sheep in this region of Normandy were special. The sheep were called "pré-salé," because of the salty flavor of their meat, acquired by grazing in the grass that grew in the salt flats surrounding Mont Saint-Michel.

"As an outsider," Massi said, "I was initially viewed with suspicion. That was until the villagers saw that I was more of an expert on their history than themselves! Books and printing presses had replaced oral traditions, and much was lost."

Massi wasn't yet in France during the war, but he related to the loss, as someone from a country that had suffered so much. He didn't resent the French people, in spite of their colonial control, only their rulers. When he came to France as a young man, it was natural for him to talk with the elders about what they knew. He didn't realize his interest was unusual. Only once the elders were gone and he was an elderly man himself did he and other people realize how much he knew.

"Mont Saint-Michel had a problem," he said, running a gnarled hand over his face and shaking his head. "In World War II, much of their recorded history was destroyed."

I sat up straighter on the futon, nearly knocking over my tea.

"Destroyed?" I repeated.

"That is the correct word for ceasing to exist, no? My English is not so perfect—"

"Your English is superb. Better than many of my college students. I understood you. I was simply surprised, because I hadn't read that anywhere."

Massi shrugged. "It's an embarrassing history, is it not? People know the truth, but it's not something they talk about."

"How did it happen?"

"Ah!" Massi said with a clap. "It happened in the most ironic of ways. During the French Revolution, the monks became concerned that their priceless illuminated manuscripts would be destroyed. Mobs of revolutionaries destroyed so much, including the statues of kings on Notre Dame Cathedral in Paris, which the mobs who opposed the monarchy had mistaken for kings of France, not religious kings of Judah as they were in truth. Books—both records of the Mont's history and precious illuminated manuscripts—were packed and moved secretly off of the Mont, taken to safe hiding places."

"I read about that," I said. "They didn't have time to remove everything, though. I wasn't able to find references to all the items left behind."

"Because during World War II," Massi said, "shortly before the allies liberated France, many of the 'safe' places were sacked. The Mont's history, housed at Saint-Lô, was destroyed."

That was our answer to why the treasure hadn't been found until now. *The records had been lost.*

"Algeria was not the only country France colonized," Massi continued. "You know of the French East India Company, and how they held trading ports along the eastern coast of India for many years?"

More of the pieces were falling into place. Just like the Englishman in the East India Company who'd written home in the letters North showed me, Frenchmen were also stationed in India. Both European powers routinely claimed treasures from India—sometimes legitimately, as gifts given to them by local rulers who wanted to gain political advantage, and sometimes by stealing them after a successful battle, as the spoils of war.

"And it was the French Revolution," Massi was saying, "that bankrupted the Company."

"Yes," I said. I knew the history well. "The French East India Company was originally abolished a couple of decades before the revolution and absorbed under the French Crown, but it's hard to destroy something so powerful. It took the Revolution to wipe them out for good."

Massi grinned, his vacant eyes creasing at the edges as they looked out at nothing and everything. "The people wouldn't stand for it."

Lane cleared his throat and shot a confused look at me. "Fascinating learning about this history, but what does that have to do with Mont Saint-Michel?"

"Ah yes," Massi said. "You see, *Le Mont* has always been a sacred spot. You know of the miracles?"

"I read about miracles attributed to this place," I said.

"Not 'attributed to,'" Massi said. "How else but for a miracle can you explain how a barren island sprung a well of pure water, and how men twelve centuries ago lifted boulders across the water to this hill?"

I could have mentioned the construction of the pyramids even earlier, but it didn't seem appropriate.

"I have seen one of the miracles with my own eyes, before losing my sight," Massi continued. "There is a stained glass window, not in the abbey. An intricate flower of glass appeared on the solid rock of the Mont, high above the quicksand. There is no way a man could have placed it there, if not for a miracle.

"Because of the sacredness of this place," Massi went on, "wealthy men have often sought favor with the monks who lived here. After the town and abbey were destroyed by a fire in 1204, dauphin Philippe-Auguste sent a large amount of gold to rebuild the Mont. He was not a very nice man, but he was pious."

Another piece clicked into place. Riches had been lavished on the Mont.

"Many other gifts were made," he said, "that were not written down. At least not in records that have survived. So numerous that the monks did not know what to do with the riches. The monks themselves lived austere lives and had no need for wealth, aside from to build the abbey and accompanying buildings here on *Le Mont*. Not everyone shared their feelings for living so simply. It wasn't only invaders who sought to rob them. They had to protect their gifts."

"So they hid them," I said, "here on the Mont."

"But during the Revolution, it was no longer safe. They removed what they could—and made sure the rest of their treasures were so well hidden that they would not be found unless someone had the secret information leading to them. The monks were clever. They didn't leave it to chance. They built in protections so their treasures would not fall into the wrong hands."

I now understood the significance of the French Revolution timing. During the Revolution, a treasure was hidden under the heavy stones on the Mont, to protect it from looting. When the monks secreted away their books, they also hid information about where treasures on the Mont were still hidden—such as the clue inside the desk Lane found at the Louvre.

But the monks didn't anticipate the Mont being converted to a prison. The old ways were gone. The knowledge was lost. That was the reason it had taken so long for anyone to even go in search of the treasure!

But during the destruction of World War II, while many things were destroyed, many things were also *looted*. That was how the information about the treasure surfaced again. North got his hands on a looted hoard from World War II, just as Lane said, and discovered a reference to this treasure at the Mont. But North lacked precise information. He knew a clue was hidden inside a desk that was now at the Louvre, so that's where he started.

"It is one of these treasures you seek, no?" Massi said.

Lane and I stared at each other.

"We're not—" Lane began.

"It's okay," I said softly to Lane before addressing Massi. "We only wish to find it to protect it from a man who wishes to steal it for himself."

Massi nodded. "Your heart is pure. You may think me superstitious to say so, but since I cannot see, I must rely on my other senses. This is how I know you speak the truth, unlike the Englishman who visited me."

Even though I expected it, it was still disappointing to hear. "That sounds like the same man."

"What did you tell him about the Mont's treasures?" Lane asked.

"The important thing is not what I told him," Massi said. "Unfortunately, it was what he already knew."

CHAPTER 29

Massi explained that the Englishman claimed to be a scholar researching the island, who had come across information that suggested there was a secret room underneath a crypt. North went to Massi because he was looking for unrecorded information and any further details to narrow down the search.

"But the details this man already has are specific enough," Massi said. "It is only a matter of time before he finds what he seeks."

I wondered how much North had uncovered about the treasure through the looted World War II records—information that had been lost to everyone else.

We said our farewells to Massi, promising to visit again to tell him how things had turned out.

When we stepped out of Massi's small cottage, the sun was setting over the bay, casting fading light across the long stretches of sand. The tide was out and I saw a few people exploring, visible only as ant-size spots walking across the treacherous beach. It wasn't yet six o'clock, but winter brought an early sunset. But instead of being greeted by darkness, floodlights clicked on around us. The lights were directed at the Mont's iconic spire, a statue of Saint Michael slaying a dragon. There were so many thoughts bouncing around my brain, but for a moment all I could do was look up at Saint Michael, the bronze figure gripping the hilt of his sword to vanquish evil.

"That was curious," I said to Lane. "Why didn't Massi suggest we simply go to the police?"

"He's from a certain time and place where he doesn't wish to involve the authorities any more than we do. But we can talk about all this later. We don't have much time."

"What are you talking about? We've already missed the last time for visiting the abbey, so we can't get back to the crypt tonight. Although I don't know what that would get us anyway. We don't have all the information North does. And apparently even he doesn't have the exact location. The crypts are huge. And there are several of them. We can't let him destroy everything!"

"I love it when you ramble, Jones," Lane said, trying to suppress a grin, "but we really don't have time." He took my hand, and we ran toward the abbey.

This time, we didn't go to the stairway entrance, but to a different section. We found people flooding out of the abbey into a walkway surrounded by gardens.

"I told you," I said as dozens of visitors pushed past us. "It's already closing time."

"I want to catch up with some new friends." Lane pulled me forward, past two workmen on one of the wide paths where tourists were leaving the abbey. He laughed and spun me around, stopping to give me a brief kiss—right in front of the two men. We got so close to them that we brushed against one of them.

"*Pardon*," Lane said, blushing as he let go of me.

The men laughed and elbowed each other. "*Bonsoir*," one said.

"*Bonsoir*." Lane pulled me out of the way of the men and tourists.

"I bet they're on their honeymoon," a woman with a Midwestern American accent whispered loudly to her husband.

Lane kissed my cheek.

"What exactly was that about?"

Lane glanced casually down the path, looked pleased by what he saw, then held up the palm of his hand so I could see what was inside:

Keys. In the palm of his hand rested a set of large keys.

"You picked his pocket," I said.

"How else were we going to get back inside the abbey after hours?"

I stared at him. A thought so natural to him would never have occurred to me.

"Come on," he continued. "We shouldn't stay here. Let's get a hotel room so we can wait until it's late enough to go back."

Our room's window faced the bay that divided the island from the mainland. Colorful timbered buildings stood below us, a staggered skyline on the hilly island. The buildings ended abruptly with the castle walls that prevented the tides from sweeping through the streets.

I covered my face with a pillow and screamed into the lumpy fabric.

"Better now?" Lane asked as I sat up and tossed the pillow aside.

"Much. Now all we need to do is figure out how we missed North's men on our scaffolding reconnaissance, get them to reveal the additional information about the treasure and its location without alerting them to the fact that we're onto them, then steal it from under their noses. Everything is just great."

"I know," Lane said.

"I was being sarcastic."

"I know that, too. But things aren't as dire as you think."

"Why not?"

"Think about why we didn't encounter them today. They don't want to be seen doing work that legitimate crews would know to be incorrect."

"They'll be working *tonight*!"

"Exactly," Lane said, fiddling with what looked like Silly Putty.

"We can spy on them and see how close they are."

"Carefully," Lane said. "Very carefully. We don't know how many of them will be there."

"What's the deal with Dante?" I asked. "He's not nearly as

smart as the rest of these guys. I thought you said North only worked with the best."

"He used to be the smartest of them all. He was doing a job for North, years ago, when something went wrong. He suffered a massive head injury."

"That's awful."

"Not that awful. I heard he was always as unpleasant as he is now. Only he used to be a *smart* unpleasant guy. Now he's a dumb one."

"But North is loyal."

"Exactly," Lane said.

"Why doesn't North just pay him off? I'm sure he's got the money to do so. Surely Dante is a liability now."

"If Dante wanted to keep working, North would honor that. But North doesn't have him do important tasks that could get him into trouble."

"For a guy who does seem to stick to this 'code' so well, killing Hugo doesn't fit his pattern."

Lane ignored me, his attention focused on the putty in his hands.

"What are you doing with that stuff?" I asked.

"I want to make sure I get a good impression."

"You're copying the keys?" I asked. "Why? You already have them."

"He'll be suspicious if the keys don't turn up eventually, and I don't know how long we'll need them. After we get in tonight, I'll leave his keys somewhere near the abbey where he easily could have dropped them."

"Wouldn't it be better to turn them in to a Lost & Found, maybe at that Tourist Information Center we saw at the entry point of the Mont?"

"It would be if the TIC opened as early as the workmen get to work. It doesn't open until 9:30."

"Oh."

Lane grimaced.

"What?" I asked.

"Nothing."

"No, really. What?"

"You're starting to think like me."

We waited until midnight, then walked to the site the back way, along the upper walkway of the ramparts. The island outside of the abbey was accessible to tourists at all hours, so we didn't need to sneak around. But after the dinner hour, most of the tourists caught the shuttle bus back to the mainland. As we walked, I didn't see another soul.

Thunder boomed in the distance as we moved like shadows across the stone periphery of the Mont. Lane took the lead when we reached the steps leading to the abbey.

"I didn't see CTV cameras," he said, "but I have no idea if there are security guards. So remember the plan."

I nodded and held up the blanket I'd carried with me as our ruse in case the guards caught us sneaking into the abbey. But it wasn't official guards I was worried about.

Using the pilfered key, Lane eased open a massive wooden door. The sound of its old hinges creaked while shadows from swaying trees danced around me. I felt like I'd stepped into the pages of one of the Gothic adventures on Lane's bookshelf. All we needed was a shadowy figure in a cape to appear on the spire above us—

"Jones," Lane whispered sharply, causing me to jump. "We're in."

Using flashlights, we crept through the abbey. We knew the men would likely be working in the crypt, but for all we knew there might be a bigger crew with some of them standing guard. It was slow going as we listened for signs of activity. Entering the outdoor cloisters, we clicked off our lights. Between the floodlights and bursts of lightening, the monastery courtyard's stone carvings were brightly illuminated. Moss-covered gargoyles looked down over the intricately carved columns, some more worn than others. Back inside, we again used our flashlights, but as we approached the crypt, Lane held up a finger to his lips and clicked off his light. I followed suit.

Enveloped in darkness, I heard a noise. Faint tapping accompanied the muffled sound of deep voices. The room wasn't pitch black, so I knew my eyes would adjust. Within minutes, Lane's shadow took form. He motioned for me to follow him toward the voices. We stopped as soon as we were close enough to hear them clearly. If memory served—which I'm not sure it did in the maze-like series of rooms—we were one room over from one of the crypts. It was closer than I wanted to be, but we needed to hear them.

With the ambient light from the rigging used by the thieves, we had enough light to make our way without stumbling. I motioned for Lane, indicating we should hide behind a thick Romanesque column for an added layer of security. He nodded in agreement. I set the blanket down on the stone floor and got as comfortable as possible. We were effectively on a stakeout, so I knew it might be a long night.

The men spoke English instead of French, as a common language, I presumed. They didn't speak much, except to grumble about the hard work, and one man who occasionally yelled at the others to be careful. His was the only voice I didn't recognize, and I assumed he was an engineer they'd brought in to help them. Since I couldn't see them from our hiding space, I couldn't tell how the work was coming along, but the new man repeatedly asked Dante if he was going to do more to help them.

If this was what a stakeout was like, it must be incredibly boring to be a cop. Oh, how I wanted to *do* something! Lane wouldn't let me talk, even to whisper, so I pulled out a notebook to write notes to him.

How long are we going to wait here?

As long as it takes to hear what they're up to.

But this isn't a TV show. They're not going to conveniently say "Here it is! We're exactly 2 hours away from finding the Lost Treasure of Napoleon"—or whatever it is—"Let's call our client, Mr. X, and tell him his illegally obtained treasure will be delivered at midnight tomorrow at the drawbridge, where we'll all stand around while we hand over the box marked "stolen treasure."

Lane snatched away the paper but didn't write anything. I grabbed it back.

Why did you do that if you weren't going to write anything?

He pressed his lips together and wrote a reply. *Because you're in danger of making me laugh.*

I blew him a kiss and wrote something practical: *Why is North here? I thought he didn't get involved.*

Odd, I agree.

Ideas?

Only that there's more going on than we understand.

I shifted position for what felt like the hundredth time. Even with the blanket, the floor was cold and hard. Lane wrapped his arm around me and I rested my head on his shoulder. His body was warm and comforting.

The next thing I knew, I jerked awake. Had I really fallen asleep? Lane stood up. Something was happening.

"Secure the pulley." North's voice echoed through the room.

The sound of shuffling feet could be heard. After a few moments, North lowered his voice. I could barely make out what he was saying, but I caught a few words. "Nothing is going according to plan."

North paused, but I couldn't hear a reply. Was he talking on his cell phone to his client? Or to someone who was speaking even more quietly?

"Yes," he said, still speaking softly. "I know, but this wasn't supposed to be about—yes, but—well, I wouldn't have written that in the letter if I knew, would I? No, it doesn't seem—Someone's coming—" North broke off, and a second louder he spoke in a louder voice. "How close are we?"

The man whose voice I didn't recognize answered in English

with a thick French accent. "With the information you've given me, how am I to know?"

"Give the man an educated guess," Marius said.

"*Mais je ne sais pas.*"

"That's not an answer."

"If he doesn't know, he doesn't know," North said. "We keep working as planned. Midnight to five. It's time to wrap up."

It didn't sound like they thought they were going to find what they were after that night. I supposed they didn't want to be buried alive, so they were working carefully.

Thank goodness for that. It was bad enough I was sitting here while thieves desecrated the historic crypt. Lane must have seen the look on my face.

Don't do it, he scribbled.

As the discontented crew wrapped up, we retreated to a spot several rooms away, but not out of the abbey. We were waiting for them to leave so we could do our own exploring.

From our hiding place several rooms away, we couldn't hear the crew clearly, so we waited nearly twenty minutes before entering the crypt. The vaulted ceilings cast eerie shadows under our flashlight beams.

"Are you sure you should be doing that?" I asked Lane as he hoisted himself onto the scaffolding. "It doesn't look very stable."

"I'm not moving anything," he said from above me. "I just want to get a closer look at the section of wall they're examining."

He walked to the far edge of the platform. The wood plank sagged under his feet. I held my breath as the metal supports groaned and Lane's flashlight beam darted across the smooth stones. I didn't like how close to the edge he was standing. Was it just my imagination, or were the bars of the scaffolding shifting?

It wasn't my imagination. And there was no stopping it. Lane realized what was happening and jumped down. But it was too late. The massive piece of construction slipped away from the wall—and landed on top of Lane.

CHAPTER 30

"I'm fine," Lane insisted.

"You're the opposite of fine."

"I'll be fine in five minutes." He stood up, his body swaying in the process. "Maybe ten." He fell unsteadily onto my shoulder.

One of the planks had split, otherwise Lane would have been trapped underneath the mess of wood and metal. His left shoulder and arm took the brunt of the weight of a metal pole.

This was bad. I hadn't thought things could get any worse than being pulled into a museum heist, seeing the blood of an ex-priest who may have been killed, and being complicit in the desecration of a historic landmark. Now on top of all that, Lane was hurt. Badly.

Supporting Lane's weight, I took stock of our surroundings.

Lane must have felt my body tense. Against my shoulder, he shook his head gently.

"There's no way they could think this was an accident," he said. "I mean a non-man-made accident." He swore and pointed. There was a thick red liquid on the piece of scaffolding that had knocked down Lane.

"Blood," I whispered.

"They'll know we were here." Lane's body faltered as he tried to walk.

I steadied him against the wall, intending to go on my own to examine the blood left behind on the renovation equipment. Lane grabbed my hand.

"You can't be serious, Jaya."

"What?"

"You can't wipe off the blood. It's too risky. That tangle of materials isn't stable. It could fall on top of you."

"Stay here," I said.

"Don't—"

"I'm not going to touch it." I removed a water bottle from my coat pocket that I'd brought along for the stakeout. Luckily I'd fallen asleep rather than gotten thirsty. Without touching the pile, I used the water to wash away the blood. I couldn't see if I'd gotten all of it, since I didn't dare touch the unstable mound. I was out of water, so I hoped it was enough.

Using all my strength, I managed to get Lane back to the hotel. I'm not sure we would have made it if I hadn't switched to flat shoes. From my jiu jitsu training I knew how to hold the weight so it wouldn't hurt my back, so I was able to support Lane with his arm draped over my shoulder. But for a skinny guy, he was damn heavy. It wasn't only because he was six feet tall. Though it didn't show, his arms and abs were firm. He carried more muscle than I'd realized.

"There's no way I can do any more work in the crypt," he said, sitting down on the hotel room bed. I helped him out of his torn jacket, and he carefully pulled off his shirt. His shoulder was swollen and beginning to turn purple. A nasty gash ran down his upper arm. I touched his shoulder gently. He winced. "I think it might be dislocated."

"You need a doctor."

"We can't go to a hospital."

"Why not? I thought they had socialized medicine here. They'll treat you."

Lane shook his head, then looked at me with such tenderness that I had to look away for fear I'd break down. I wished we were anywhere but here. Or that we were here but on a romantic vacation instead of plotting to foil the theft of a French treasure.

"We can't do that," he said, "because now North will be looking for us."

I groaned. Then paced. I had to get hold of myself. "House calls! We can find a doctor who makes house calls."

"We have to get off the island, Jaya. If North thinks it's us who caused that scaffolding to fall, in a few hours they'll come looking. We don't want to be here when that happens."

"Where can we go?"

"It doesn't matter." Lane winced. "We need to leave."

"You're in no shape to make it across the causeway to the mainland."

"No, but we can request a shuttle at any time, and the room is already paid for. From the shuttle stop, we can call a taxi. I'll figure out somewhere to go—"

"You know people here in France." I paced across the uneven floorboards. "Are any of them nearby?"

"We can't risk going to anyone I know."

"Because of North?"

Lane nodded. "I don't know who I can trust not to tell him."

"I have an idea."

"What is it?"

"If I take the bag, are you up for a taxi and train ride?"

"I'm fine. I can even carry the bag on my other shoulder." He swore as he attempted to lift it.

"Give that to me." My fingers touched his as he handed me the backpack. His eyes met mine and the pain left his face, replaced with worry.

"I'm sorry, Jones. This isn't your mess to clean up. We'll get you on a plane home and—"

"What are you talking about? Of course this is my mess. It's my fault you went through with the stupid plan of robbing the Louvre. Without having me to use as leverage—"

"This isn't your fight. I'm the one—"

"That's not what this is about. We were both misled. This is bigger than a trinket for a collector. Not only a piece of history, but—"

"Hugo," Lane said, closing his eyes. "Part of me wonders if we should go to the police, regardless of what happens to me."

"That's the blood loss talking. Let's get you out of here."

I called to request an off-hours shuttle and did a three-minute sweep of the hotel room for anything that could identify us.

"We don't have anywhere to go, Jones," Lane said.

"Yes, we do. After the shuttle drops us off, we'll get a cab to take us back to Rennes. From that hub we can catch a train to where we need to go."

"Where are we going?"

"To see a friend."

Chapter 31

North didn't know about Sanjay's friend Sébastien, since Sanjay's message had been in code. He was the only person I could think to turn to. We could have gone to a hotel, but I felt more comfortable going somewhere private. I was hoping Sébastien knew a doctor we could trust. Based on the information from Sanjay, I found Sébastien's address. He was something of an institution in Nantes.

I had no choice but to throw away Lane's bloody jacket, wrapping it in a shopping bag before tossing it in a trash can. There was no way he'd fit into my coat, so I bundled him in my bulky sweater, which became a formfitting fashion statement on his lengthy torso. He looked paler after squeezing into it, but I wanted to make sure he kept warm until we could get him to a doctor.

"Maybe we can stay after all," Lane said in a French accent as he hobbled down the cobble-stone walkway. "Get me a cane and I've got a perfect disguise. Nobody would recognize me."

"Not funny."

The sun was beginning to rise when a taxi dropped us off at the train station hub in Rennes shortly after eight o'clock. Using Lane's stash of euros, I booked tickets on a train to Nantes that was departing shortly.

I wanted to go over what we'd learned, but Lane promptly fell asleep. I poked his side when we were a few minutes outside of Nantes.

"I thought we should talk before we get to Sébastien's," I said. "You slept enough."

He opened his eyes. "I'm injured. My body needs the rest."

"We'll find you a doctor who makes house calls as soon as we arrive."

"Tell me again how you know this guy?"

"He's a magician friend of Sanjay's. He's not a magician himself exactly. He's the behind-the-scenes guy. He's ninety years old, and he helps stage magicians come up with mechanized illusions."

"And he knows who you are?"

"Sanjay has certainly mentioned him to me." I didn't want to tell Lane that I'd reached out to Sanjay in code since arriving in France. Instead, I told the truth, except for saying *when* I learned about Sébastien. "Your invitation to Paris—which I now know was North's invitation—didn't give me any way to contact you. I wasn't sure what was going on. It was too good an opportunity to pass up a trip to France, but I thought I might need more to do. Sanjay said Sébastien was an amazing guy."

It was midmorning when the high speed TGV train pulled into Nantes. I hadn't expected it to be such a big city. We took another taxi to the house. Lane's cash was running low.

"You sure this is the right address?" Lane asked after the driver stopped on a dirt road.

"*Oui, monsieur.* This is the Renaud circus."

We were outside of the central part of the city. Most likely outside of the city limits, based on the look of things. The driver lifted our bags out of the trunk as Lane and I stared at our surroundings.

We stood at the edge of a scraggly vineyard. We were near the heart of wine country, yet this field looked like it hadn't been watered or harvested in years. In the distance, two motorcycles kicked up clouds of dust as they sprinted through the vines. Neither the dead vineyard nor the joyriders were what Lane was commenting on. His gaze was fixed elsewhere. Next to the vineyard were two structures, a barn and a house. At least that's what we had to assume they were. Neither of them looked like a normal house or barn.

The wooden beams that made up the barn's structure looked as if they had been put together like pieces in a game of Tetris. Their placement looked haphazard at first glance, as if a large child had constructed the building like a toy built out of dominoes. But the differently-shaped geometric beams fit together perfectly.

"If you're sure," Lane said. I nodded and he paid the driver, who disappeared in a cloud of dust down the dirt road.

Next to the barn was a two-story house. The underlying structure was a simple French Norman-style house, with a sloping roof that dominated the building. It looked normal except for the added metalwork on the door, windows, and roof.

I pressed what I hoped was the doorbell. What sounded next wasn't a bell or buzzer, but a whirring noise, followed by a loud chirping that sounded like a dragon-sized bird was sweeping down on the house.

"What the—" Lane began.

I couldn't help laughing. "I'm certain this is Sanjay's friend."

We watched as a mechanical bird moved along the rain gutter at the side of the house to a spot perched above the door. The bird chirped, and was joined by a second bird that ran along the gutter from the other side of the house. When the second bird reached the first, they chirped a short song together.

When the sound of chirping ceased, a three-inch peep hole in the front door sprung open. It wasn't a person who had pulled open the small window. Instead, I stumbled backward as a clawed metal hand squeezed through the small opening in the door. The well-oiled fingers clutched a cloth. Once the hand was all the way through the opening, the fingers opened their grasp. The cloth fluttered to the ground.

I picked it up. Words had been painted on the white cloth.

Find me in the studio →

"Definitely Sanjay's friend," I said. "Come on."

I dropped our bags in front of the door, picked up the cloth message that had dropped from the door, and walked to the studio. The arrow on the cloth was less than helpful since it had fallen to the ground, but there was only one other structure near the house.

The converted barn didn't have a discernible doorway. In between the house and barn sat a beautiful picnic table of solid wood with two benches that looked like sanded tree stumps. Upon closer inspection, that's exactly what they were.

"Stay here," I said to Lane.

"My pleasure." He sat on one of the stumps.

Failing to spot a door, I circled the barn. As I rounded the side, two startlingly large lop-eared rabbits hopped in front of me, one white and one gray. As I walked further, the fuzzy creatures turned and followed me. Confused, I stopped. The braver bunny—the gray one—sniffed my foot. He looked up at me with his black eyes. I could have sworn he scowled at me.

I continued walking, and a movement in the distance caught my eye. I turned to see a dozen rabbits scampering away. I had to find Sébastien before I went completely insane.

At the back of the barn was a wooden deck that led to what did *not* look like a door. However, when I stepped onto the first step, I felt my weight shift ever so slightly. A click sounded. The wooden paneling of the barn began to shift, and within a few seconds, a doorway opened. I climbed the remaining few steps and walked inside. The interior of the barn was as bright as the outside, so it took my eyes no time at all to adjust. I rather wished they had. I was greeted by an eight foot man made entirely of metal.

A tall, spry man stepped out from behind the contraption. Bright white hair framed a thin, almost bony, face. Even brighter blue eyes looked at me through small round glasses. His movements made him appear younger than ninety, but this must be Sébastien Renaud.

"Ah!" he said, pulling off thin cloth gloves. "I know who you must be! Sanjay told me I might see you, Mlle. Jones. English is best, yes?"

"Thank you. We wouldn't get very far with my French."

Sébastien's knobby hands belied a firm handshake. "I'm delighted you could make it to my humble home. I hoped you would visit, but I did not wish to presume. I was unsure if Sanjay spoke only with his own desires that we should meet, or if you truly wished to see me."

"I'm very happy to meet you."

His smile turned to a frown as his gaze fell to the object in my left hand.

"*Merde*," he said. "The message did not remain in the hand?"

"It fell." I handed him the cloth the doorbell had triggered. "It's very ingenious."

"What good is ingenious if it doesn't work? Ah well. Please, come inside."

"I'm not alone," I said.

"No? When I spoke with Sanjay, I believed him to be in the States."

"I'm here with another friend."

"An invisible one?"

"He's outside sitting on a bench. He's not, uh, feeling well."

"We should go to the main house, then! Jeeves will make us tea."

He hurried past me, leaving me to wonder why, if he had a butler, the man hadn't answered the door.

Before turning back, I couldn't resist taking another look behind Sébastien, now that he was no longer blocking the view. I could have sworn I'd stepped through a time warp to another century, although oddly, I wasn't sure if that century was in the past or in the future.

Mechanized contraptions of all shapes and sizes filled the barn. I'd seen some of them in history books—automatons from the 1800s. And some of them in science fiction movies—a bird with wings of wood that must have stretched at least fifteen feet and hovered close to the ceiling high above. Was the bird's beak opening and closing? I found myself compelled to get a closer look.

Sébastien popped his head back inside. "Whenever you're ready, your friend and I will be in the main house."

I trotted after Sébastien, stopping one last time to look at the bird. Its head was definitely moving, its eyes following me. I walked more quickly.

Sébastien and Lane were already seated on the couch. A wheelchair-bound robotic man wheeled its way toward the two men, carrying a tray with teacups and a steaming pot of tea. Ah. This mechanical man must be Jeeves.

Lane grinned at me.

"Feeling better?" I asked.

"A doctor is on the way," Sébastien said.

"Was I gone that long?" I asked.

"Not at all," Sébastien said. "I am efficient. Unlike the dangerous *voyou*—the hooligans who ride their motorbikes through the vineyards."

"They came out of nowhere," Lane said. "I was telling Sébastien how I tried to get out of the way in time, but fell." He avoided meeting my eye, but I knew him well enough to go along with his story. I remembered seeing the two motorcycles weaving between the rows of shriveled grapes, making it a plausible story.

The doctor arrived before we were done with our tea. The water the robotic Jeeves brought us wasn't quite steaming, but I forgave him. Chocolate-covered cookies also adorned the tray.

I was expecting a jovial country doctor approaching Sébastien's age. The kind of man I'd seen in a black and white movie. He was, after all, making house calls. The only part of my expectation that proved true was the style of the black leather medical bag in the doctor's hand.

"*Bonjour*, Monsieur Renaud," she said, kissing the air next to Sébastien's cheeks in greeting.

She looked around my age. In high heels, she was only an inch or so taller than me. She wore a skirt that made it clear she weighed at least ten pounds less than me. It made her appear almost skeletal, like one of the specimens she must have studied in medical school. But balancing out her tiny body was a warm, wide smile.

"Ah!" she exclaimed as her eyes found Lane. "Sébastien, *montrez-moi où je peux examiner le patient.*"

Sébastien and I helped Lane up from the couch.

"*Parlez vous français?*" the doctor asked Lane.

"*Oui.*"

"*Très bon. Mon anglais n'est pas bon.*"

Sébastien showed the two of them through an arched doorway.

"Thank you," I said to Sébastien.

"Of course." He smiled and took a bite of cookie. "Jacqueline is a superb doctor. She will see to your friend."

Sébastien and I finished our tea and cookies in companionable silence while my eyes wandered around the room. My wide-eyed wonder must have made me look like an eight-year-old child.

It was as if the laws of physics didn't apply here in Sébastien Renaud's house. Stepping inside from the unkempt farmland must have been how Alice felt going down the rabbit hole. The house created the feeling of being at least twice as large as it looked from the outside. It was an illusion, I knew, but that didn't stop it from feeling real.

Unlike the shriveled grape plants next to the house, the inside was filled with thriving plants of all kinds. They were all miniature, which helped give the house the appearance of being larger. In between living plants were mechanized contraptions. These weren't works in progress, like the creations in the barn studio next door, but completed works of art.

I wanted to ask Sébastien about the items that surrounded us, but I couldn't decide where to start. Before I could make up my mind, he spoke.

"Would you like more tea or cookies?"

"This was enough, thank you."

"*Merci beaucoup,* Jeeves," Sébastien said, carefully enunciating the words. "*C'est tout.*"

The robot bowed its head. The wheelchair backed up, its wheels squeaking ever so softly.

"Brilliant," I whispered. "Jeeves—and all this—it's absolutely brilliant."

"You are friends with The Hindi Houdini, I presumed you would appreciate this. I am confused about two things, though."

"Yes?"

"From the way Sanjay spoke of you, I assumed the two of you were...what is the English expression? I thought you two were 'an item.' But this man here, Lane. The two of you have feelings for each other. This much is clear."

I felt my face flush. I still didn't know what to make of the brief moment Sanjay and I had shared, but the more time I spent with Lane, the more certain I was about where my passion lay.

"Sanjay and I aren't romantically involved," I answered quickly. "He's my best friend, and he feels the same about me. You must have misunderstood the nature of his affection."

"As you say," Sébastien said, but he didn't look like he believed it.

"What was your second question?" I asked in an attempt to change the subject.

"Ah, yes. About the nature of your visit, and your friend's injury. Why don't you tell me the truth about what has happened and why you are *really* here?"

CHAPTER 32

"We shouldn't have intruded," I said, standing up. "As soon as the doctor is done with Lane, we'll be on our way. We'll take care of paying her."

"Sit down, sit down." He motioned with such emphasis that I could hardly refuse. "I am very happy you have come, and I would be even happier if you would tell me the truth. I can see something is happening. No, no, do not worry. Mlle. Jacqueline will not notice anything is amiss. She is a very good doctor, but only observant in the ways of the body. I see more."

"Magicians," I mumbled.

"Yes, we magicians notice details," he said. His hearing was better than mine. "How do you think it is possible for me to bring these mechanized wonders back to life and to create new ones? Precision requires paying attention to the details. All things are revealed in the details."

"Lane was injured in an embarrassing way," I ad-libbed. "We thought it was easier to tell you it was something straightforward. I apologize for the deception. You've been so hospitable—"

"I will continue to be so. Sanjay is one of my favorites, you know. He has both the mind and the heart for stage magic. He cares for you. Therefore I know you're worthy of help. You have no need to hold up this pretense."

I didn't know if I was holding onto the pretense for Sébastien or for myself. North would have discovered the wrecked scaffolding by now. I wanted to believe he'd think it was a natural landslide, as was common on the Mont, but was I fooling myself?

Before I could decide how to respond, the doctor emerged from the other room, with her medical bag in hand but without Lane. She spoke a few words of French to Sébastien, gave me a bony-but-firm handshake accompanied by a genial smile, and departed. She chuckled as she stepped through the door with the metal hand still sticking out. The poor thing looked like it was hanging on for dear life.

"Your friend sleeps," Sébastien said. "He will recover. We will wake him in a few hours."

"Thank you."

"*C'est rien.* Now, about the truth."

Sanjay trusted Sébastien. Should I?

It wasn't only Sébastien I didn't know if I could trust. I didn't trust myself. Part of me wanted to call a cab and run to the airport. I could be safely home in my apartment in less than a day, have a drink with Nadia or Tamarind that night, and go back to teaching classes and playing tabla with Sanjay the following day. I didn't want to think about what Naveen was teaching to my students. Probably about how my whole approach to history was wrong.

But at the same time, the thought of leaving to return to my comfortable life left me feeling empty. How could I leave Lane? How could I live with myself knowing his friend might have been murdered and the killer not apprehended? How could I be complicit in a huge treasure being stolen? And most of all, how could I go back to my sheltered, normal life, when I was in the middle of France inside a magical artist's studio on a treasure hunt?

Sébastien saw the hesitation on my face. "Why don't I give you a proper tour first? I can see you're interested in my creations."

"That might be the understatement of the century."

He laughed. "Flattery will get you everywhere."

I stopped in front of a framed black and white photograph behind a tree made of metal. The trunk of the tree was a combination of intertwined metals that had been curled over one another like roots, and its branches stretched five feet wide. A solitary copper bird sat atop one of the highest branches.

I looked more closely at the photograph on the wall. "Is that you?"

"You recognize me?"

"Your eyes," I said, "and the shape of your face. It hasn't changed. But I didn't realize you were a magician. Sanjay said you were a behind-the-scenes guy."

"For as long as Sanjay has known me, yes. That photograph was taken in London, more than sixty years ago, during my brief career as a stage magician. I began as a clockmaker."

I looked more closely at the handsome young man in the photograph. Even then, he didn't look like someone who would be contented to sit behind a desk.

"I see your surprise," Sébastien continued. "It is a similar occupation, if you look at the mechanics. Many famous magicians got their start as clockmakers. It is a natural progression. After seeing magic shows as a boy, I was not satisfied with my clockmaking business. It was interesting, yet I felt pulled toward something more."

"You performed at the Lyceum," I said. "So you were good. But you gave it up?"

"I may have been good, but I didn't enjoy the stage. Some people, such as Sanjay, they enjoy the adoration. I found it overwhelming. Within a short time, I was...what is the English expression? Burnt out?"

I nodded. "You decided to help other magicians create illusions instead."

"Not right away. I focused on building a clockmaking business for many years. My hobby became acquiring and fixing up old automatons." He swept his hand across the room.

I continued a few paces, stopping at a large magic show poster. Though it was an illustration, I again recognized Sébastien. He was with another man. Each flanked the edge of the poster, shown in silhouette as they faced a levitating woman in the center of the poster. A smaller black and white photograph of the two men was next to the poster.

"That was my partner, Christo."

"Nobody asked you to come back to the stage?" I asked.

He smiled wistfully. "For many years, I didn't wish to be found. I was contented. Christo and I had a wonderful life in the countryside."

"Building automatons together?"

Sébastien chuckled. "No. Christo was good at sleight of hand, but I was the one interested in how these mechanisms work."

"I'm surprised nobody tracked you down for that reason."

"It wasn't as easy to find people in those days. It was years before a young magician found me and asked for my assistance. I agreed, and this is when I found my life's calling. With young stage magicians, I helped them create set pieces for their performances. Word spread. I have always appreciated my privacy. I think it is for the same reason I also hated the stage. I tried to retire when I turned seventy five, shortly after Christo passed away, but retirement was a living death. I stared at my old creations. They stared back at me. This is when I built Jeeves. Then, several years ago, for the centennial anniversary of the death of author Jules Verne, I was invited to be part of a project that was being developed here in Nantes."

He pointed to a poster on the wall showing a mammoth-size mechanical elephant. "It was here I found my calling in retirement. There are many inventors like me here in this city. I stayed on and worked in the workshop of *Les Machines de L'Île*. There is a shared workspace there, but it is not enough space. Mainly I work here at my own home studio."

"How did you build that crazy barn next to the house?"

"A magician cannot give away all of his secrets! Now, come. I will give you the full tour. Then perhaps you will take me into your confidence and tell me a few secrets of your own."

We stepped from the living room area into a den with a freestanding iron furnace in the center. Something warm and soft brushed against my foot. It bit my shoe. I clamped my hand over my mouth to stop myself from screaming.

"Ah!" Sébastien clapped his hands together once. "Démon! *Non!*"

I looked down at a gray lop-eared rabbit that looked suspiciously similar to the one I'd seen outside. "I could have sworn you called that thing a demon."

"Yes, that's his name. Démon. He's a devilish one. Impossible to train."

"You can train rabbits?"

"Not well. That's how I ended up with rabbits in the first place. Magicians often think rabbits can be a good addition to their shows. Women love them. But when you've been bitten by *un lapin* so many times..." He shrugged. "This is when a magician I knew gave me his rabbit."

"I thought I saw a lot more rabbits than that outside."

"The magician told a friend that I had taken his rabbit. Shortly thereafter, I was given another one. Two rabbits quickly became fifty. Most of them are happy to be wild rabbits. They find their own way. But the ones that choose to stay close, I feed and train. It's nice to have company."

I stepped further into the room, careful to step over the fiendish bunny.

"Don't worry about him," Sébastien said. "Jeeves has taught him to get out of the way if he doesn't want his tail caught."

This room was less crowded than the main room. It was large but cozy. Against the far wall was a painted mannequin with a turban on his head, sitting at a desk with a chess set. Why did it look familiar?

"The Turk!" I said.

"You recognize him?"

"The famous chess playing illusion from the eighteenth century."

"My version isn't the original, of course. And," Sébastien paused and gave me a sly smile, "mine works."

The Turk made me think again of Tipu Sultan's famous tiger, and the similarities between his tiger and the illuminated manuscript painting from the Louvre. Tipu's impressive automaton was at a museum in London, and it didn't have anything to do with an elephant. Yet I was sure there was something tying them together. But in Sébastien's magical house, I didn't want to think about the stolen treasures of India. I wanted to soak up the wonder.

I walked closer to Sébastien's rendering of the chess-playing Turk, who himself wore an enigmatic smile on his plastic face. "Being in this place makes it tempting to turn my back on everything going on around me and ask you if I can be your apprentice. I'd even put up with Démon destroying my shoes. I can't believe you don't have people beating down your door."

"The world has changed," he said. "Simple creations like this create so much wonder, but in this modern age we forget that until we experience it firsthand." He sighed. "Now, are you ready to tell me what you're running from?"

"Are you sure you want to know?"

Half an hour later, with the story spilled out of me, we woke up Lane.

"He knows," I told him.

"What do you mean *he knows*?" Lane looked at me sharply.

"That's the trouble with magicians. They see things beyond the obvious."

Lane groaned.

"We can trust him," I added. "Sanjay trusts him completely."

"And you trust Sanjay."

"He knows *everything*," I said, enunciating the words in hopes Lane would catch my meaning. "He knows about how you were coerced by the associate of your wealthy father's into being part of a theft, which is why we can't go to the authorities."

Lane didn't acknowledge the "truth" I'd summarized, which of course left out things I wasn't ready to trust Sébastien with. Under other circumstances I would have expected Lane to give me a look or a nod, but I was pretty sure he assumed, like me, that Sébastien would have picked up on it. There wouldn't be any secret glances if we didn't want Sébastien to know something was up.

I wasn't worried about Sébastien thinking we were lying, because we weren't. We merely left out irrelevant details.

"It is preferable we make a plan before returning to *Le Mont*," Sébastien said.

Lane and I looked at each other, neither of us sure what to say.

"I have outlived all the people who meant the most to me," Sébastien said. "What good is it to be alive for nearly a century if I cannot do the things I wish to do? And today, I wish to help you."

CHAPTER 33

"What we need," Sébastien said, "is a ruse to create misdirection."

"As you may have noticed," Lane said, "I'm in no shape to create a ruse."

"*Précisément*. It is this condition that has given me the idea for your ruse."

Lane and I glanced at each other.

"You wish this man North to believe that you and Jaya had nothing to do with the minor mudslide that took place at the Mont. You wish him to believe you don't suspect he had a hand in your friend's death, and that you do not believe he is searching for a treasure at Mont Saint-Michel. You therefore wish him to believe you are having a romantic holiday to recover from your traumatic experience." Sébastien paused and looked at us expectantly. "Don't you see? It's simplicity itself! You shall give him exactly what he wants."

"I thought you didn't want us to give up," I said.

"Young people these days have no imagination. Did you not notice the small bone structure of Mlle. Jacqueline?"

"The doctor?" Lane said.

"*Oui*. Jacqueline will play the part of Jaya while you rest to recover from your injuries. Lane and Jacqueline will book a suite at a Loire Valley chateaux that is also a hotel, using Lane's credit card. This man who searches for you will be able to find you this way, I presume."

"Yes," Lane said, "which is the whole reason we can't use any credit cards."

"We *want* him to find you," Sébastien said. "He's a busy man, so he will not appear himself. Yet he will check to make sure it's the two of you at the hotel. A tall American man who speaks to the hotel staff in French while his petite, dark-haired girlfriend remains silent because she does not speak French. The two of them will not emerge from their suite much, but they will indeed be present over a hundred kilometers from Mont Saint-Michel."

A smile spread across Lane's face. "To the outside world, we're on a romantic getaway, but in reality Jacqueline is there as my doctor. But what makes you think she'll drop everything and do it?"

"She's unemployed. She moved home to care for her father—an old friend of mine—last year. He fell and broke his hip, but he has recovered. She has been doing house calls while she searches for employment."

"Hang on," I said. "Lane isn't that badly hurt. He doesn't need a doctor. If your idea is to hide somewhere safe until Lane is well enough for—whatever the new plan is—then why wouldn't I be the one to go with him?"

"Because," Sébastien said, "we are not merely waiting. We are *acting*. You have said time is of the essence. This means we cannot wait. While Jacqueline and Lane create a diversion, Jaya and I will be stealing the treasure from under North's nose."

My mouth fell open, but it took me a few moments to find my voice. Lane must have had the same reaction. We both began to object at once. Lane tried to stand up to object more forcefully, but he faltered and sank back down onto the couch.

"I was with you until that last part," Lane said, gripping the cushion.

"Sébastien's an engineer," I said, my eyes sweeping over his ingenious creations. "Unlike the messy job we did at the site, and the unskilled job North's crew is doing, I bet Sébastien could rig something to find the secret room. That's what you're thinking, isn't it?"

The lines around Sébastien's eyes crinkled and his white eyebrows scrunched together as he smiled. "I don't miss the stage, but I do miss a challenge."

"This isn't a theoretical exercise," Lane said. "You can't put Jaya in danger like that."

"Nobody is *putting* me in danger. We already decided it was worth the risk to stop this theft and bring North to justice."

"That was before I got hurt. Before we showed our hand. They might already be on to us. That was never part of the plan. We were supposed to make it look like a work crew innocently found the treasure."

"With Sébastien," I said, "that's still possible. They don't know him. Since he's offered—"

"I don't like the idea of you going back there," Lane said. "Not before we know what they think happened last night."

"I'll be careful. I learned from the best." I realized, too late, that I was saying too much in front of Sébastien.

"What are we going to tell Jacqueline?" Lane asked. His face was impassive, but I knew he would have shot me a withering look if not for Sébastien looking on. Instead, he'd changed the subject. Classic misdirection.

"What did you tell her already?" Sébastien asked.

"The same thing I told you, that I was in an accident involving motorbikes."

"She suspected nothing?"

"No."

"*Alors,* then we can keep it that way. I will merely tell her that her services are required to nurse you back to health while Jaya attends to urgent business."

I didn't like the sound of a woman who looked superficially like me nursing Lane back to health, but that was the least of my concerns about this plan. "She only speaks French," I pointed out, "so if North follows up on Lane's credit card charge, he'll find out Lane is with a French woman, not me."

"I'll tell her I want to practice my French," Lane said. "Then it'll make perfect sense for me to be the one speaking to the hotel staff."

"I thought you didn't like this plan!"

"It's growing on me."

I threw my hands in the air and lay down on the couch opposite Lane and Sébastien. "While you two are living it up at a fancy hotel, Sébastien and I will be conducting reconnaissance at Mont Saint-Michel to see what North knows and for Sébastien to figure out how to rig something to get to the treasure. Is that the plan?"

They both nodded at me.

"Since I need to stay out of sight, what's the point of me being there at all?"

"We don't know how quickly we'll need to act," Lane said. "I need to be far away for North to not be suspicious. We can use the burner phones to be in touch without North knowing what we're up to. But that gives me another idea. In case North doesn't find me right away through my credit card, we'll make it easy for him. You can call Sanjay on your own phone."

"To feed him the line about you and me going on a romantic trip together. While the reality is that I'll be stuck inside a hotel room somewhere near Mont Saint-Michel."

Lane reached into his pocket and pulled out an object smaller than the tip of his pinkie finger. "You won't be blind. Sébastien can wear this on his collar."

"This is the camera you used at—"

"Yes," Lane cut me off. "You know I love my gadgets."

Lane handed the tiny camera to Sébastien.

"*C'est magnifique,*" Sébastien said softly. "I have never seen a camera so small. This would be perfect for a magician...Jaya will see and hear what the camera picks up?"

"Only see it, I'm afraid," Lane said.

"No matter. This is better that I imagined would be possible. She won't let me forget anything I see when I report back."

"This is the only way she'll stay in the room," Lane said.

"I'm right here, you know."

"Shall we call Sanjay and Jacqueline?" Sébastien asked. "I was led to believe you were in a rush."

Sébastien called Jacqueline first, to make sure the plan would work. She was happy to accept the job of personal doctor for a few days, especially since it involved accommodation at a luxury chateaux.

Calling Sanjay was more complicated. Lane decided we would put the sim card back into my own phone for me to do so, figuring North was still tracking it. But he insisted on waiting until we left Nantes, just in case North's spyware also had location-tracking that could pinpoint our location.

"Do we need to call a cab?" Lane asked.

"I can drive," Sébastien said.

"Uh..." Lane began. We'd both seen the mud-covered VW van in front of the house that looked like it hadn't been driven in decades.

"Follow me," Sébastien said.

We had to run to keep up as Sébastien led us around the house. Behind the main house was a half-covered garage. In it sat two silver cars. Unlike the mud-encrusted van in front, these two sports cars had been polished so brightly I could see myself in the reflection.

"Wow," I said. I hadn't appreciated cars before I'd inherited my Roadster. But after driving a car with such an engine, I'd come to understand why people enjoy fast cars.

"Which one do you prefer?" Sébastien asked. "The Porsche Boxter or the Porsche Panamera? Ah, how thoughtless of me! The decision makes itself. We are four. We will take the four-seated Panamera."

"This car looks brand new," I said.

"As I said, what good is it to live so long if one cannot do what one pleases? I appreciate nice cars. My skills have been sought out by many magicians, enabling me to buy my toys."

I ran my hand over the side mirror, not realizing I was doing it until I saw a grin on Sébastien's face. I shoved my hands into the pocket of my jeans.

"Once this is over, you must drive her," Sébastien said. "For now, I know where we're going. I'll drive. Grab your bags. It's time."

CHAPTER 34

On the way to the train station, we stopped to buy an additional prepaid cell phone for Sébastien.

I called Sanjay from the train station in Rennes, on my old phone. Jacqueline waited in the car while Lane and Sébastien hovered around me. Storm clouds gathered above, and a rumble of thunder filled the air.

"I hope I didn't wake you," I said when Sanjay picked up, realizing it was six or seven o'clock in the morning in San Francisco.

"I'm up, but this isn't a good time. Can you call me back in a few?"

"Who is it?" a female voice asked.

"It's Jaya," Sanjay said. "Give me a minute, Tempest."

"Tempest is over there?"

"We're practicing a new illusion."

"At seven o' clock in the morning?"

"It's only six, actually. You know I hate to go to bed until I get something right. And you know Tempest. She's even more of a perfectionist than I am. We haven't gotten it right yet."

"Sanjay!" I heard Tempest's voice in the background.

"You told me Tempest doesn't play well with others. Why did she agree to help you?"

Lane and Sébastien gave me funny looks. "What are you doing?" Lane whispered.

"Never mind," I said. "I won't keep you two. I just thought someone at home should know that I changed my plans. I'm no longer in Paris. I'm going to be at a Loire Valley wine country castle hotel for the rest of the week. With Lane."

Sanjay didn't respond immediately.

"Sanjay?"

"I heard you. Thanks for letting me know. Sorry I can't talk now. Tempest has me kind of tied up. Have fun." The phone clicked off. What was that about? And what was his magician friend Tempest Mendez—stage name The Tempest—doing there?

"Bye," I said to dead air.

Lane gave me the briefest of kisses goodbye before he and Jacqueline disappeared through the sliding doors of the train station. And with that, both of the men in my life disappeared with other women.

After we dropped Lane and Jacqueline at the train station in Rennes, Sébastien and I drove on to Mont Saint-Michel. The clouds opened up and blanketed us in rain, but the deluge only lasted for ten minutes. Though the road was slick from the downpour, Sébastien knew how to handle the car. Part of me wished we'd have been able to take the convertible Boxter. Sébastien's wild white hair seemed to be calling out for wind to whip through it.

"The last admission to the abbey is at five o'clock," I said. "Do you think we can make it in time?"

He shifted gears smoothly as we exited a roundabout on the outskirts of Rennes. "But of course."

Lane had given Sébastien the copied abbey key he'd made, so it would be possible to get into the abbey after hours. But it would be easier for Sébastien to get the lay of the land if he could do so openly first.

We drove without speaking for a few minutes as we left Rennes behind us. The air between us was a combination of companionable silence and nervous apprehension. But as soon as we passed the ring road that circled the city, Sébastien's shoulders relaxed.

"I have never liked cities. This," he said, hitting the accelerator, "is much better."

My head pressed into the back of the comfortable seat as the car took off. With Lane and Sébastien on my side, I felt like anything was possible.

"How did you meet him?" Sébastien asked.

"Sanjay?"

"I already know that story. He saw your tabla drum case in the boot of your car. He thought you were the most beautiful woman he'd ever seen, so he made flowers magically appear for you."

"That can't be what he said."

"No." Sébastien said, glancing at me as we passed green plots of farmland. "He didn't say that, but I could hear it in his voice. That boy is in love with you."

I gawked at Sébastien. "Magicians can't actually read minds, you know."

"If you insist." A wicked grin flashed across his face, but he kept his eyes on the road. "*Alors*, I meant for you to answer how you met Lane."

"He's an art historian. Our work overlaps, so I sought his help with a research project last year."

"The two of you are very alike, you must realize. In a more fundamental way than you and Sanjay."

"What do you mean?"

"Lane is an observer of human nature, and therefore is good at adapting."

I thought of how North called Lane The Chameleon, but I didn't express my thoughts out loud. Vineyards passed by in a blur as we sped down the highway.

"It's a quality that reminds me of how I was in my day," Sébastien continued. "But Sanjay...The boy charges forward without thinking. His ego outweighs caution."

I laughed.

"You agree?" he asked.

"That's definitely Sanjay."

"That quality is why he's a masterful stage performer in a way I never was. I prefer the sidelines, as does your friend Lane. Yet—"

"What?"

"Both of these men in your life, they are both illusionists."

I'd never thought about it like that before, but Sébastien was right. Was he also right about Sanjay's feelings for me? Was that why Sanjay had acted strangely on the phone just now?

The drive was only supposed to take a little over an hour, but I expected it would take longer due to the storm. Instead, the earlier heavy rains seemed to be keeping people off the road. When the castle-like crest of Mont Saint-Michel came into view through the mist, it was shortly before five o'clock, less than an hour after we departed Rennes.

Since cars weren't permitted to drive onto the island, we were forced to park at the parking lot next to the shuttle bus station and ride the shuttle bus along with the rest of the tourists. It was late enough in the day that there were fewer tourists heading toward the island. Most of them were headed the other direction, leaving for home at the end of their day as modern pilgrims. We passed crowded shuttle buses heading back to the mainland.

Sébastien and I were to go straight to a hotel we booked on the phone on our way there, with Sébastien doing all the talking. Since it was off-season, we had our pick of rooms. To remain secreted away, we selected a cabin high on the Mont, several steep alleys away from the main tourist street. The abbey would be closing shortly, so we hurried on the cobblestones. I wore my heels in the car, but switched to flat shoes before we trekked up the steep Mont.

"Why did you insist on bringing so much luggage?" I asked, lugging one of the two large bags Sébastien insisted on taking to the island. "You said we weren't going to bring too many of your engineering supplies until you saw what we were up against."

"Ah, I was wondering when you'd ask."

"You're not going to answer?"

"Isn't a little mystery a good thing?"

Ten minutes later, Sébastien and I had made our way up the narrow streets and were inside a hotel room similar to the one Lane and I had shared the night before. I dropped the heavy bag Sébastien had given me onto the sloping hardwood floor just inside the door, pulling off the hat and glasses that were the bulk of my disguise. I tossed the hat and glasses onto the closest bed and surveyed the room. Even though the twin beds were smaller than the standard American twin beds I was used to, they filled more than half of the room. The thick, timbered beams along the ceiling were low enough that Sébastien had to duck his head to reach the window. He pulled open the curtains.

"We should probably keep those closed," I said, rushing to his side.

"*Pourquoi*? Ah! Of course." He pulled the curtains closed. "Forgive me, I'm not used to this type of illusion."

We hurried to the abbey, going over our plan. If either of us was caught doing something we shouldn't be, we were to act like tourists who had become separated. He was my elderly French grandfather showing me the sites of France, and I was his impetuous American granddaughter who was more interested in chasing handsome Frenchmen than spending time with her frail grandfather. I was getting over a breakup with my American fiancé, thus the escape to France to see a grandfather I hardly knew.

A lie, like an illusion, is believable because of the details, Sébastien said. He taught me to say *"J'ai perdu mon grandpère"* — I lost my grandfather — but aside from that it was perfectly reasonable that I spoke no French, as it was perfectly reasonable that I would know so little about my grandfather based on the story we'd set up.

We made it to the ticket counter at a few minutes before five o'clock and bought tickets to enter the abbey. I thought things were finally going our way—until we reached the crypt.

Unlike the previous day, when the scaffolding sat unused, North now stood a few yards in front of me.

CHAPTER 35

I jumped back and flattened myself against a column, motioning for Sébastien to get out of their line of sight. I was far enough across the room that I didn't think North and his men had seen me. More than a dozen other tourists ambled through the room, their attention drawn not to the black-haired American woman who was acting oddly, but to the vaulted ceilings of thick stone.

"It's them?" Sébastien asked, his voice low.

I nodded, my heart pounding. "We need to go."

"Now's your chance."

A toddler wailed at the other end of the crypt, claiming the attention of anyone who could hear.

With Sébastien at my side, I made a hasty retreat out of the crypt. He fell into step beside me. We didn't stop until we were back in the cloisters.

"Slow down." He wheezed and braced himself against a column.

"Oh Sébastien! I'm so sorry. Are you all right?"

He stood up straight and grinned. "I was convincing?"

I stared, dumbfounded.

"*D'accord*. I think I will have a chat with your friends."

"You can't be serious."

"I do hate to be serious, but in this case it's for the best." He raised a hand to his ear. When he removed it, a small piece of hearing aide was showing.

"I think your hearing aide is falling out." I hadn't noticed before that he wore one.

"*Très bon*. Very good. It looks like an assisted hearing device, no?"

"It's not?"

"Look at your phone."

A choppy video feed illuminated the screen—currently showing my own surprised expression.

"The video camera!" I said, before remembering to lower my voice. I needn't have bothered. Half the tourists in the cloisters held cameras in their hands, while the other half stood to pose for pictures. "Isn't the camera a little too visible?"

"I'd say it's showing just enough. It *needs* to be visible. *That* is the misdirection. If I were to wear it on my sweater or coat as a pin, that would arouse suspicion by those who would be looking for such things. But a device to help an old man hear? This, nobody will question." He tapped a key on the cell phone Lane had given him.

"But you can't just—" I broke off as the phone buzzed. "You're calling me?"

"Aren't you going to answer?"

I answered the phone. At least that meant I didn't have to keep looking at my own frustrated face on the phone's screen.

"*Allô?* Jaya? Is that you?" Sébastien's eyes twinkled.

I rolled my eyes. "*Oui, grandpère?*"

"*Bon.* The camera has no sound, so we must maintain phone contact as well. Stay here. My phone remains on in my pocket so you can both see and hear everything I do."

"This isn't the plan. You can't—"

Before I could finish my thought, he turned on his heel and trotted back in the direction of the crypt. I lunged to grab his arm, but he sensed it and dodged out of the way. He was faster than I gave him credit for. Short of tackling him and making a scene, there wasn't anything I could do.

In the seconds before he left my line of sight, I watched his spry step change to the feeble steps of an elderly man as he disappeared around the corner. I stopped, as he knew I would. I wouldn't risk entering the section of rooms where the men were working.

Damn illusionists.

I pulled my scarf and hat more firmly around my head, and slipped an earbud into my ear so I could listen to Sébastien's phone while I watched the video. I held the phone in my cold hands, listening to ambient noise and watching the video bounce to the rhythm of Sébastien's steps. He walked through the stone rooms at a slow pace, playing the role of a harmless, infirm old man.

My throat caught when North came into view. *This was really happening.* Sébastien was going to confront him. My instinctive reaction was to call Lane, but I didn't do it. There was nothing he could have done.

North was with both Marius and Dante, along with another man I didn't recognize. The new man was the only one dressed in workman's clothing. A lock of Sébastien's white hair fell over his ear, obscuring half the lens. I was still able to see most of what was happening. The new man pointed animatedly at the scaffolding as North shook his head. Both Marius and Dante stood a few feet away, their arms crossed across their chests.

The sound coming through the phone echoed ominously as Sébastien walked deeper into the crypt. I caught snippets of conversation coming from the people Sébastien passed. He stopped a few feet away from North, but his head was turned toward a stone column that must have been five feet wide, one of the many impressive architectural features that kept the abbey's floors from caving in.

I could no longer see the thieves, because of the angle of Sébastien's head, but they were close enough that I could hear them. I recognized the voice of the man who hadn't looked familiar. It was the new man who'd been in the crypt the previous night. He spoke in French with North. I didn't understand most of what they said, but I caught several recognizable words, including "accident." Did that mean they didn't suspect Lane and I had been poking around?

I didn't have time to think more about it. Sébastien turned his head toward the men. His voice came through loud and clear as he spoke rapidly in French. Sébastien's words tumbled over one another.

What was he doing? Was he nervous? This was a horrible idea. He'd told me he hated being on stage. And here he was walking into the spotlight.

A moment later, I realized I was wrong. I understood what he was doing. He wasn't nervous. He was playing a role. He wanted them to ask him to switch to English, no doubt so I could understand the conversation. Which is exactly what North did.

"There is a problem?" Sébastien asked.

North's scowl turned into a salesman's plastic grin. "Not at all! I'm a history buff, and I was asking this man about the renovations going on here. He's an excitable fellow, that's all."

Sébastien tilted his head in time for me to see the unfamiliar man rub his neck nervously. A crucifix hung from his neck. When he was done rubbing his neck, his hand went to the crucifix.

"You are the engineer?" Sébastien asked the fidgety man. "I was an engineer in my day. I can see this scaffolding isn't safe."

"No, *monsieur*. There was a small accident. That is all. There are frequently tremors, and sometimes tourists go where they should not..." He rubbed the crucifix. Even on the small screen, dark circles stood out under his eyes. "This scaffolding is set to be moved, so I will make sure it is secure before anyone uses it."

"May I be of assistance?"

"*Merci, monsieur*, but we—I mean *I*—I mean *nobody* will be working here until tomorrow. We will fix it then. *Maintenant*, it's nearly time to leave."

"I didn't realize renovations were taking place in this part of the abbey," Sébastien said.

He was pushing his luck...

"There are very many sections being renovated," the fidgety man said. "And many rooms are simply being checked for structural damage."

"That's what's going on here? Checking the walls for structural damage?"

Sébastien, for the love of God, don't say anything else.

"Oui, monsieur."

Sébastien took a step forward, but he was looking up as he did so. He lost his balance and stumbled into North.

The video feed went fuzzy, but the sound remained strong. A grunt and hurried footsteps. The video returned a moment later, pointed upward at an angle.

"Pardon," Sébastien said. "How clumsy of me. This body of mine is not what it used to be."

"Don't worry, sir," North said. "May my friends and I help you back to your room? We were getting ready to leave."

"I'm meeting my granddaughter in a few minutes. But thank you."

Though I could only see their disembodied heads and the vaulted ceiling braces on the video screen, it looked like he extended his hand for North to shake. The smile never leaving his face, North shook Sébastien's hand, then waved goodbye.

Sébastien reached me less than a minute later.

"This is terrible!" he exclaimed.

"You can tell me about it later. We should hurry."

"Yes, I believe they were telling the truth that they, too, are leaving."

It was a good thing Sébastien was as fit as he was. We ran through the abbey, not looking back. Because of the vast rooms and courtyards, we had to be sure to stay well ahead of North and his men. Once we reached the cobblestone paths outside the abbey, we slowed down, but not by much.

"Having trouble keeping up with me?" Sébastien asked when I paused to look behind us.

"I was thinking," I said, "that I'd love to take you home with me so you can be my jogging partner."

"I might take you up on that one day. But first—"

"Let's get out of here."

By the time we let ourselves into our hotel room, the impact of what we'd seen had caught up with me.

"That was stupid," I said. "Really stupid. We can't change plans like that."

"We learned they do not suspect you and Lane to have damaged their equipment."

"I'm glad to know it for my peace of mind, but it doesn't change anything. Don't do anything like that without consulting me first, okay? It's too risky."

"Even if it means this?" He held up the clay impression of a key.

"We already have the keys to get into the abbey later tonight. You know that."

"You said you wished to get inside and see the documents that are keeping him one step ahead of us, no?"

"Of course I do. But blowing our cover isn't how I'd like to get there."

"This," Sébastien said, making the lump of clay disappear and reappear in his hand, "is an impression of the key to North's hotel room."

CHAPTER 36

Even if Sébastien could make a key from the impression—which he informed me he could—I knew we'd have to wait until after midnight before sneaking into North's room.

Our best information told us they'd be sticking to their plan of searching for the treasure between midnight and five a.m. What were they doing there at the end of the legitimate work day?

"I'm going to go crazy waiting," I declared, peeking out the window. The floodlights had clicked on, giving me a beautiful view of the tiny village and the lapping tide below. "I feel like things are so close to making sense, but at the same time I can't imagine what's going on."

"The awkward man," Sébastien said. "He was a real workman here on the Mont."

"The fidgety guy with the crucifix? You think so?"

"Their inside man. That's how you would say it, no?"

"Oh! That explains why North is there during the day to check things out. If their accomplice is a real workman who was working today, he would have seen that the scaffolding had been disturbed. He must have told them, so they wanted to check it out."

"After his own full day's work."

"Which explains why he looked so tired."

"This whole operation," Sébastien said, shaking his head. "These men have some good ideas, but haphazardly executed. They are behaving like amateurs. You led me to believe they were professionals."

"They are. Even a few days ago, they were behaving more professionally. Something is going on. They're desperate. But why?"

"Is it not simply the fact that renovations will be over soon?" Sébastien suggested. "The crypts are too big to examine quickly, and if they don't know where they should look..."

"I need to see what's in North's room."

"Patience. I will get you inside in a few hours."

"If you suggest I take a nap, I might strangle you."

"A nap? Of course not. Naps are for the Spanish and the Italians. As for the French? We are revived by food and wine."

"I wish we could go out to dinner, too, but this island is too small. It's not safe."

"That's not what I had in mind." Sébastien unzipped a boxy suitcase. "Perhaps this will help take your mind off things for a couple of hours." Inside sat a picnic basket with two icepacks on top. Inside the wicker basket was an assortment of French treats including scones and chocolate-covered croissants.

"Where did you get all this?" I asked. "You were only inside the house by yourself for five minutes while we were packing up the car."

"I like to keep Jeeves busy." He winked before diving back into the picnic basket, leaving me to wonder about the wheelchair-bound automaton that had brought me tea the previous day.

It was an even more elaborate spread than I thought. In addition to the pastries on top, Sébastien pulled out roasted chicken, two baguettes, an assortment of cheeses, a bag of salad, a box of chocolates, and, of course, a bottle of wine.

Instead of china dishes, the serving plates, trays, cups, and bowls were all stainless steel that looked suspiciously like they were from thali sets—the Indian style of a large serving plate with smaller bowls on top for various dishes.

"I know the thali plates aren't traditional picnic fare," Sébastien said, "but they're so much lighter than china. When I reached my eighties, I thought it was a good idea to take better care of my back. My friend Samir was changing the style of dishes he used at his restaurant. *Alors,* he gave these to me. Wine?"

"I'd better not. I want a clear head later."

"Wise," Sébastien said, pouring himself a glass. "It's in my blood. Without a glass of Burgundy, I might as well lie down and die. Which is not the plan for this evening. But I will only have one glass. We must stop those men!"

"What did you think of them? Your impression, as a keen observer of human nature."

"Desperate men do desperate things, Jaya. Are you sure you want to go through with this?"

"How can I stop? They might destroy the Mont in search of their treasure. I don't have enough evidence to get them arrested. At least, not without implicating myself."

"A bad situation indeed."

While waiting for midnight to approach, I called Lane to let him know North's men knew about the disturbed scaffolding but didn't think it was due to the two of us, and that Sébastien had pilfered North's room key.

"Don't do it," Lane said. "I can be there tomorrow." Even when he was angry, it was comforting to hear his voice.

"I didn't call to ask for your permission."

"Please, Jones. You know what North is capable of."

"We're waiting until we're sure he's not there."

"You don't get it, Jones. He'll have the room booby trapped in some way."

I sat down on the floor and swore. "Really?"

"Wait for me to get there tomorrow. Jacqueline and I have made a fuss with the hotel staff, so if North heard the call you made to Sanjay and is following our movements, he'll know that you and I are vacationing here together already. I can come back—"

"And your shoulder?"

There was a pause on the other end of the line. "Jacqueline can drive me."

"You need to recover. Tell me what to expect from North. That way we can be careful."

"You don't want to—"

"I do, and I am. So you can either tell me what to look for, or you can leave it to me and Sébastien."

At a quarter to midnight, Sébastien insisted on departing by himself to spy on North's hotel room. From the keychain he'd lifted and promptly returned, we knew in which establishment North was staying. It was too dark out for me to see much on the video feed, but I heard rustling as Sébastien got as comfortable as he could in a shaded nook in front of the door leading to North's room.

At two minutes after midnight, I was wondering if Sébastien had fallen asleep when I heard his sharp intake of breath, followed by the faint sound of knocking.

"They're leaving," he whispered. His voice was so soft that I barely heard it over the phone.

He waited a few minutes, then stood up. A few minutes later, he was back in our room.

"Was it all four of them?" I asked him.

"The real workman knocked on the door, then the other three joined him. The muscular Italian—Darius?"

"Dante."

"Yes, Dante. Does he always look so angry?"

"Unfortunately, yes. He suffered an injury that was North's fault, so North feels guilty and insists on working with him."

"Unfortunate, indeed...*Alors,* I watched until they were far on their way to the abbey. It's safe for us to proceed."

"You really think you'll be able to spot any booby traps they've set in their room?" I asked.

"Yes, now that I know to look for them. Shall we?"

I bundled in my coat, hat, and scarf, and we headed out into the chilly night. The stormy skies were kicking up a ferocious wind, but weren't letting loose with rain or snow.

Sébastien led the way to North's room. Hotels on the Mont weren't arranged as large blocks. There wasn't room for that. Instead, the hotels all had main offices on the main road, but most of the rooms were spread out in small houses and cabins up winding cobblestone paths.

North's room was a few zig-zags away from our own cluster. When we reached a main door that was an entry point to a small grouping of four rooms, Sébastien carefully inspected the solid door before we slipped into the small lobby.

"I don't see..." Sébastien whispered. "Ah!"

"Shh."

"Your friend was right," Sébastien whispered. He pointed at a small box next to the door frame that I never would have noticed. "Portable trip wire. Step over this line when we enter the room."

I gulped and did as he said, stepping carefully over the foot-high trip wire.

Inside, my nervousness was quickly forgotten as I laid eyes on a leather folder I recognized.

"That's it," I said. "That's North's."

I rushed to the desk and picked up the folder that looked like an artist's portfolio. But I knew what would be inside. The letters North had shown me a portion of.

"It's them," I whispered. "There's got to be a dozen letters here. Sébastien! He ripped this letter in half himself! I'm going to kill him!"

"I'm sure the offense is worth contemplating murder, but shall we discuss it back at the room? Take pictures and place the folder back where you found it."

"What are you doing?" I asked.

"I could have sworn I heard voices."

"Probably the neighbors up late."

"Probably..." He slipped out the door, careful to step over the trip wire.

It took all my self-control to take pictures of the letters rather than reading them right then.

"Jaya!" Sébastien whispered sharply. "Pack up. Put everything back exactly as you found it."

"They're coming back already?"

"Hurry!"

I snapped a last picture, then replaced the letters into the folder, sitting it squarely on the desk exactly as I'd found it.

We slipped out the front door and rounded the corner, pressing ourselves flat against the wall. And just in time.

"Did you hear something?" It was North's voice, loud enough that he must have been only a few feet away from us.

"What?" Dante asked, his voice agitated. "One of the ghosts?"

"No." North's tone told me he spoke through gritted teeth. "I thought I heard footsteps—of real people, not ghosts—but it's the wind shaking the sign to the *auberge*."

"But the legends say—"

"Forget I said anything. Let's get the schematic Gilbert asked for. I don't see why he couldn't have remembered he needed it before we climbed all the way up to the abbey." The sound of their voices ceased as they stepped into their room.

I let out a sigh of relief. We hadn't set off the trip wire. They'd merely forgotten something. Sébastien and I dashed down the path toward our own room.

"We made it!" I flung myself down onto my bed and reached up to pull off my hat, when I made a terrible discovery. "My hat. Where's my hat?"

"Your hat?"

"Sébastien," I said. "I had my hat with me when we went to North's room. It's gone."

CHAPTER 37

"It's windy outside," Sébastien pointed out. "Your hat may have blown away."

"Do you believe that?"

"Wait here."

"Where are you going?"

"I'm an old man with insomnia. I'm going on a walk. It doesn't matter if they see me."

"It would be better if they didn't."

"Yes, but this is a situation where we need to know. If they find evidence their room was searched, then it's no longer safe for you to be here on the Mont."

I groaned. How could I have been so careless?

"Wait here."

I couldn't bring myself to do anything besides pace anxiously while I waited for his return.

Five minutes later, one of the sweetest images I'd ever seen in my life stepped through the door. With hair that had been swept into an even more extreme mad-scientist coif by the fierce wind, Sébastien held my hat in his strong, wrinkled hands.

"It fell," he said, "a few meters from their room, next to the wall where we hid." He tossed the hat to me. "I admit you had me worried."

"You and me both."

"Are you ready to look at these letters that you think are so important?"

I pulled up the images on the laptop screen. Indignation again filled me as I flipped to the letter that had been ripped in half. I knew that one must be important, because he showed part of it to me, but he didn't want me to see what was written at the bottom.

"I'm going to kill him," I said again.

"At least he did not destroy these letters after he got what he wanted from them."

"Are you always this cheery after breaking and entering?"

"I haven't had this much fun in years."

"We almost got caught!" But as I spoke the words, I knew that if I was being truthful, I'd say I felt the exact same way.

Sébastien pointed back to the screen. "I don't want to distract you."

"Right! Right. Give me a minute. I shouldn't speculate until I've read everything."

But the more I read, the more confused I became.

"These letters are written by the same man," I said, "but they're so different from each other."

Sébastien looked over my shoulder as I scrolled slowly through the images.

"A descent into madness," Sébastien murmured. "As if his stay in India were driving him insane."

"Opium. I've seen this change before. Opium addiction was a big problem for East India Company soldiers."

"The English," Sébastien said.

"I'm surprised North took these letters seriously. You weren't exaggerating when you said these were the ramblings of a madman. Look here. In the portion of this letter North didn't show me, Trenton Smith goes on and on about Clive of India's famous gold treasures that were lost at sea. But Clive had been dead for decades when this letter was written in the 1790s. Yet Smith writes of a mysterious Frenchman who had the treasures of both Clive and an Indian sultan."

"Yet you believe him to be lucid," Sébastien said thoughtfully, "and that there's a treasure hidden here on the Mont."

"The local historian I spoke with gave me the missing pieces of the puzzle about how the treasure ended up here, and why it has never been found. Wealthy Frenchmen who wanted to gain favor either politically or with God often donated their riches to this site of spiritual significance, which explains the gift. And the fact that the Mont's historical records were hidden during the French Revolution and destroyed during World War II explains why the knowledge about its location was lost. But none of those facts tell us what we'll find."

"You have your suspicions."

"Tipu Sultan's secret treasures," I said. "Most were lost to history when his alliance with the French wasn't enough to save him from being crushed by the English. Unfortunately, we only have the ramblings of a madman to lead us to the answer."

CHAPTER 38

I slept for three hours. A few minutes before five o'clock in the morning, the ancient hotel room door creaked open. I shot awake.

"Don't trouble yourself," Sébastien said in the darkness.

"You were outside? Where did you go?"

"I wanted to see when they would return."

"You didn't get any sleep?"

"I've never wished to spend time sleeping."

"So you waited outside their rooms."

"They returned to get some sleep. But we only have a few hours before the legitimate workmen will be arriving for the day."

"Then let's go."

The floodlights lit our walk along the winding paths from our cabin hotel room up to the abbey. A thick fog had descended in the few hours during which I'd slept. I was tempted to believe Dante's story of ghosts who roamed these walkways. It was the perfect atmosphere for them. My heart skipped a beat as we rounded a corner and came upon the tiny St. Pierre church and cemetery. Standing outside the church, a statue of Joan of Arc looked eerily real through the hazy fog.

We walked on. The sound of a creaking gate caused us both to stop in our tracks.

"The wind," Sébastien whispered. He pointed at the low iron fence that encircled the tiny cemetery of the church, as its squeaking gate clattered shut.

"Then why are you whispering?"

"This would make a perfect backdrop for a horror movie, no?"

"If I were superstitious, I'd slap you. Come on. Let's keep going."

A scream rang out.

I clutched Sébastien's sleeve. I felt his body tense as well. He pulled me down, hiding us in the shadows of a low wall.

"Please tell me I imagined that," I said. In the dead of night, sounds echoed through the empty streets. I couldn't tell if the scream came from a man or a woman. In the foggy darkness in front of a cemetery, there was something else about the voice I didn't want to admit to myself. It sounded almost inhuman.

"I regret to say," Sébastien whispered back, "you did not imagine that cry."

The wail came again.

Sébastien put his head in his hands. "*Un chat!*"

"What?"

He lifted his head. He was laughing. "A cat, Jaya. It's a cat."

"But..." He was right. If a feral cat had cried out back home in Golden Gate Park, I wouldn't have thought twice about it. But here, inside this remote fortress on the coast of France that had survived for over 1,000 years, in front of a cemetery shrouded in fog, surrounded by quicksand and the ocean's unrelenting tides, the simplest explanation of a 21st century cat hardly seemed the most appropriate.

Wiping tears of laughter from his eyes, Sébastien stood up and offered me his elbow. "Let's get out of here."

It wasn't a fear of ghosts that had my heart racing as we neared the abbey. On the quest for a historic treasure from the country of my birth, with the promise of also achieving justice for Lane's missing friend, I felt more alive than I had in months. Back at home, Naveen Krishnan was no doubt doing irreparable harm to my carefully constructed courses, yet being here seemed so much more important. Teaching history was the life I'd worked so hard to achieve. Why wasn't it enough?

Lost in my thoughts, I didn't notice any more inhuman howls from cats or other creatures. Before I knew it, we were back at the abbey and Sébastien was opening the main door with the extra key Lane had made.

We didn't know the shortcuts between rooms in the labyrinthine abbey, so we stuck to the main route. I paused on the west terrace that looked out over both the ocean and the mainland. The fog stretched as far as the eye could see. I could barely see the sandy ground beneath us. I realized why. Water now encircled the Mont. I hadn't paid attention to the tide tables, but the warning sign at the base of the Mont wasn't easily forgotten. It gave the high and low tides of each day, because the height of the tides varied greatly throughout the month.

With a last glance at the ocean, I led the way into the abbey.

The fog was thick enough to obscure some of the floodlights, so we used flashlights the whole way. I wasn't sure if it was only my imagination or whether the fog also made the shuffling sound of our footsteps echo more loudly that night.

Stepping into the outdoor cloisters, I stopped abruptly, in awe of the sight before me. Fog had seeped into the garden that lay at the center of the contemplative square, above which ancient gargoyles looked on protectively.

I turned my flashlight upward. The light shone across the intricate limestone carvings above the miniature granite columns that braced the cloister's walkways.

I hadn't noticed before how few of the carvings were still intact. The jagged remains of stone carvings had been preserved. I smiled to myself, pleased that "renovation" didn't mean a modernization that forgot the past.

Sébastien cleared his throat.

"It's nearly impossible for a historian to pull away," I said.

"I wish we had more time. It will be daylight soon."

We continued onward, walking with purpose until we reached the crypt where we'd found North the previous day shortly before closing time.

"*Zut!*" Sébastien cried out. He set his small black backpack on the floor.

"What's the matter?"

"This scaffolding is in a different place than where they were working yesterday."

"I noticed that. But that's a *good* thing. It means they don't know where exactly to find their buried treasure. It means we have more time—"

"Perhaps," Sébastien murmured, rubbing his chin.

"What are you thinking?"

"This is but one of at least three crypts, and they do not have the engineering equipment to properly determine where secret hiding places might be."

"That's exactly why we thought we could find the treasure before them," I pointed out, "with your engineering knowledge." I motioned to the backpack he'd brought, which contained basic engineering measurement equipment.

He nodded but didn't look at me. He pointed his flashlight around the vaulted ceiling, his thoughts obviously elsewhere.

"The entrance to a secret room could even be inside one of these massive columns." I lay down on the stone floor and spread my arms and legs as if I was making a snow angel, illustrating my point. "These things are almost as wide I am tall."

"It could be anywhere," Sébastien mumbled to himself.

I sat up and leaned against the column. "Shouldn't we get to work, then?"

"Jaya," Sébastien said, coming over to sit next to me. "If the thieves had narrowed down the search for us, then yes, I could most likely use my knowledge and tools to find a false wall. But even if we assume this *Gros Piliers* crypt is the correct one, it is simply not possible to cover so much space in this grand a room. Not in the amount of time that we have."

I sat up. "There has to be a way. I can't let them get away with whatever they did to Hugo and destroy the Mont in search of this treasure."

"That's not what I'm most afraid of."

"What do you mean?"

"These are smart men," Sébastien said. "They, too, must realize the futility of their situation. As I've said before, desperate men do desperate things. I've lived for nearly nine decades. I have seen both the best and the worst in men. Most men are not truly bad. But under the right circumstances...Almost anyone can be forced to act in desperate ways."

"We're not giving up."

"No. But this requires a different plan."

"Do you have one in mind?"

"If you're up for driving the Porsche while I catch a wink of sleep, I do."

CHAPTER 39

The round-the-clock shuttle bus deposited us at Sébastien's Porsche shortly before daybreak. After stepping into the passenger seat, he typed an address into his phone, then set the phone into a dashboard dock.

"Follow these directions," he said, "and we'll be there in less than two hours."

There wasn't much traffic on the road, so I opened up the engine and we flew through the French countryside. Sébastien rolled up his coat to use as a pillow, and promptly fell asleep. Shifting gears in bare feet and passing a tractor, I didn't even need coffee to feel awake.

As we approached our destination, I thought for a moment that we were returning to Sébastien's house. But instead, the GPS system led me a different direction, out of a roundabout. We were heading toward central Nantes.

I glanced at Sébastien, who was snoring softly. Asleep in the reclined seat, he looked older. Though I still didn't think he looked ninety, without the facial expressions that showed his joie de vivre, the deep lines on his face showed him to be the elderly man that he was.

Traffic slowed as we approached the center of the city. In the stop-and-go traffic, Sébastien stirred.

"She likes you," he said, returning his seat to an upright position. He ran a hand through his wild hair, resulting in an even taller white bouffant.

"The car? I like her, too."

The navigator led me alongside the Loire river that ran through the center of the city. We had approached from the north, so I drove along the north side of the river until I could cut across on a narrow bridge. In spite of the chilly weather, there were just as many bicycles as cars on the road.

"*C'est bon*," Sébastien said. "We're almost home." With those joyous words, he again looked decades younger than his years.

"Unless there's a vortex inside that carousel ahead, we're nowhere near your house."

"That carousel marks the beginning of my second home."

"In an industrial warehouse?"

"You don't recognize it yet, from the photographs at my house?"

A moment later, the creature that appeared showed me where we were. I slammed on the breaks as a forty-foot elephant came into view.

Luckily, the bridge was nearly empty of cars. Though I'd seen the photographs and illustrations of the giant mechanized elephant at Sébastien's house, the images didn't do justice to the wooden elephant that roamed the park. Far more detailed than a statue on wheels, the animal was made up of hundreds of separate sections of wood, intertwined to replicate the real movements of an elephant.

"The Grand Elephant," Sébastien said. "If you return to driving, you may park up ahead."

I put the car in gear and cruised by the elephant just as it roared and blew a burst of steam from its trunk, much to the delight of a small group of children running alongside it.

"No need to rush," Sébastien said, as I zoomed into a parking space, the tires squealing. "You'll have plenty of time with the elephant. It will take several hours to gather what we need from this studio. My barn is my personal studio. As an emeritus staff member at *Les Machines de L'Île:* The Machines of the Island, I have access to this shared studio. There's much more equipment here."

"What *is* this place?" I asked on the short walk back to the path of the elephant. The area looked like a combination of old warehouses, a Victorian carousel, a wondrous arboretum, and a Twilight Zone episode with children trailing the surreal elephant.

"This area used to be shipyards," Sébastien explained. "It is the project I told you about at my house that revived the area. After years of disuse, a group of engineers and artists got together and created this testament to the meaning of life. The animals are man-made creations, yet with simple materials and engineering—not computers—they move and interact with us. One of my greatest joys is watching the expressions on people's faces as they watch the animals come to life."

"We missed the elephant." I heard the disappointment in my voice as we reached the front of an open warehouse.

"He'll be back shortly. He likes to walk through the whole park."

"Are there more mechanical animals like him?" Now that we were closer, I could see that the warehouse was more than it seemed. A mechanical tree filled with real plants stood next to a gift shop and café, and a strange assortment of plants peeked out from behind closed doors. Families stood in line in front of an entrance to get inside.

"None of the creations are quite like the Grand Elephant, but yes, there are others. A giant heron made of wood and steel, not quite as large as the elephant, flies through this building, carrying two children with it."

"So there are mechanical people, too?"

"Ah, no. The children are very real. There are two baskets the heron carries as it flies through the sky."

I shook my head. I knew I should be thinking about foiling North's plans, but in this wonderland I felt as if I'd left the real world far behind.

"It's as if I'm in another time," I said, "but not one that exists."

"As you young people might say, it is a 'mashup' of Jules Verne and Leonardo da Vinci's imaginations. It began with an exhibition called The Clever Mechanicals that toured the world in the early

2000s, and the idea caught on. Inventors came here to continue thinking up modern versions of classic creations, and to have it all be sustainable. I was asked to consult, and I never left."

"I can see why."

"*Bof!*"

"What is it?"

"The elephant in The Clever Mechanicals exhibition," he said. "I haven't thought of that original elephant in quite some time. But with you here, it reminded me—he was called *The Sultan's Elephant*. This country of mine has had a long history entangled with India. *Alors!*" He rubbed his hands together. "We don't have time to sit around speaking of the philosophical implications of colonization. I must get to work. There's an extra bed in the studio, if you'd like to get some sleep while I gather materials."

I shook my head. "What I need is to go for a run. I don't think I've ever been somewhere more perfect for it."

I donned my running clothing and shoes, and set off to explore the Machines of the Island.

One side of the old warehouse had been converted into the theme park of mechanized animals and self-sustaining plants, leaving the other side as a working studio for the dozens of artists and engineers whose ingenuity made these creations a reality. But I wasn't ready to be indoors.

Instead, I followed the path of the Great Elephant, whose slow progression was trailed by children clapping with glee. I caught up with it as it rounded the back of the park. It was even larger than it looked from the car. Many times the size of a real elephant, this mechanical animal transported not one but dozens of people on an elephant ride. His leather ears flapped in the wind, as his jigsaw-puzzle trunk twirled and blew steam at the children on the ground. Wheels and a motor were visible on the back side of the creature, but if you stayed in front of it, you could imagine that the intertwined pieces of wood making up its legs had brought the wooden beast to life.

Passing the elephant, I ran onward, circling the large concrete park. On the far side stood a three-story carousel, grander than the small one I'd seen on our approach. Winding around it, I caught glimpses of the fantastical creations that spun slowly around. Instead of horses, this carousel was full of piranha skeletons and sea monsters.

I was tempted to stop and get myself a ticket, but I had too much pent-up energy. I continued running until I was too tired to worry about anything besides getting myself a snack.

I ordered a baguette sandwich in the café next to the warehouse and thought about what to do while waiting for Sébastien. I called Lane on our burner phones, but he didn't answer. I was tempted to check email, but I half expected that using the modern invention would set off a series of alarms here in this fantasyland. As I ate my sandwich, savoring the delicious sweet pickles the menu called cornichons, the Grand Elephant passed by. Watching the ingenious creation, I felt that anything was possible.

I entered the exhibit hall and was about to watch the heron come to life, when I caught a glimpse of Sébastien's untamable hair. He ran into the room and grabbed me. He was running so quickly that he skidded on the concrete floor as he came to a stop.

"No time to explain," he said, his voice out of breath. "Head for the car. Get it running. I'll meet you there."

"What are you—"

"Run, Jaya," he said. "For the love of God. Please. *Run.*"

CHAPTER 40

With my heart thudding in my chest, I sat in the car, revving the engine. Whenever Sébastien arrived, I'd be ready to go. Thankful I'd stopped to fill up the tank with gas on the way, I tried to stay positive, but I couldn't help worrying that North was onto us. How had that happened? I was positive nobody had followed us from the Mont. We were the only people on the pre-dawn shuttle bus to the car park. Even if North had figured out what we were up to, how had he found us at the Machines of the Island of Nantes? I'd called Lane from our burner phones. We'd done everything right. Hadn't we?

I didn't have to wait much longer for my answer. Two minutes later, Sébastien appeared. He walked as quickly as a man could walk without breaking into a run. Under one arm he carried a bulging canvas bag. Over his other shoulder hung a duffle bag.

"Open the boot!" he called.

I located the switch and popped the trunk. Sébastien dumped his gear into the trunk and slid into the passenger seat.

"Drive," he said.

"Where are we going?"

"Anywhere that isn't here."

I peeled out of the parking spot and gunned the engine. As we left the mechanical wonderland in our wake, I heard the sound of sirens. Sirens? North wouldn't have called the police.

"Are those for us?" I asked.

"Indeed."

"You'd better fill me in on what's going on." I shifted gears to avoid losing control as I spun around a roundabout.

"It's my fault. I didn't think through the necessity of being secretive."

"You *told people* what we're doing?"

"The contrary. Which was the problem. We're a collaborative group. That's why the studio is an open floor plan. When I began to collect equipment secretively..."

"One of your co-workers thought you were trying to steal something and called the police?"

"Worse."

"What's worse than that?"

"Years ago, one of my misguided colleagues thought it would be a good idea to test out his engineering skills by robbing a bank vault. He rigged equipment that would allow him to both detect weaknesses in the walls and take advantage of that weakness to get inside. His first, experimental piece of equipment is still here. I removed it from storage."

I groaned and shifted gears to avoid maiming a family of bicyclists. "So now the *police* are after you?"

Sébastien waved his hand. "Claude has always been prone to fits of exaggeration. As soon as the police talk with him and others, they will see there is no reason to suspect I'm robbing a bank."

"Then why did you run?"

"We don't have time to convince the police and my colleagues of our intentions. Do you have any idea how long the police would have kept us?"

He had a point. "Did you have a chance to get what we need?"

"I'm not sure if *anything* will be enough, but when Claude interrupted me, I was working on adapting the machine in the boot to detect differences in stone. I did not have time to make calculations for the specific materials on the Mont—the different stones and bonding materials such as quicklime. *Alors*, I hope it's enough to find our secret room."

"And as soon as we've located the room, we can alert the

authorities, rather than damaging it ourselves or waiting for the thieves to damage it."

"*Précisément.*"

Winter days were short in northern France. The late afternoon sun was close to the horizon as we approached Mont Saint-Michel once again.

The plan was for Sébastien to try out his equipment after the abbey was closed but before North's midnight digging resumed.

At eight o'clock, the two of us got to work. The safest thing to do was split up. I was to wait one level above the crypts, by the abbey church. From that more central location, I could watch out for anyone aroused by the noise. The abbey church was for more than the tourists. It was a functioning church, so it was possible that someone from the present-day order might be wandering around this early in the evening.

As Sébastien headed for the crypt with the miniature video camera, I got comfortable in a sheltered walkway outside the church. Well, as comfortable as one can get on a chilly night while leaning against a rough stone wall and hoping not to be discovered. Though I hadn't slept much in days, adrenaline kept me going. I wasn't the slightest bit tired, and I could have sworn I didn't hear or see a thing.

It was only the video feed on my phone that alerted me there was something wrong.

I watched helplessly as North's angry face filled the screen of my phone—before the feed went dark.

CHAPTER 41

This was all my fault. How had I agreed to let an elderly friend of Sanjay's help with such a risky plan?

My hands shook so badly that I was having trouble hitting the buttons to call Lane. The phone slipped from my hand and clattered to the stones below.

That was all I needed, to smash my cell phone while I was trapped on freezing, foggy Mont Saint-Michel in the middle of the night below a clandestine treasure hunt operation in which my partner had just been captured and my sort-of boyfriend was off with a beautiful doctor hundreds of miles away.

I scooped up the phone. It was badly scratched but still functional. I was about to will my fingers to work and call Lane, when the phone rang. The screen showed as Sébastien's number, but after what I'd just seen, it couldn't be him. I desperately hoped I wasn't about to speak with the person I was guessing now possessed the phone.

I sank down onto the stone floor and answered the phone.

"I hope," the English voice said, "that I'm not speaking with whom I believe this to be."

"Don't say anything!" A voice in the background called out. It was Sébastien's voice. Relief flooded through me as I realized he was alive—followed by dread.

North now had a hostage.

"Would somebody put a gag on him?" North's muffled voice said.

"North," I said.

"Well, this is unfortunate. I was led to believe you were vacationing with Lane at a Loire Valley chateaux. I wonder who Lane ordered dozens of roses for then. Any ideas? No matter. I hoped you had forgotten all about me by now, but it seems I was misinformed."

"How could I forget you, North?"

"As charming as you are, I hoped we wouldn't encounter one another again."

"Let the Frenchman go," I said. "He has nothing to do with this."

"Feisty from afar. I'm afraid you have no bargaining chip at the moment. I'm the one who has Sébastien Renaud."

My breath caught.

"Oh yes, I know who he is. He wasn't foolish enough to have any identification on him, but he was once quite well-known. It appears he didn't think anyone would still recognize him after all these years. Such a shame he's so humble."

I closed my eyes. If I could have sunk any lower onto the cold stone floor, I would have. "That's how you found us?"

"That's part of it. I wasn't sure about the collapse in the crypt. There are minor tremors periodically, which is what the other crews believed happened."

"But you're too smart for that."

"Flattery will normally get you everywhere, but not today. No, I couldn't be sure, so I checked up on your whereabouts. By the way, that was very nicely played, my dear. I never suspected you two had split up. I'm not taking any more chances. I know you're not far. Why don't you and Lane meet me in the Devil's Dungeon in one hour?"

"Why would we do that?"

"Your combination of cunning and innocence really is quite charming, Jaya, but I'm tired. I haven't slept much in days. This project is behind schedule, and I've had to pitch in myself. Me! You can understand why I'm not feeling especially generous."

"Lane is farther away than that. Even if I could reach him—"

"I'm a reasonable man. You have an hour and a half."

"That's not enough—"

"If you try my patience, I might be forced to do something I've never done before. I'd hate to harm Sébastien."

"You didn't have the same qualms about Hugo."

North didn't answer right away, but I heard his heavy breathing. He was flustered. I should have taken it as a sign I was pushing him too far, but I didn't think that was it. Whenever we mentioned Hugo, he seemed genuinely upset. "I *didn't* hurt Hugo," he said.

I didn't know what to say. I had to stall for time. I had no idea how soon Lane would be there.

"Remember," North continued, his voice forceful, "I can make each of your lives so miserable you will wish you were dead. I'll start with you. I still have that information that will ruin your life. One phone call from me is all it would take."

"I don't care," I said, my voice shaking to such an extent I barely recognized it.

"Of course you care. Now is not a good time to call my bluff."

"I'm not bluffing. Stay on the line." I muted North and started tapping in a new phone number. I hoped I knew how to use the phone well enough that I was putting the two lines on with each other while leaving North muted.

Though it was late evening in France, it was only early afternoon in San Francisco. I hoped the dean would answer his phone. Or I hoped he didn't. God, I had no idea what I wanted.

He answered.

"Dean," I said.

"Jaya, is that you? I almost didn't answer the phone. I didn't recognize the number."

"I'm afraid something has come up in France."

"You need a few more days? I'm sure Naveen would be more than happy to cover for you."

"I need more than a few days, actually. Naveen can take over my classes." I took a deep breath, feeling my teeth chatter from both cold and fear. "I'm resigning."

"We must have a bad connection." I could almost hear his disapproving frown.

"You heard me properly. I'll send in my formal resignation as soon as I can. I'm sorry."

I clicked off, and clicked back over to North. He was swearing with such creativity that I almost muted him again.

"That," North said, breathing hard, "was a *very* stupid thing to do. I'm still going to send them the information on your misdeeds. This won't be the end of your grief."

"It doesn't matter any more," I said. "Sébastien's career is long over. Lane's new career ended last year. And now my career is finished. Lane and I can disappear together. I'm calling the police now. You can't hurt us. You have nothing to threaten us with."

North laughed. "Oh yes. I most certainly do. Thanks for staying on the line with me. I knew you weren't far. Dante? Will you escort Jaya to the dungeon while I send along proof of Jaya's plagiarism?"

I'd been so focused on the conversation that I hadn't been paying attention to my surroundings. Dante stepped into the walkway directly in front of me.

North had played me. This whole time, he knew I was close by. All he had to do was keep me talking until they could find me.

I tried to scramble up from my seated position, but Dante was too close. He held an object in his hand that made my mouth go dry. A thick, black club. Even more frightening were his angry eyes that glared at me with such hatred that you'd think I'd kicked his puppy. The last thought I had before everything went dark, was that I'd given up everything in my life for nothing.

CHAPTER 42

I woke up in a dark, damp room with my head feeling like it was twice the size it should have been.

"Jaya, thank God."

The hand on my back startled me. I sat up and immediately wished I hadn't. If I'd eaten anything recently, I would have thrown it up.

"Lie back down," Sébastien said. "Here, use my coat as a pillow."

"I'd rather use it as a coat," I mumbled, lying back down and letting darkness envelope me again.

When I came to a second time, my head felt only slightly bigger than it should have. I carefully eased myself up.

"Where are we?" I asked, looking around the dim room. Sébastien sat next to me on the rocky floor, his back against the stone wall.

"Not in the Devil's Dungeon. That's actually on a map. This place where we are..."

"Are we still on the Mont?"

"Yes, but far beneath the abbey. Where we are, nobody will find us."

My eyes took a few moments to focus. There was very little light in the room. A single oil lamp hung in one corner.

The sound of a heavy door creaking echoed through the dungeon.

Lane stumbled into the room. "Jones," he said, rushing to my side.

"He's here to rescue you," a posh voice said from the doorway.

I was certain North was going to take a step back and lock us in. Instead, *someone else* shut the door, leaving North inside with us. North closed his eyes and leaned against the solid door, his fists clenched.

"What's going on?" I said. "Did Dante get a bit confused?"

North opened his eyes and glared at us. "This is what I get for refusing to kill you lot."

I looked from North's uncharacteristically disheveled hair, to the narrow ceiling made of rock, to the oil lamp flickering in the corner.

It all made sense now.

North wasn't the one pulling the strings. He never was.

That's why nothing had made sense about Hugo's strange disappearance, why North hadn't been able to change plans midstream, and why it had degenerated from a smooth operation to a botched one.

North was the smooth talker. The con man. But he wasn't a mastermind.

Whereas Dante, the unpleasant man with cold eyes who was a liability for North to keep around—*that* was a man who would commit murder. For someone so intelligent and evil, it would be easy—maybe even fun, in a sick way—to play the role of a brain-damaged sidekick.

"It was never you," I said. "It was *Dante*. This whole time, you were his front."

North's excuse for keeping Dante around was that he was in Dante's debt after Dante suffered a head injury on a job gone wrong. But that was all a lie. The nasty man was there because he was the one pulling the strings.

The conversation Lane and I had overheard made sense now. North was complaining to Dante that he didn't like what he was being forced to do on this job. He'd been kept in the dark about the nature of the treasure at first, too, which is why he said he never would have written about a related subject in his fake letter to me.

North mentioned the East India Company to entice me to come to France, in case an invitation from Lane wasn't enough to get me there. But like much of Western Europe, so much of France's past was caught up with their colonial history that there was a good chance any long-lost treasure would involve a colonial connection.

A strange expression crossed North's face. His angry glower disappeared, replaced with resignation.

"Yes," he said, "and now that you know the truth, I'm in more danger than I was before. Thank you for that. And in case you couldn't tell, that was *sarcasm*." He stepped away from the door and rubbed his arms. "God, it's freezing in here."

Lane had remained suspiciously silent. Now he let go of my shoulder and rushed at North.

"Hey!" North said, ducking as Lane punched him.

Lane was aiming for North's nose, but North was able to move slightly, so Lane's punch only caught the edge of his jaw.

Sébastien attempted to pull Lane off, but I had no such inclination. If Lane wanted to punch North, that was fine by me. The man had it coming.

"We're all in this together now," Sébastien said. "Let's use our energy to find our way out of here."

"We're not in this together," Lane said, straightening up and shaking out his hand. "Is there any rope around here?"

I found an old piece of rope in a corner of the dungeon that I could use to tie North's hands behind his back.

"I hardly think that's sanitary," North said.

"You should have thought about that before you lied to me," Lane said. He stretched the fingers of his hand. He would no doubt end up with a nasty bruise from punching North. But not nearly as bad as the bruise on his opposite shoulder.

"You need me," North said, backing away from me and the rope.

"Why is that?" I asked.

"I'm the only one who knows where Hugo is."

Lane's breath caught. "Hugo is alive?"

"Weren't you listening to me a minute ago? I'm not a killer. I'm a trained forger who's a decent thief and a brilliant con man. A general-purpose rogue, if you will. But not a killer."

"Where are you keeping Hugo?" Lane said. "Here on Mont Saint-Michel?"

North shook his head. "Too risky. After Hugo approached you at the Louvre, it was clear he wanted to tell you what was really going on. I was asked to take care of him in a way I disapproved of. I kidnapped him instead."

"There was so much blood," I said.

"Yes," North said with a sigh. "I've never done a kidnapping before. It turns out people don't go willingly, even if you insist it's for their own good."

Lane scoffed.

"He'd be dead right now if it wasn't for me," North snapped. "And he will be in a few days if I don't get out of here. He's only got enough food and water to last another couple of days."

Lane's hand was balled into another fist.

"Don't waste your energy," I said.

Lane circled North, but relaxed his fist. "This could be a trick. He's a con man, you know."

"You're about to tie me up with a mildewy rope," North said. "How could that possibly be part of my plan?"

I'd forgotten about the rope in my hand when he mentioned Hugo. "Thanks for the reminder."

"See, I'm a helpful guy."

Sébastien took the rope from my hands. "I can tie a knot that nobody can escape from. Not even Houdini."

North's face fell. "I knew you were trouble the moment I saw you, Mr. Renaud."

Sébastien wrapped the rope around North's wrists.

"Ouch. Does it have to be so tight? Are you upset that I recognized you? It's your fault for being too modest. The night of our encounter, I thought it looked like someone had searched my room. The trip wire hadn't been activated, and nothing in particular was different. Only that vague feeling you get when something isn't quite the way you left it. Just like a skilled illusionist would have been able to accomplish. That's when I remembered your face. It took me a little time to track down your name, but you were too famous in your day to be forgotten. Once I had your name, it was easy to connect you to Jaya through her friend Sanjay."

"*Merde*," Sébastien muttered.

"I can't feel my hands," North said.

"*Bon*."

"It's not my fault you're full of false modesty," North retorted. "Look where it's got you."

"Don't blame yourself, Sébastien," Lane said. "None of us could have known this would happen."

The old magician nodded and turned toward the wall. He ran his fingers along the stone.

"You know this place," I said to North, "and you're supposedly the expert on contingency plans. That means there's another way out of this dungeon."

North laughed mirthlessly. "This dungeon *is* the contingency plan. The idea of last resort. Remember, nobody was supposed to get hurt. Nobody is ever supposed to get hurt."

Sébastien clapped his hands together. "Finally! Now that I have your attention, may I point something out? This room is so damp, for the same reason it's not on a map of *Le Mont Saint-Michel*: the tide fills this room with water. Look at the floor. It has already begun. Unless we get out of here, in a matter of hours, we will drown."

CHAPTER 43

Sébastien showed us the base of the wall where water was seeping in.

"This must have been why they abandoned this level," he said. "The tremors shifted the land, cracking the rock and letting the ocean water in. I suspect that we've been left in here to drown."

North cleared his throat. "I hate to say this, but you're absolutely right. That was the plan I refused to participate in. Your deaths are supposed to look natural, like you were stupid tourists who didn't pay attention to the tide warnings. After drowning in here in the salt water, your bodies were to be released into the tides."

"If water is getting in," I said, "that means there must be a way out."

Sébastien shook his head. "Only if you're three inches high and can swim in the opposite direction of a fierce tide."

"The light," I said, pointing at the oil lamp hung in the corner. "The fact that light still works means the water won't rise to the top! All we have to do is tread water and wait for the tide to go back down."

"And pray we don't get hypothermia," Lane said.

"It's worse than that, I'm afraid," North said. "We brought that lamp with us. It hasn't been sitting here through another high tide."

"And these water marks," Sébastien added, pointing at the low ceiling. "The tide will fill this entire room."

We stared at each other.

"Well, then," Lane said. "Let's get to work finding a way out."

With four of us, we could each take one wall. Two were made of solid rock, and two of mortared stone blocks. Sébastien untied North, and instructed us to use small fragments of wood we found strewn across the floor to look for cracks in the rock and trace the mortar in between the stones, looking for weak spots.

"There's got to be something more we can do," North said as the rotted piece of wood in his hand snapped in two.

"If I'm going to die," I said, "you can at least tell me what's so important about this treasure that's getting us killed."

"I thought you'd already figured it out."

"I think so, but there are still a few missing pieces. You acquired those letters from the British East India Company clerk at an estate sale, where you were looking for art for your legitimate business. But at the time, you didn't believe the ravings of an addict. It wasn't until you found a corroborating reference that you believed the rumors he spoke of. Based on where the Mont Saint-Michel treasures and records were hidden during the French Revolution, and then destroyed or stolen during WWII, I'm guessing it was Nazi plunder that led you to your corroborating evidence. Am I right so far?"

"I knew you were smart, but I didn't realize *how* smart," North said, giving me a nod of admiration. "That's my downfall, isn't it?" He sighed and turned back to his wall.

"When you learned directions to a secret room had been hidden inside a desk from the monastery scriptorium, you sought out the desk." As I spoke, I continued to tap my piece of broken wood into the spaces between stones. "That's when you discovered that most objects from Mont Saint-Michel had been removed during the Revolution. The Louvre had acquired the scriptorium desk that contained the clue."

"I'm the one who made that connection," North said. "Even though I'm not the one running this operation, my knowledge of art comes in handy."

"But," I said, "you still didn't want to act before you had more proof that the treasure was real, *and* that it hadn't already been discovered. That's where Hugo came in. With the connection to Mont Saint-Michel, you knew he'd be able to tell you if your speculations were correct. But because of the religious significance of the Mont, Hugo wouldn't have anything to do with it. Being a smart business man, you would have backed off then, wouldn't you? Only you weren't the one calling the shots."

"Quite. Once I found the desk at the Louvre, I considered keeping the information to myself and calling the whole thing off. I know I'm good at setting up a successful con, but *Louvre* good? I'm not that arrogant. But I knew one person with the skills to pull it off. That's when I brought in Lane. With him, I knew we could do this."

Lane swore. I glanced at him and saw he'd broken his wooden stick. He looked around for another one.

"What I still don't understand, though, is why part of Tipu Sultan's treasure is so important for you to risk all this."

North spun around. "Tipu Sultan? Who the hell is Tipu Sultan? It's Clive of India's lost treasures that are here. You got a look at the full extent of the letters when you broke into my room, didn't you? You know what this is about."

"I read the letters. Clive's lost treasure *isn't* what this is about."

"That Company clerk clearly mentioned Clive's treasures!"

"Yes," I said, "but you're forgetting the additional clue in the illuminated manuscript page the monks left us."

"*Sequere cementarium claustri ad cryptam.* How could I forget? Follow the stonemasons of the cloisters to the crypt. All that told us was directions to their hiding place. And not even specific directions, at that. As you may have noticed, there's more than one crypt, each of them larger than you'd think would be found on this damned rock."

"You didn't have the parchment authenticated to see when the writing and illustration were added?"

"Funny enough," North said, "Hugo refused to cooperate at that point. And we were in a hurry. Our information was solid.

Even though I'm not an expert on illuminated manuscripts, I know forgeries. The parchment wasn't a fake. And since it has been hidden inside the desk at the Louvre since the 1790s, even if I was mistaken, there's no way it could be a modern fake."

"You didn't notice the painted illustration of a tiger attacking a man that was in a much brighter paint than the words? It looked like the tiger was painted much more recently than the Latin script."

"That's what the monks did, Jaya." North let out an exasperated sigh. "They painted pictures of people and animals in their manuscripts. That's what they're known for at the Mont. The beautiful illustrations praised God and also helped illiterate people understand the subjects of the books. That's why they're called *illuminated* manuscripts as opposed to plain old manuscripts. Really, I thought you'd have more of a general education."

"I knew all that," I snapped. "I've never heard of an illuminated manuscript that included an illustration of a gruesome automaton made famous by Tipu Sultan, the Tiger of Mysore."

"But that doesn't—it doesn't—how—"

"The English clerk talks of a Frenchman who was rumored to have amassed a treasure in India that he wanted to return to France, a treasure that included an automaton as well as treasure taken from Clive. But it's the tiger and an elephant painted on the parchment. *That's* the portion of his treasure that's here at the Mont."

"I don't believe it," North said. "This has to be about Clive's treasures. It has to be."

"Even if you're right," I said, "why is Clive's treasure more important than anything else you've gone after before?"

North frowned.

"The treasure doesn't matter, you two," Lane said. "Come over here. I think I've found something." He pointed up at a crack running along the joint of the wall and ceiling. "The rock is weak here. Sébastien, do you think this room will collapse if we dig here?"

Sébastien stood back and looked around the room. We watched him in silence for several minutes. Without anything to do but wait, the damp cold felt more oppressive.

"Find whatever materials you can," Sébastien said, wiping his dusty brow with his sleeve. "We dig."

We couldn't all fit around the weakened rock, so Lane and I continued checking the other walls for possibilities while Sébastien and North dug. North grumbled under his breath about fake injuries preventing Lane from taking his place.

Half an hour later, neither Lane nor I had found another weakness in the walls, and Sébastien and North had only managed to dig out a narrow opening of about a foot. Icy water sloshed around my ankles. Only my heightened alertness from fear prevented the chill from defeating me.

"I have it!" Sébastien said, pushing forward. I rushed over to where he stood. A sprinkling of dirt fell on his arms, and when he pulled them back, I saw that he'd broken through the wall.

Instead of being elated, he shook his head. "It's no use."

"But we're through," I said.

"The rest of the rock is too solid. All we have is this small opening. Nobody could fit through that."

I looked at the hole, then down to my hips. "Nobody besides me."

"You can't go alone," Lane said.

"What choice do we have?"

Nobody said anything.

I looked around for something I could take with me as a weapon. The wood fragments were too small to be of use, so I scooped up the discarded rope.

"Lane," I said, "can you lift me up? Why isn't anybody moving? This is our best shot. They're not right outside the door, because the hallway must be filling with water, too. I'll make my way out, then come back with help. North, how dangerous is the engineer you employed?"

"Don't worry about him. He's not helping with anything like

this. He doesn't even know we're down here." North looked up to the heavens and shook his head. "Your beau doesn't appear to be moving. Would you like a hand up?"

North boosted me up to the narrow opening. I squeezed through, feet first, willing myself not to think too far ahead. I was getting out of the dungeon. That's all that mattered.

I nearly slipped on the uneven floor as I landed on the other side of the prison wall. Water lapped at my feet. I oriented myself in the faint light from the hole I'd come through. The dungeon door was a few yards away. I ran to it and tried the handle. It didn't budge. A shiny new padlock the size of the palm of my hand kept the door shut. Without keys or a sledgehammer, I wasn't getting into that room. I stood there for a few moments, my hand pressed flat against the door. Lane was only a few feet away from me, but it might as well have been a thousand miles.

A dim light shone ahead. If there was a window slit overlooking the ocean that I could squeeze through, I could swim to safety. I ran forward toward the light. The path sloped upward, leading me away from the tidal waters. But hope made me reckless. I tripped on an uneven rock and tumbled forward. Pain shot through my arm. Ever since I'd broken it two years before, it hurt when I applied too much force.

Even worse than the pain was the realization that the light I'd been running toward was moving. It wasn't light from a window to freedom. It was a flashlight. A flashlight clenched in Dante's hand.

CHAPTER 44

Dante gave a start. This time around, he wasn't expecting to see me.

"How did you get out?" He pointed his flashlight at my face.

I bit my lip and shrugged. "It's not too late, Dante. You haven't killed anyone yet." I began backing away slowly.

"Stop moving. Does he know you're out?"

I stopped backing away, more from surprise than from Dante's request. Was Lane right that North's imprisonment had been a ruse?

"You can pretend you never saw me," I said.

"It's too late for that." He raised a fist.

I knew I was no match for his size, but I wasn't much of a match for anyone when it came to size. I like jiu jitsu because it focuses on ground combat, where height and bulk are less important than intelligence and keeping your head.

I lunged at Dante. Not for his face or midsection, but for his legs. I wanted to knock him to the floor, where I'd have the advantage of surprise.

He wasn't expecting me to go for his knees. The force of my weight against his legs threw him off balance. The flashlight flew out of his hand and he fell to the hard stone floor with a thud. The flashlight rolled to a stop, the fragmented light casting a harsh shadow across Dante's face. Though stunned, he didn't take time to catch his breath before he was on his knees and on top of me.

Underneath him, I vaulted my hips into a bridge pose, again knocking him off his center of gravity by tipping him over the top of my head so he was forced to balance on his hands. I gripped his elbow to pull away the last of his control. He grunted as I tossed him over and slid out from under him. His head knocked against the stone floor. While he was dazed, I used the rope I'd brought with me to tie him up. He groaned softly as I rolled him over, wrapped the rope around his wrists, and ripped off a piece of his shirt to gag his mouth.

Satisfied that he wasn't going anywhere, I searched him for keys. I pulled out at least two purses' worth of junk from his coat, shirt, and slacks pockets, but the only key was to a car. As I stared helplessly at the useless car key, Dante's eyes popped open. Unable to speak through his gag, he grunted at me and thrashed around in his bonds. But as the realization quickly sunk in that he wouldn't be able to break free, his body grew still. The look of loathing on his face gave me a bigger chill than the frigid ocean water I'd escaped.

I picked up his fallen flashlight and ran.

I had no idea where I was, or where I was going. We were in some old section that everyone had forgotten about, and the records were lost. My plan had been to go *up*. If I could find a way.

The beam bounced wildly against the walls, a combination of dirt and stone. The light flickered. I stopped. The light flickered again.

I turned it back off to conserve the battery's life, hoping that was the cause of the flicker and not that it wasn't broken from the fall. With the flashlight off, the darkness that surrounded me was as black as tar. The stale air felt thick, as if I was breathing in the blackness around me.

I waited a moment for my eyes to adjust. They didn't. There was no light for my eyes to adjust to.

As I sat in the darkness and tried to think, I breathed deeply, the scent of decay filling my lungs. What I wouldn't give for a window and a light switch. There had been an oil lamp in the dungeon and Dante had been using a flashlight, so I knew electric lights were too much to hope for. My only hope to find one was to keep going and make my way up.

I reached my hand out in front of me. The simple act was more frightening than I imagined it could ever be.

Feeling the rough stone wall, I made my way by touch. I trudged along for what felt like hours, but was probably a much shorter period of time. Slowly feeling my way by touch, the surface of the wall gave way to metal. I jumped back and turned the flickering flashlight back on. I stood in front of a jail cell. This lower level must have been for prisoners, before it was breached and the area flooded. Unless— I shuddered at a horrific thought. It was only my *hope* that the prisoners had been moved once this level began to flood.

The flashlight beam remained steady, for the time being, so I hurried along, rushing as quickly as I could without tripping. I cried out in joy as the beam of light shone over a set of stairs. That's what I'd been looking for. A way up.

I scrambled up the stairs, tripping over my own feet in my rush. The flashlight flickered. I shook it. "Come on, flashlight. You don't have to hold out much longer." I'd only been alone in the dark for a short time, and already I was talking to myself.

When I reached the top of the stairs, I stopped in my tracks. The beam of the flashlight illuminated a decaying skeleton.

Whoever had been imprisoned here had been left here to rot, never receiving a proper burial. I wondered if anyone even knew he'd died. Would anyone know that I'd died down here?

I felt my breathing become labored. I wasn't sure if it was from stale air or from fear. Things couldn't possibly get any worse.

The flashlight went out.

It took all my will to continue. Again feeling my way with raw fingertips, I walked forward, past the skeleton. The only sound was my own breath. Not even rats were here to keep me company.

Up ahead, I saw a faint light. A window! I must have climbed high enough to reach a window.

A flash of hope washed over me—only to be lost a moment later. The light was *red*. Light from either the rising sun or from the nighttime floodlights wouldn't be red. I must have been hallucinating. Still, I walked closer to the light. It strengthened. I could see my hand stretched out in front of me. I wasn't imagining it.

I followed the light, my hesitant steps turning into a run as it grew brighter. Rounding a corner, I found the source of the colored light. High in a corner of a small room was a narrow slit in the rock that formed a window. Set into the slender opening was the most beautiful stained glass window I'd ever seen.

It wasn't like the pieces I'd seen in churches, with religious figures. This one was a mosaic flower. Springing out of an ocean of blues and greens, a yellow stem wound upward. The sky was filled with red flower petals. I stepped closer. Hundreds of tiny shards made up the piece. I couldn't imagine how long it had taken to create, but the result was a piece of art. It was as beautiful as anything in the Louvre, and it was here, buried deep under Mont Saint-Michel, forgotten.

This was the miracle Massi had mentioned. How had it come to be here?

In the soft glow of warm light, I took in the beauty found in this unexpected place. Looking around the room, another surprise greeted me. *This was a prison cell.*

A portion of rock wall had been carved out, creating a narrow work space. Shards of colorful glass lay across the makeshift desk. A prisoner had used leftover stained glass to create beautiful art. I picked up a shard of bright blue glass that fit in the palm of my hand.

I looked back at the exquisite window. If that prisoner could make something beautiful in this godforsaken place deep beneath the abbey, so could I. I was getting us out of there.

The sound of footsteps echoed in the silent space. Could it be someone outside? I had no idea what time it was. The light from the high narrow window could have been from floodlights or from the sun.

A bright light shone behind me. I whipped around, looking for somewhere to hide.

Before I could act, a man stepped into the room. And I knew that I'd been wrong about everything.

"You," Marius said, "have been making my life very difficult. It's time for you to come with me."

Dante appeared behind him, carrying the rope I'd used to tie him up. With a malicious smirk on his face, he stepped forward and bound my wrists.

CHAPTER 45

The door of the dungeon opened and I was thrown back inside. I stumbled and landed in the water. It was now two feet high.

"Thank God," North declared, as Lane rushed to my side and began untying my wrists.

"I thought you were on our side now," I snapped, shivering in the cold water.

"For the last hour," Lane said, "all he could talk about was how you must be dead. I was about to put a gag on him."

"I was only gone for an hour?"

"Feels like much longer when you're on the run, doesn't it?" North said.

A scraping sound caused us all to turn our heads. In the opening I'd squeezed through, a boulder appeared, covering the hole.

"Are you all right?" Lane asked me, noticing my bleeding fingers as he finished untying my wrists. "What happened?"

"I knocked out Dante, but his flashlight conked out on me. I had to make my way along the walls in the dark. I got far enough up to find a window, but they caught up with me."

"They're good," North said. "I wouldn't work with them otherwise."

"I liked you better when you put a positive spin on everything," Lane said. "Too bad you're a pessimist at heart."

"He's also a liar," I said. With the rope gone from my wrists, I grabbed North's collar. "It's your fault I'm back in here."

"I'm not lying! We're in this together."

"It's *Marius* who's your boss."

"What?" Lane cut in, pulling me away from North. It was a halfhearted attempt. If I'd put up a fight, he wouldn't have succeeded in stopping me.

"If North had been honest about Marius being in charge, I would have been more careful to look out for him just now!"

"Shouldn't you have been careful regardless?" North admonished.

I opened my mouth to yell, but was stopped by Sébastien.

"Fighting isn't helping." His authoritative voice came from the corner of the room, where he was tracing the edge of the stones on the wall with his fingers. "If we don't find a way out soon, we'll either die from hypothermia or drowning." He took a step. The water was above his knees.

"Have you found anything else?" I asked.

Sébastien shook his head. "I'm three quarters done. There is only the small opening we sent Jaya through, and the hole at the bottom of the room where water is flooding in from the ocean. The lower hole is bigger than I thought, but now it's full of water."

"The hole at the bottom," I said. "I bet I can fit through it and swim to safety."

"Too risky," Sébastien said. "We don't know how quickly you would push through. You might drown before you reach the other side of the rock."

"We should make North swim through the hole," Lane said. "I'm sure we can make enough room to get him through."

"If only I could swim," North replied. "Alas, if you send me, you won't be saving yourselves. All you'd be doing is murdering me."

"That doesn't sound like a bad idea right now," Lane said. "*Marius?* Really? Why didn't you tell us?"

"I was planning on getting out of here alive. It didn't seem prudent to rat out my boss. When Jaya suggested Dante was faking his personality, I simply failed to correct her. How did you figure it out?"

"Dante was the one who caught me first," I said. "He wasn't any smarter than he was before. Meaning he wasn't acting. I was easily able to get the upper hand when we fought, and what he said made me question my assumption. But when Marius found me, so much more made sense. His desperation doesn't have as much to do with the treasure you think you'll find here. He's tired of living in the shadows. He was telling me and Lane about the book he's writing. He's unhappy with the current state of affairs. It's made him unstable, more willing to take risks in favor of a bigger payoff, like a famous treasure. I bet he no longer cares if you get caught."

North sighed. "Neither of us thought I'd be as successful in this role as I was when we started working together years ago."

"Good for you," I snapped.

"There's no need to be nasty because I'm an overachiever."

"I'm taking away all your gold stars for never learning to swim."

"I'll go," Sébastien said softly. "I'm a strong swimmer. I have a chance at making it. If one of us is to risk going through that hole to bring us all to safety, it should be me."

"You can't," I said. "Of all of us, you're the one who was dragged into this blindly. You're the last person who should risk their life—"

"I'm an old man, Jaya." He took my shivering hands in his. "I've lived a good life. Yours is just beginning. Let me do this for you."

CHAPTER 46

"We're all getting out of here," I said. "You're not risking it, Sébastien. There has to be another way."

Sébastien smiled weakly. "What would Sanjay think of me if I didn't do everything within my power to help you out of here?"

"You can help. But not by being a martyr."

"This is your last chance. Soon, my body will be too cold to swim. All of ours will be."

"Can't you reason with Marius?" I asked North, trying not to focus on the freezing feeling taking over my body. "If you're telling the truth that Hugo is still alive—"

"I am."

"Then you can convince Marius he doesn't have to do this."

"You weren't wrong that he's gone off the deep end." Water sloshed against North's waist. It was rising more quickly now. "Bad choice of words under our present circumstances," he added, his teeth chattering.

I slipped as a new surge of water forced its way into the room. My head dunked under water, but I was able to right myself. The water was now nearly to my chest. I expected Lane to make sure I was all right after I'd fallen below the water, but looking around the dim room, I didn't see him.

"Lane?" I called out. "Lane!"

Sébastien recited a poetic verse in French under his breath. I wasn't sure if he was reciting a poem or saying a prayer.

"We're buggered," North whispered. "What good's a conscience now?"

"Lane!" I ducked my head under the water, attempting to find him. The solitary lamp in the room didn't provide enough light to see under water. The salt water stung my eyes, and all I could see was near blackness. It was no use. I returned to a standing position and rubbed my eyes.

Lane's head splashed out, and he coughed up salt water.

"Were you stuck on something?" I asked, making my way to him.

"Not exactly. The water knocked me off my feet, but it also gave me an idea. The water is coming in forcefully enough that I'm betting it's the ocean directly on the other side of this room. If we time it with the next surge, we could go underwater and pull on the rock next to where the water is coming in."

"The water pressure," Sébastien said. His voice was weak, and he steadied himself against the wall as he spoke. "We can use the water pressure to our advantage."

I wasn't sure if it was a trick of the light or if everyone's lips were turning blue. Either way, we didn't have much time. The water now filled more than half of the room.

Lane used his watch to time the surges of water. Once we were sure of the timing, we knew when we had to act.

"Show time," Lane said. We all ducked our heads under the water and pulled at the stones next to the low hole.

As I tugged, I felt a great force pushing me away. I tried to hold on, but it was no use. The water was too strong. It flung me backward. Carried along by the force of the water, I crashed into the back wall.

My head throbbed from being hit yet again, so it took me a moment to realize I was clutching a piece of rock in my hands. Did that mean...

"Jaya!" Sébastien shouted. "It worked. Let's go."

I was still dazed as Lane swam up to me and led me back to the hole that was now large enough for us all to fit through. "Are you up for holding your breath for a few seconds?" he asked. "We should go before the next rush of water."

I nodded and took a deep breath.

Heavy water swirling around me, I lost all sense of direction. Was I feeling sandy ocean floor or a rough rock wall? Panic seized me. My arms flailed, desperately grabbing for anything real to hold onto.

A strong hand found mine. It pulled me upward. Cold air hit my face. I opened my eyes to see a starry night sky above and Lane Peters at my side. Braced against the rock face, I was able to stand. The water was up to my chest, and the tide was still rising. I looked around. Solid rock on one side of me, the ocean on the other.

"Swim this way," Sébastien's voice called out. "The tide is shallow here." Next to him, North was coughing profusely.

Half walking and half swimming, Lane and I made our way toward Sébastien.

"Don't step too quickly," he added.

"Why on earth not?" North asked. "We need to get out of here."

"Quicksand," Sébastien said. "Don't forget the quicksand."

"Bloody hell," North mumbled.

Since I could no longer feel my fingers or toes, being sucked under quicksand didn't sound like the worst thing that could happen to me. Still, I heeded his words. Stepping slowly and carefully went against everything my survival instincts were screaming at me, but I was so close to reaching the safety of the shore. I couldn't fail when I was so close to success.

"Good," Sébastien said as Lane and I reached the more solid footing where he and North stood. "Very, very good."

"Are you all right?" I asked. He looked as if he was about to fall over. A second later, he did exactly that.

Lane caught him before he could go underwater.

"I'm sorry," Sébastien whispered through chattering teeth. "The cold has seeped into my bones."

"Hold on," Lane said. "We're almost there." He heaved Sébastien into a standing position, wincing at the effort. His shoulder wasn't ready for this. "Jones, I'm going to lead Sébastien to shore. Follow where we step. That way you'll stay safe."

With a semiconscious Sébastien at his side, Lane led the way to shore.

The tide kept coming. Whenever it approached, we stood still, planting our legs in the sand for stability. We were out of the deepest areas, so I wasn't expecting the strength of the wave that approached. The warning signs weren't kidding about strong tides that looked deceptively calm.

North cried out beside me. The burst of water knocked him off his feet.

"Help!" he cried out. "I can't swim."

I waded back to him. "Then stand up."

"But the water!" He flailed his arms. "It's higher now!"

"North, look at me. I'm standing right next to you. The water is below my waist."

"Oh. Why didn't you say so in the first place?" He took my hand and stood up.

Lane and Sébastien were several dozen yards ahead of us now. They had almost reached the edge of the sand line.

"We're falling behind," I said. "I can't tell what path they took to reach the shore safely."

"Ladies first."

I was so busy scowling at North that I didn't see it coming. All I saw was the expression on North's face. His eyes opened wide with terror. Before I could turn to see what he was looking at, I was knocked over and forced underwater.

My first thought was that the tide had come from the wrong direction.

Strong hands closed around my neck. This wasn't the tide.

I hadn't expected it, so I hadn't taken a breath of air. I couldn't stay underwater long. My body begged me for a breath of air. Even underwater, the rote responses from my self-defense training kicked in. Unfortunately, I'd never trained underwater, so my natural offensive moves didn't work without solid ground. I tucked my arms to my sides, where they could give me more strength. But it was no use. The hands that choked me were too strong. Failing to secure my release with my arms, I switched my focus to my legs. Slowed and blinded by the water, I couldn't find a weak spot.

Suddenly, the hands relaxed. Both of us were pushed aside. Was someone trying to pull off my attacker? Lane was too far away. Even though he couldn't swim, it had to be North. His heroic action gave me the opening I needed to make my escape.

I wrapped my foot around my attacker's leg to throw him off balance. The move worked. As he attempted to regain his balance, he loosened his hold on my neck even more. It was my opening to squeeze my arms between his. That broke his hold completely.

I pulled free and jumped up, gasping for air. Marius stood directly in front of me, his face contorted with rage.

Behind him, the tiniest hint of sunlight was beginning to peek above the horizon, bringing with it a faint cast of yellow. Soon, a beautiful view would be visible from the Mont. The sight reminded me of something important I'd forgotten. Something that might help me live to see that tableau. Inside the pocket of my jeans was the fragment of stained glass.

"Peters!" North shouted. "We could use a little help here!"

As Marius stepped toward me, I grasped the fragment of glass. With one more step, he was upon me. I raised my arm and cut him with the glass. Blood rushed from his cheek as the glass slashed his face.

He clutched his cheek and stepped back, screaming with frustration.

"Jaya!" Lane called out from a distance. "Hold on!"

But I knew he was too far away to help. Moving through the tidal waters would take him too long.

I clung to the shard of glass so tightly that I felt it pierce the skin of my palm. I wondered if I had it in me to go for his neck the next time Marius came at me.

I prepared myself for whatever came next, but the seconds stretched on. The expression on Marius's face changed from anger to confusion. He took a step toward me, but he didn't advance. He hadn't been that short before, had he? The water was up to his neck. I stared at him. He wasn't shrinking. He'd stepped in quicksand.

"Please," Marius said, his arms flailing wildly as he realized his predicament. "I'm stuck. Help me. I won't hurt you. I promise."

"I refuse," North said, "to work for such an ungentlemanly employer." He stepped forward toward Marius, his arm outstretched. I watched in horror, certain he was about to push Marius's head under the water.

"North," I said, "don't—"

Before he could act, a massive wave swept over us, knocking us off our feet. The force of the water pushed me into something solid. It grunted.

"We have to go back for him, Lane," I said in between coughs. My mouth tasted like I'd swallowed a salt shaker.

"Let him go, Jones. The water is rising too quickly."

I looked back. The tide swallowed up the rest of Marius's head.

North floated past us. "A little help?"

I reached out and grabbed his hand.

"Thank you, my dear. Thank you."

My hands linked with Lane and North, we made our way to shore.

CHAPTER 47

The sunrise couldn't have been more heavenly. The storm clouds had passed, and the sun rose above the ocean with Saint Michael watching over us. We stood on solid concrete, wearing dry clothing, warming ourselves in front of a bonfire.

While Lane, North, and I were making our way back to shore, Sébastien found the energy to let himself into a construction trailer and find clothing we could change into to stave off hypothermia. He also found a phone from which to call the authorities.

Using scrap wood, North started a bonfire inside a metal trash can. The four of us gathered around the fire and watched the sunrise.

"Tell us where Hugo is," Lane said.

"I'm not revealing his location, but he'll be free by the day's end. I give you my word."

"You think your word is good enough any more?"

"Isn't it? I risked my neck for you lot, and if you didn't notice, I saved your girlfriend from Marius in the tides. At great personal risk, mind you."

"I was doing just fine myself," I said.

"That's gratitude for you."

"Thank you, North," I said. "I'm being serious now. I know what you did. You knocked Marius into the water, giving me the opening I needed to get free." I leaned over and kissed him on the cheek.

"Well, there's no need for that."

"Shouldn't we be looking for Dante?" I asked.

"He's gone," North said.

"What do you mean *he's gone*?"

"Didn't you see him on shore? He's smarter than any of us gave him credit for. He saw that all was lost. Unlike Marius, he let it go. The last I saw, he was walking toward the mainland. Just like I'll be doing as soon as I'm warm enough to walk properly."

"The police will be here any minute," Sébastien said.

"I'm sure they will," North said. "I take it you're all intelligent enough to realize it wouldn't be prudent to turn me over to them, or to mention me at all. After all, I'm not the one who recently robbed the Louvre. It would be such a shame for them to find out who did."

Lane locked his eyes on North's. "Wouldn't it, though," he said, matching North's accent perfectly.

"You won't have to worry about me again. I'm not going to ruin your lives. I'm even going to let you have this treasure."

"It's not any of our treasures," I said. "The proper authorities will locate it, without doing damage to the Mont. I'm sure you'll be able to read about it in the papers, then visit it in a museum."

"*Nobody* is going to find it, dear girl," North said. "You're welcome to use the papers in my room—I know you already have a key. By the way, that was very nice work, Mr. Renaud."

"Thank you," Sébastien said. "It was good to practice my sleight of hand. I was afraid I might be rusty."

"I doubt the information will lead anywhere," North added. "I'm starting to think the whole thing was a hoax. Expecting anyone to find a secret room through one of the thousands of stones across three crypts? The clue was probably the work of a bored monk having a laugh."

"I don't think so," I said. "I figured out where it's hidden. And I think I know what we'll find."

Lane and North both raised an eyebrow at me. Only Sébastien seemed unconcerned about the treasure.

"What will you do now?" I asked North.

"Your concern is touching."

Sirens sounded in the distance.

"That's my cue," North said. "Have a wonderful life."

Lane pulled me against him and we huddled close to the fire, watching North walk down the causeway to the mainland.

"What an odd fellow," Sébastien commented.

We spent half the day explaining to the police what had happened. We suggested Sébastien go to a hospital to make sure he was okay after collapsing from his earlier chill, but he wouldn't have it. He said all he needed was an extra hot double espresso. I could have used about five coffees and an equal number of croissants. I was pleased the French police agreed.

It was surprisingly easy to tell the truth. By omitting the fact that the parchment clue came from a secret hiding place at the Louvre, it was easy to explain that a criminal had gotten his hands on Nazi plunder that suggested a lost treasure was hidden on Mont Saint-Michel, and that he'd kidnapped us when we tried to stop him. Regional police knew the history of the Mont, so they believed the story. Especially when they learned an Englishman was involved.

We told them there was a Frenchman involved, too, who had perished after getting stuck in the quicksand. They were used to hearing this news. Every year, dozens of people drowned in the perilous tides.

Last, they asked for the specifics about the treasure. I told them there was one last piece of information I needed, and that then I could show them where it was hidden.

When they said we were free to leave, I knew where I needed to go. But first, we had two stops to make: North's hotel room, and our own. Using the key Sébastien had copied, we retrieved the complete set of documents related to the treasure, then stopped in the room Sébastien and I had rented to take hot showers and dress in the changes of clothes we'd brought with us. My sneakers were ruined, but I happily slipped on my high heels. Now we were ready.

In the cloisters, I located what I needed. I was now certain I was right, but there was one last thing I needed to put it all together. We climbed to the top of the Mont to see Massi Bruel.

The blind historian was cooking a lamb stew for lunch when we knocked on his door. He generously invited us inside to share his meal. I didn't think I could eat another bite after the number of croissants I'd devoured, but with the scent of the sweet fruits and savory spices in the stew, I again found myself hungry.

"Justice," he said at the conclusion of our story. "The man who perished in the quicksand deserved his fate."

It had taken the entire meal for us to tell Massi what had happened. We now sat in the living room, drinking Maghrebi mint tea. Sébastien watched in awe as Massi poured the steaming liquid from high above the teacups as expertly as he had before.

"It's amazing that the knowledge of the lower level of rooms has been lost for so long," Massi said.

"I wish the hoard from Saint-Lô that North purchased contained all the missing records," I said, "but it doesn't look like that's the case."

"It's the illuminated manuscript clue for which you need my assistance?" Massi asked.

"It is. *Sequere cementarium claustri ad cryptam.* Follow the stonemasons of the cloisters to the crypt."

"My Latin isn't nearly as good as my English, but I don't believe you came to me for a translation. How may I be of assistance?"

"I think the clue refers to the stonemasons themselves."

Massi shook his head. "The names of nearly all of the architects and masons are lost. If that's what you seek, I'm afraid I must disappoint you."

"Two stonemasons from the 12th century carved their likenesses into the cloisters. The revolutionaries didn't destroy their carvings during the French Revolution. Therefore there are *literally* stonemasons sitting in the cloisters. I believe they want to tell us something."

"*C'est vrai.*" Massi's cloudy eyes widened. "This is true."

After the meal, Massi walked with us to the cloisters. "It's nice to have a beautiful lady on my arm," he said, patting my elbow.

"How do you know I'm beautiful?"

"A man can sense these things."

"Here they are," I said, stopping in front of the carving.

Lane set down the stepping stool we'd acquired for this purpose, helped Massi up, and placed his hands over the carving. I was hoping a blind man's hands would be more sensitive to slight variations in the worn stone.

"Their hands are pointing down," I said, "but I'm hoping there's some sort of number or marking that indicates a specific stone."

"A 'jobbers mark,' you mean?" Massi asked.

"Exactly. I hope."

"You brought paper?"

I handed him a pad of paper and pencil. He took it in his hands and made a sketch of a symbol that looked similar to two number eights, or a double infinity symbol.

"If we find this symbol on a single stone in the floor of one of the crypts," I said, "we'll find our treasure."

CHAPTER 48

In the *Crypt des Gros Piliers*, we found a solitary stone in the floor with the infinity symbol the stonemasons in the cloisters had pointed us to.

The head of renovations at the Mont was so intrigued by learning of the fabled treasure that might be buried under his nose that he insisted on removing the stone right away. Removing one stone from the floor wouldn't cause any structural problems, and would, in his estimation, give a more thorough understanding of the layout of the Mont that might in fact help with the renovations. I thought that was a stretch, but it was his prerogative. Who was I to say no to a man who was a huge fan of treasure hunt movies? I wanted to see the treasure dug up too.

I was fairly confident that I was right, but I couldn't be sure until the treasure was revealed. The foreman scheduled the rock to be removed the following day.

In the meantime, Lane booked a room on the Mont. I moved my things into his room, giving Sébastien our old room to himself. As soon as it was late enough to call California, I phoned Sanjay from the room to tell him what was going on.

Once I'd filled him in, the silence on the other end of the line nearly killed me. Either I'd been speaking to a lost connection or he'd had a heart attack and lost the ability to speak.

"Did Sébastien put you up to this call?" he said finally. "Is this a gag about one of his new automatons? Did he build something even cooler than Jeeves?"

After I convinced Sanjay I wasn't joking, he yelled at me for several minutes. Then there was another pause.

"You really think you're going to find a version of Tipu's Tiger in France?" he asked.

"You know about Tipu's Tiger?"

"I'm a magician, Jaya. How could I not? It's one of the most famous automatons in the world. It has a crank organ inside its belly that mimics the sounds of both a screaming man and raging tiger. It was very much ahead of its time. It was a Frenchman who created it in India. I never heard of anything else like it, but if he survived the various wars there, it stands to reason he'd have created other similar beasts. I wonder what he put into the belly of this one."

North was true to his word. By nightfall, Lane received a phone call from Hugo. He was safe, and not too worse for wear. He had a bump on the head and a deep cut on his hand, which is where all the blood came from that I saw at his apartment.

North had supplied him with every comfort, aside from freedom. He thought he'd even gained a couple of pounds during his few days of captivity. He wasn't far, so he wanted to meet us on the Mont and be there for the discovery of the treasure the next day.

Hugo arrived as we were sitting down to dinner at Mère Poulard. He greeted me with two kisses on my cheeks and a warm hug. Over two bottles of wine, the four of us talked until we were the last people in the restaurant and the wait staff began to hover.

Back at the hotel room, I stepped into the bathroom to freshen up after the hectic day. When I emerged, Lane was fast asleep.

In the morning, the foreman oversaw the careful cleaning out of the mortar around the heavy stone and then its removal. Beneath it, we found a narrow staircase.

A room approximately ten feet in each dimension lay at the bottom of the stairway. The room was stuffed with treasures. On two sides, simple wooden tables held stacks of breathtaking antique books.

The item in the center sent an even bigger thrill through me. There lay Tipu's Tiger, only not. Here in the secret room at Mont Saint-Michel lay a six-foot elephant with a wooden man wrapped in its trunk. At their feet, a tiger crouched, ready to pounce.

The same man who created Tipu Sultan's Tiger, now housed at the Victoria and Albert Museum, must have created this. Except this one was even more impressive. Unlike the one at the museum, this elephant and tiger hadn't been poked and prodded for centuries by enthusiastic spectators.

Trenton Smith's ravings hadn't been completely accurate, though. The creation was made of wood, not gold.

The foreman stepped toward the automaton, his hand reaching out to a piece of thick, darkened paper in the tiger's mouth.

"Don't touch it!" I cried. "It could crumble if it's not handled properly."

"She's right," Hugo said. "*Attendez*, Jaya, what are you doing?"

"Just because we can't touch it," I said, "doesn't mean we can't read what the man wrote."

Standing inches from the tiger, I read the visible portions of the paper in the tiger's mouth. Or, I tried to. "It's in French!"

Hugo laughed and traded places with me. "This man, Devereaux, served as an officer in the French East India Company. He wished to donate his treasures to France, and what better place than Mont Saint-Michel. He hoped that this fortune stolen from British officers in India would honor the French. Ah! Such a rivalry! This is why, as the centerpiece of his gift, Devereaux wished to bequeath an automaton made for Tipu Sultan, the Tiger of Mysore, of an elephant and tiger eating an Englishman. *Mais*, this is all I can see without touching the letter."

After photographing the treasures and finding archival storage bags and gloves, we removed the letter and learned the rest of the story.

To the Sultan, this grand automaton was neither ferocious enough, nor was the tiger central enough. He asked the creator to make him another one, with only a tiger. The sultan discarded this one, giving it back to the French creator. With some of the riches Devereaux had already acquired in India, he purchased the automaton from the French inventor.

As for his earlier riches, he claimed that he'd beaten Robert Clive, aka Clive of India, in a game of chess, and had won a portion of Clive's treasures. But based on the dates and location of this man's station in India, I was skeptical.

Regardless of where he found them, he wanted his treasures to go to the French, to serve God and country.

"Hold on," I said. "If this is like Tipu's Tiger, then it's an automaton with moving pieces that does something."

"Like what?" Hugo asked.

"Tipu's Tiger has an organ that makes sounds to imitate a roaring tiger and a screaming man."

"You've gotta love the French," Lane said loudly enough for only me to hear.

"Sébastien," I said. "I can't see where this opens. Maybe this isn't an automaton. It was made earlier than Tipu's Tiger."

"Hmm..." Sébastien said, crouching down like the tiger. "The tusk appears to be a lever." He pulled on the tusk of the elephant. It moved. Everyone in that small room held their breath. I hoped he knew what he was doing.

Hugo let out a low whistle.

"Well, what do you know," Lane whispered.

Inside the mouth of the elephant sat a stack of gold coins.

"Clive's gold coins, thought to have disappeared at the bottom of the ocean when the Doddington sank," I said. "North and I were *both* right."

*   *   *

With that unexpected discovery, I was ready for another celebratory night—when the bad news came in. The tide had gone down and the bay searched. No body had been found.

With the strong tides in the area, the authorities expected the body was swept out to sea. I wasn't so sure...

But I knew that if I ever crossed paths with Marius again, I would recognize him by the scar across his face from where I'd slashed him with stained glass.

CHAPTER 49

It was time to go home. Home to a plagiarism scandal and a job I no longer had after resigning.

Since Lane and I didn't think it prudent to tell of our involvement in the theft at the Louvre or tell any details about North that would incriminate Lane, I wouldn't be able to explain how North forged the documents that showed me to be a plagiarist. With that door closed, I had to figure out what else I could do with my life. Besides being a historian, the only other things I knew how to do well were play the tabla and waitress. Perhaps I could get a job as a waitress at the Tandoori Palace during the lunch hour and play tabla in the evenings. I sighed and took a sip of tepid tea.

As I stood in Sébastien's kitchen, drinking tea prepared by Jeeves and looking at a framed poster of The Sultan's Elephant from The Clever Mechanicals exhibition, I contemplated my options. Sébastien was busy chopping shallots as part of a feast he was preparing to celebrate everything we'd accomplished. I was staying at his magical house for a last night in France before flying back to San Francisco.

My phone rang, showing a familiar number. Someone was calling from the university. Tamarind was the most likely person to be calling me, but she would have called from her cell phone, not a university phone. I stepped out of the kitchen to answer the call.

"Jaya!" The dean. I scrunched my eyes shut.

"Listen," he continued. "About this call you made—I know all about what was behind it."

"Um—"

"How a rival was trying to sabotage you by accusing you of plagiarism."

"A rival?"

"I understand why you acted hastily and tried to resign. You didn't want to cause a scandal for the university."

"Wait, what do you mean *tried to* resign?"

"I can't take a decision you made for the greater good of the university as final, can I?"

"But you received proof of plagiarism."

Démon, the opinionated rabbit, narrowed his eyes at me as I raised my voice.

"I did indeed," the dean said. "I needed an extra dose of acid reflux medicine that night, I can tell you. It was such a relief to learn the proof had been faked."

"How did you find out it was a sham?" I stepped around the bunny, who was sniffing my heel with interest.

"Naveen Krishnan."

"Naveen?"

"He didn't believe it when he saw it. He knows you, and said you'd never stoop to plagiarism. He dug a little deeper. Discovered the documents were faked."

I didn't think he had it in him, but Naveen came through for me. He was a pompous jerk, but he had scruples. He wanted to beat me, but he wanted to do it fairly.

After catching up with the dean for a few more minutes, I hung up, knowing that my job was waiting for me at home.

The bigger question was what else I had waiting for me at home. With the threat of North gone, Lane could return to California—if he wanted to.

Lane said he had a couple of things to take care of in France before meeting me there. He wasn't sure how quickly he could be there, but he promised he'd come.

I didn't turn down the first class ticket he bought me to fly nonstop from Paris to San Francisco. But again, I couldn't quite enjoy the luxury around me. What would I find back home?

CHAPTER 50

After my flight landed at SFO, I caught a cab to my house, where I was looking forward to sleeping for several days. When I reached the foot of the stairs leading up to my attic apartment, someone was waiting for me. For a split second, I thought it might have been Miles. Nobody else I knew in San Francisco would wait on my stairs like that.

But it wasn't Miles. Lane Peters sat on the steps, reading a paperback novel, a duffel bag at his feet.

"I don't have anywhere to stay right now," he said, standing up. "I thought maybe..."

"Yes," I said. "Most definitely, yes."

"We can pick up where we left off."

"At long last," I said, "with some privacy."

Lane and I dropped our bags on the landing outside my door while I fished for my keys. I was *finally* going to have some time alone with Lane that didn't involve the stress of a master criminal coercing our actions. I figured we could put our feet up, order takeout, and possibly do other things we hadn't yet had the opportunity to do...

"Do you hear that?" I asked.

"The music?" Lane said. "Isn't it coming from Nadia's place downstairs? It was playing when I arrived a few minutes ago."

"Weird," I said. "I didn't know she had any bhangra music."

I turned my key and pushed open the door.

"Surprise!" a group of people shouted over the music.

I stumbled backward, indeed surprised. Lane caught me. He laughed and kissed the top of my head.

Tamarind, Nadia, and Sanjay were there. Even Naveen was at my apartment. The even bigger surprise was that he was dressed casually. Well, casually for Naveen. He wore a crisply pressed dress shirt tucked into jeans.

Sanjay and Tamarind hugged me, Naveen shook my hand and congratulated me, and Nadia raised a glass my way.

"You must be Lane Peters," Sanjay said, sticking out his hand for Lane to shake.

"Sanjay Rai," Lane said, shaking his outstretched hand. "It's good to officially meet you. Really good."

As I extricated myself from a second hug from Tamarind, a knock at the door sounded.

"You invited someone else?" I asked.

"Just us," Tamarind said. "This party isn't rowdy enough for someone to have called the cops. That reminds me, I'd better turn the music up."

I opened the door to find Miles. His hands were especially ink-stained today.

"Sorry," he said, "I didn't know you had people over."

"You want to come in? It's sort of a welcome home party."

"I don't want to intrude. I was just wondering if I left a book of poetry over here the other day."

"I remember it. Tamarind borrowed it. She's here. Come on in." I closed the door behind Miles as the music went up several decibels. "Hey, Tamarind? Do you have that poetry book you borrowed?"

But the normally uninhibited Tamarind was speechless. Staring at Miles, her lips parted and a blush formed on her cheeks.

I looked from her to Miles. A shy smile formed on his face as he looked at Tamarind. Well, well, well...

"Champagne, anyone?" Sanjay said, raising his voice above the music as he popped a cork and carefully poured the champagne over a pyramid of glasses stacked on a silver platter.

"Showoff," I said.

"Hey, I'm celebrating, too. I got my new traveling illusion to work right. Hey, why don't we play some live music? I've got my sitar in my truck."

"Looks like time alone will have to wait, Jones," Lane whispered in my ear.

Author's Note

On May 3, 1998, I was a 22-year-old recent college graduate backpacking through Europe. I was visiting the Louvre on a crowded Sunday afternoon—at the same time an enterprising thief brazenly stole the Corot painting Le Chemin de Sevres.

The art heist in *Quicksand* is completely fictional, but the response of journalists and the authorities is based on my experience trapped inside the Louvre. What I found most fascinating about the ordeal was the fact that what the press reported was far from the truth. Though the museum was locked down as soon as the theft was discovered, there were far too many museum visitors to search each of us thoroughly. It didn't happen. And as I write this sixteen years after the theft, the painting has never been found.

On that day so many years ago, I didn't yet know I would become a mystery novelist. But once I began writing the Jaya Jones Treasure Hunt Mystery Series, I knew I would one day write about that experience.

A few additional notes on fact versus fiction in *Quicksand*:

As with all of my treasure hunt mysteries, the historical context is completely true, but the specific treasure itself is fictional.

The history of Mont Saint-Michel over the centuries is factual. Sadly, it's also true that many of the Mont's historical records were destroyed. At the start of the French Revolution, the monks moved many of their illuminated manuscripts to the town of Avranches, where the books remained safe. Historical documents were transported to a different town, Saint-Lô, where they were destroyed during WWII shortly before the war ended. Through this destruction, most of the architectural records of the Mont were lost. But some of the history can be found in the stones themselves. "Jobbers marks" are real, and a carving of 11th century stonemasons exists in the cloisters. That particular carving was spared defacing by the revolutionaries, and barebones information about these men was discovered in a manuscript and is therefore able to be recounted by the Mont's wonderful tour guides. The secret rooms in QUICKSAND are fictional—as far as I know. But because so much of the architectural history is merely speculation, it's entirely possible there are some secret rooms that have been forgotten.

Tipu Sultan and Robert Clive are real historical figures, but the lowly East India Company men in *Quicksand* are fictional.

As described in the book, Tipu Sultan, aka the Tiger of Mysore (1750-1799), was a grand figure in the south Indian kingdom of Mysore. A poet and scholar in addition to a soldier, Tipu formed alliances with the French against the English, and led armies into battle to protect his homeland. He adopted the tiger as his personal emblem, and collected and commissioned a treasure trove of tigers. Tipu's Tiger is a real automaton that you can visit at the Victoria & Albert Museum in London. Any additional automatons he may have created are the products of my imagination. He died in battle, defending Mysore, when he was forty-eight.

Robert Clive, aka Clive of India (1725-1774), is one of the most celebrated figures of the British East India Company, because his military prowess enabled Britain to secure a stronghold in India. He acquired a vast array of treasures in India, the origins of which are debated. Some of his gold sank on the Doddington, and many of his treasures have been auctioned off by his descendants. It's generally believed that he committed suicide, possibly with an overdose of opium, when he was forty-nine.

The present-day characters in *Quicksand* are fictional—though the rabbit Démon is based on a pet I once had.

Les Machines de L'Île is a real amusement park in Nantes, France. It's every bit as magical as I describe it. The Grand Elephant roams the park and is a wondrous sight for children of all ages. The park's official materials describe it as a combination of Jules Verne's "imagined worlds," Leonardo da Vinci's mechanical universe, and Nantes' industrial history. If you ever find yourself in France, I highly recommend detours to both Mont Saint-Michel and Nantes.

GIGI PANDIAN

USA Today bestselling author Gigi Pandian is the child of cultural anthropologists from New Mexico and the southern tip of India. After being dragged around the world during her childhood, she tried to escape her fate when she left a PhD program for art school. But adventurous academic characters wouldn't stay out of her head. Thus was born the Jaya Jones Treasure Hunt Mystery Series. The first book in the series, *Artifact*, was awarded a Malice Domestic Grant and named a "Best of 2012" debut novel by *Suspense Magazine*. Gigi's short fiction has been short-listed for Agatha and Macavity awards. Find her online at www.gigipandian.com.

In Case You Missed the 1st Book in the Series

ARTIFACT

Gigi Pandian

A Jaya Jones Treasure Hunt Mystery (#1)

Historian Jaya Jones discovers the secrets of a lost Indian treasure may be hidden in a Scottish legend from the days of the British Raj. But she's not the only one on the trail...

From San Francisco to London to the Highlands of Scotland, Jaya must evade a shadowy stalker as she follows hints from the hastily scrawled note of her dead lover to a remote archaeological dig. Helping her decipher the cryptic clues are her magician best friend, a devastatingly handsome art historian with something to hide, and a charming archaeologist running for his life.

Available at booksellers nationwide and online

Visit www.henerypress.com for details

In Case You Missed the 2nd Book in the Series

PIRATE VISHNU

Gigi Pandian

A Jaya Jones Treasure Hunt Mystery (#2)

A century-old treasure map of San Francisco's Barbary Coast.
Sacred riches from India. Two murders, one hundred years apart.
And a love triangle. Historian Jaya Jones has her work cut out for
her.

1906. Shortly before the Great San Francisco Earthquake, Pirate
Vishnu strikes the San Francisco Bay. An ancestor of Jaya's who
immigrated to the U.S. from India draws a treasure map...

Present Day. Over a century later, the cryptic treasure map remains
undeciphererd. From San Francisco to the southern tip of India,
Jaya pieces together her ancestor's secrets, maneuvers a
complicated love life she didn't anticipate, and puts herself in the
path of a killer to restore a revered treasure.

Available at booksellers nationwide and online

Visit www.henerypress.com for details

Be sure to check out Jaya's prequel novella
FOOL'S GOLD featured in

OTHER PEOPLE'S BAGGAGE

Kendel Lynn, Gigi Pandian, Diane Vallere

Baggage claim can be terminal. These are the stories of what happened after three women with a knack for solving mysteries each grabbed the wrong bag.

MIDNIGHT ICE by Diane Vallere: When interior decorator Madison Night crosses the country to distance herself from a recent breakup, she learns it's harder to escape her past than she thought, and diamonds are rarely a girl's best friend.

SWITCH BACK by Kendel Lynn: Ballantyne Foundation director Elliott Lisbon travels to Texas after inheriting an entire town, but when she learns the benefactor was murdered, she must unlock the small town's big secrets or she'll never get out alive.

FOOL'S GOLD by Gigi Pandian: When a world-famous chess set is stolen from a locked room during the Edinburgh Fringe Festival, historian Jaya Jones and her magician best friend must outwit actresses and alchemists to solve the baffling crime.

Available at booksellers nationwide and online

Visit www.henerypress.com for details

Henery Press Mystery Books

And finally, before you go...
Here are a few other mysteries
you might enjoy:

NUN TOO SOON

Alice Loweecey

A Giulia Driscoll Mystery (#1)

Giulia Falcone-Driscoll has just taken on her first impossible client: The Silk Tie Killer. He's hired Driscoll Investigations to prove his innocence and they have only thirteen days to accomplish it. Talk about being tried in the media. Everyone in town is sure Roger Fitch strangled his girlfriend with one of his silk neckties. And then there's the local TMZ wannabes—The Scoop—stalking Giulia and her client for sleazy sound bites.

On top of all that, her assistant's first baby is due any second, her scary smart admin still doesn't relate well to humans, and her police detective husband insists her client is guilty. About this marriage thing—it's unknown territory, but it sure beats ten years of living with 150 nuns.

Giulia's ownership of Driscoll Investigations hasn't changed her passion for justice from her convent years. But the more dirt she digs up, the more she's worried her efforts will help a murderer escape. As the client accuses DI of dragging its heels on purpose, Giulia thinks The Silk Tie Killer might be choosing one of his ties for her own neck.

Available at booksellers nationwide and online

Visit www.henerypress.com for details

THE AMBITIOUS CARD

John Gaspard

An Eli Marks Mystery (#1)

The life of a magician isn't all kiddie shows and card tricks. Sometimes it's murder. Especially when magician Eli Marks very publicly debunks a famed psychic, and said psychic ends up dead. The evidence, including a bloody King of Diamonds playing card (one from Eli's own Ambitious Card routine), directs the police right to Eli.

As more psychics are slain, and more King cards rise to the top, Eli can't escape suspicion. Things get really complicated when romance blooms with a beautiful psychic, and Eli discovers she's the next target for murder, and he's scheduled to die with her. Now Eli must use every trick he knows to keep them both alive and reveal the true killer.

Available at booksellers nationwide and online

Visit www.henerypress.com for details

FINDING SKY

Susan O'Brien

A Nicki Valentine Mystery

Suburban widow and P.I. in training Nicki Valentine can barely keep track of her two kids, never mind anyone else. But when her best friend's adoption plan is jeopardized by the young birth mother's disappearance, Nicki is persuaded to help. Nearly everyone else believes the teenager ran away, but Nicki trusts her BFF's judgment, and the feeling is mutual.

The case leads where few moms go (teen parties, gang shootings) and places they can't avoid (preschool parties, OB-GYNs' offices). Nicki has everything to lose and much to gain — including the attention of her unnervingly hot P.I. instructor. Thankfully, Nicki is armed with her pesky conscience, occasional babysitters, a fully stocked minivan, and nature's best defense system: women's intuition.

Available at booksellers nationwide and online

Visit www.henerypress.com for details

BOARD STIFF

Kendel Lynn

An Elliott Lisbon Mystery (#1)

As director of the Ballantyne Foundation on Sea Pine Island, SC, Elliott Lisbon scratches her detective itch by performing discreet inquiries for Foundation donors. Usually nothing more serious than retrieving a pilfered Pomeranian. Until Jane Hatting, Ballantyne board chair, is accused of murder. The Ballantyne's reputation tanks, Jane's headed to a jail cell, and Elliott's sexy ex is the new lieutenant in town.

Armed with moxie and her Mini Coop, Elliott uncovers a trail of blackmail schemes, gambling debts, illicit affairs, and investment scams. But the deeper she digs to clear Jane's name, the guiltier Jane looks. The closer she gets to the truth, the more treacherous her investigation becomes. With victims piling up faster than shells at a clambake, Elliott realizes she's next on the killer's list.

Available at booksellers nationwide and online

Visit www.henerypress.com for details

PILLOW STALK

Diane Vallere

A Mad for Mod Mystery (#1)

Interior Decorator Madison Night has modeled her life after a character in a Doris Day movie, but when a killer targets women dressed like the bubbly actress, Madison's signature sixties style places her in the middle of a homicide investigation.

The local detective connects the new crimes to a twenty-year-old cold case, and Madison's long-trusted contractor emerges as the leading suspect. As the body count piles up like a stack of plush pillows, Madison uncovers a Soviet spy, a campaign to destroy all Doris Day movies, and six minutes of film that will change her life forever.

Available at booksellers nationwide and online

Visit www.henerypress.com for details

3 1901 06187 4931

CPSIA information can be obtained
at www.ICGtesting.com
Printed in the USA
LVHW021753160220
647103LV00009B/137